Z JEFFRIES

Chase: The Boy Who Hid

This novel is entirely a work of fiction. The names, characters and incidents portrayed in it are the work of the author's imagination. Any resemblance to actual persons, living or dead, events or localities is entirely coincidental.

First edition

Editing by Charlie Knight
Cover art by Mikki Noble of Paracoze Designs
Proofreading by Pamela Willson

This book was professionally typeset on Reedsy.
Find out more at reedsy.com

For Richard. I wish you could have seen it.

Chase: The Boy Who Hid

Book One of the Hide & Seek Chronicles
By Z Jeffries

I

Part One

Night of the Navigator

Chapter 1

There was one place in the garage I was totally safe from everyone. If I pushed out Dad's big rolling tool chest, he couldn't see me seated behind it, and I could work in peace. Or in this case, avoid a funeral in peace.

"Chase, you cain't hide from this!" His accent stretched his words.

Dad could yell all day, I wasn't budging. We all knew that casket was empty, even if I was the only one with enough brains to realize Grandad was still alive. And Dad didn't seem that broken up for a guy who was so positive his dad had passed.

Besides, Mom said I didn't have to go to the funeral. I just had to wait for her to tell him that.

So by the light of my smartphone, I adjusted the magnets on the old floatboard for the millionth time, trying to get it running again before Grandad showed back up. He'd be impressed, it was just his style — a flashy improvement on an overhyped vehicle like the Hoverboard. I just had to get these magnetic panels to align perfectly, and then there it was — silence from the living room. Never a good sign. That meant they were talking quietly, which meant Mom was talking. I tightened the bolts holding the magnets on the salvaged skateboard deck.

As I gently placed the board to float above the base, magnets repelling in perfect balance, Dad bellowed again, "We be home late, and that homework better be done. And we signin' you up for indoor soccer this week, boy. No excuses."

"We love you, and we're here if you want to talk." Mom added before of course saying, "Lock the doors behind us, please."

"And don't spend all night fiddlin' with your electronic crap! Do something productive." The door slammed, the magnet slipped again, and I kicked the deck across my room.

"Fudgeknuckles," I automatically muttered. The swearword substitute suddenly felt hollow. It was a Grandadism, one of lots of alternatives to cussing, often shouted at prototypes failing their test runs. My room was full of those prototypes; heck the whole house was. Everywhere I looked was something that reminded me of him, everything was some memory staring at me like it was making fun. Everything but that dang shipping container abandoned in the driveway.

Someone had to find him.

This house and this tiny, nothing-town where I was stuck were the only places I knew he wasn't. I just felt so helpless. Nobody would listen to me. Of course he wasn't killed in a test piloting accident; he wasn't a pilot. Why would the engineer be *inside* the jet he engineered? It made no sense. And didn't they always have test footage? Why wasn't there any test footage? And why couldn't they find a body? And even if he was in the jet and it had crashed — no, I wouldn't think about that.

CLANG!

Throwing rocks at a shipping container didn't fix anything, but it sure felt good.

CLANG!

My pocket vibrated. Another text to see if I was okay. I considered throwing my phone, but the prospect of asking Dad for a new one changed my mind.

I chucked another rock instead.

CLANG!

All the adults who pretended to care so much: the counselors and teachers (pretty much anybody who didn't cost my parents any money), were constantly checking in, telling me it was okay to be angry or sad. But I didn't want to talk about feelings, or cry, or go to some stupid funeral with an empty casket.

CLANG!

I wanted Grandad back. To help him repair sprinklers, rebuild computers, and work on his car.

CLANG!

Or just talk, ask him about countries he's been to, or about new technologies. Or literally *anything*.

CLANG!

And if I couldn't have that, I wanted to throw rocks at the big red crate blocking our gravel driveway.

With a grunt, I heaved another.

PING!

The high-pitched noise, different from a clang, about made me jump. I'd hit the corrugated metal alright, but instead of ricocheting off the broad side of the shipping container, the rock "pinged" off a corrugated metal rectangle of a door.

A door that wasn't there before.

I froze. My eyes darted to the neighbor's houses before remembering they were all at the service, too.

We didn't know where the shipping container had come from; didn't know who owned it. Mom and Dad had been arguing about the danged thing ever since it showed up a couple months back. Heck, I could be in trouble just for activating whatever doohickey made the door appear. Maybe I broke it. Fudgeknuckles. I imagined Dad in his recliner getting a bill and calling me to stand in front of him and explain. He'd have to pay for it. I'd have to work it off.

BOOM!

I jumped at the sound resonating from within the shipping container—an impact echoed by a deep, low rumble. I couldn't suppress my curiosity. Driveway gravel crunched under my old Skechers as I approached slowly.

The outline of the door was lit from behind like there was an orange light inside. Taking a deep breath, I reached out to touch the red metal. The door opened by itself to release a flood of warmth and light and the source of the rumble. A cube the size of a smart car was suspended in the air within the crate, with plugs, wires, and cables coming off it like hair on its head.

The cube had fine gridlines on it like it was covered in tiles or made up of smaller cubes. Each tile was about four inches by four inches, matte black and shimmering with a rainbow spectrum. Black, white, and clear hoses, and multi-colored wires were all hooked to the cube, which was hovering impossibly in the middle of the shipping container.

Along the walls were built-in desk terminals with screens, gauges, and panels of lights, everything powered down. Brand names boasting computing power were stenciled onto computer towers; there were microprocessors not available for public purchase, custom technology from Powers, Limited I'd only read about on wired.com. Everything looked like it cost a million bucks.

The equipment seemed so important, I felt in trouble just being there. But, I'd probably never get a chance to see tech like this again, so I figured if I was going to get in trouble just for being there, why not have a look around? In for a nickel, in for a dime.

I whispered, "Sweet Molasses," to myself. I'd learned long ago not to cuss; Grandad said not to give anyone a reason to think I was stupid.

The box's interior came to life. Lights flickered on, the computers booted up, and the floating cube quieted, now bobbing in the air, held up, I guessed, by the hoses and wires. Then I heard a voice that stopped me in my tracks and caught my breath in my throat.

"Hey there, kiddo."

That voice. He was alive! My heart about leapt up my throat. I spun around, calling out, "Grandad?"

Chapter 2

B ut he wasn't there, not really. His familiar wrinkled, pale face filled each of the monitors, his smile topped by his silvery push-broom of a mustache. Even though he wasn't there next to me, I smiled and blinked back hot tears.

"From one inventor to another, Chase, I'd like to show you something. This is the Throne."

At that word, the cube's wires, cables, and tubes cast off, spitting hisses of steam and showers of sparks. The device, *floating in the air,* rotated as Grandad continued talking from the monitors.

"Cutting edge technology. This device runs on science still hypothetical. It's built on theories of theories. My theories. This is my legacy for you, Chase. The Throne is your inheritance."

He stared at me, paused on the monitors, the smile under his mustache frozen in time. I recognized the expression on his face, the one that said he was proud of me. But this Grandad didn't clear his throat or scratch his mustache. This Grandad wasn't real.

The real Grandad was missing out there somewhere and still owed me twenty dollars. That was always the deal, twenty dollars for every new invention. With him gone, it was selfish to think, but my mind kept going to the twenty bucks for the floatboard.

When Hoverboards made by Swagtron came out—those sideways skateboards steered by leaning forward?—Grandad and I both dogged on them pretty bad, mostly for not being as awesome as Back to the Future 2 promised post-2015 tech would be. Then one day, next to the Best Buy dumpster, in a beat-up box with the barcode scribbled out, I found a Hoverboard. Fixing it took minutes, just loose connections, and I immediately saw the potential for something much cooler. After months of work, I made something special. I named it the floatboard.

It was a simple enough design—a magnetized metal sheet repelled a charged Hoverboard base. So the rider hovered a foot in the air and steered by leaning their weight. I thought I was as cool as Marty McFly. Well, minus the girlfriend.

I screwed up by taking it to school way back last April in 8th grade, planning on only showing the science geeks out behind the lab. But at a boring school in a town where nothing happens, a hovering skateboard attracted a lot of attention.

Of course, the bros wanted to try. With their trendy names and expensive clothes (they could probably afford Swagtron Hoverboards of their own), they took it from me and shoved each other for a turn.

One didn't have the balance to stand on it. Another was better, but got flustered when he fell off. They were getting frustrated, restless. It was like watching primates.

"Give it back," I pleaded. "I have to show it to my Grandad."

This led to a chorus of "Gay Morty" jokes. Then another guy got thrown off the board, which led him to pick up the original Hoverboard base and smash it because, "The name floatboard is stupid."

Chad or Brad or someone tore a wheel off, then somebody stepped on the metal sheet and bent it. Someone else punched me, but luckily I blocked it with my face.

There was no use standing up to the bros; the floatboard was totaled and I'd be going to a different high school in a couple months anyway. But still, it wasn't my fault the name "Hoverboard" was already taken by a board that didn't hover.

When I got home that day with a black eye and busted pieces of my floatboard, I was hoping a bag of frozen peas would fix one thing and Grandad the other. But Grandad never showed.

That was six months ago.

So instead of building and inventing, I spent my summer doing chores and fending off Dad's insistence I play sports. Grandad used to be the buffer to keep me off the playing fields, so without him I had to get creative. Once, Dad found out I faked sick to avoid track tryouts and yelled for about an hour, then asked if I wanted to live the rest of my life like a little girl.

That night, I couldn't sleep, dreading I'd have to join some sport and shower with all of the guys, and I'd get embarrassed and made fun of, called gay my whole high school career.

The next day I woke up to find our driveway blocked by the big red shipping container. Coincidentally, that was also when Dad stopped nagging me about try-outs.

* * *

10

The walls and ceiling of the container opened, the crate around me blossoming with a loud creak. The lid and sides hit the gravel, letting out clouds of dust. Frozen in my Sketchers, I suppressed the instinct to run as the dust settled. For a moment, I worried about my folks and neighbors seeing until I remembered they were all at the memorial service. I was alone outside with the supercomputer terminals and the "Throne."

The "Throne" was a floating cube made up of smaller pieces, like a big block of black Rubik's Cubes. It shuddered to life, and the smaller blocks separated from each other, revealing lines of light between them, thin at first, like a grid, then wider and wider until the orange glow was blinding.

Again Grandad's voice spoke, but this time it didn't sound like him. It was his voice, but unnatural. Robotic. "Introduction Tutorial: Basic shapes. Command: Throne."

Not something Grandad would say.

The orange glow subsided, revealing the cube had rearranged and morphed to become a floating chair. Intricately carved with plush red velvet on the seat, back, and arms, what had been a futuristic cube was now an antique chair.

This was the 'Throne'? I always thought of thrones as grand seats on pedestals made of gold or melted swords. But this weird old chair floated without jets, magnetic panels, wires or anything else to keep it in the air.

"Go ahead, kiddo. Get on." The voice was wearing on me. It was off. Grandad drawled more when he spoke. And the image was too healthy. Grandad always looked tired and gaunt, from traveling and working too much. The digital doppelganger didn't even have the dark bags under the old man's green eyes.

I couldn't take it anymore and said to either the chair or the computers, "Stop using his voice."

My hands were balled into fists, and I was shaking.

The monitors went blank. A feminine voice, small and calm, said, "Is this more acceptable?"

"Better," I responded.

The female voice said, "Please ascend for introduction tutorial."

I climbed onto the Throne, the cushion just as uncomfortable as I thought an antique chair would be. Sitting back, I felt important while grasping the armrests.

"Prepare for take-off," the voice emanating from the Throne said.

"Take-off?" My voice cracked. "Does this thing have seatbelts?" I asked, looking around. And just like that, a seatbelt crossed my chest, securing me down, although I couldn't see where the seatbelt was attached.

"Prepare for take-off," it repeated.

Prepare how? Not knowing how to prepare for take-off, I searched for controls around the plush red velvet arms and the silky pillows propped behind me. Whatever this old chair was supposed to do, I had no idea how to make it happen. Breathing deeply, I thought about take-offs and what pilots would do. But I'd never been on a plane; what did pilots actually do?

A countdown felt appropriate, so I mustered confidence, leaned forward, and began, "Ten…"

Before I even made it to nine, the Throne shot up into the air at a forty-five degree angle. Launched like a missile. My house, my neighborhood, and then the entire dang town shrank below my feet.

It was difficult to breathe. Everything went cold. My

fingernails dug into the wood of the armrests as the force pinned me to the back of the chair. Suddenly, in literal mid-air, the chair stopped. My head jerked forward when the Throne hit the brakes, and I might have peed a little.

My eyes were scrunched shut so hard it hurt. Once I was certain the Throne was indeed still, I caught my breath and peeked open my eyes.

Around me the evening skies stretched out forever, reds and yellows dying to one side, dark grey creeping up the other horizon. Between my dangling sneakers, I saw yellow light from street lamps coming on, and rolling hills full of trees that from this height looked like broccoli.

I reminded myself to breathe.

The Throne announced, "Piloting tutorial engaged."

The wind whistled, tousled my hair, and pulled at my clothes. But nothing happened. I sat on the chair a hundred feet up. Whatever the piloting tutorial was, the Throne was waiting for me to start.

I cleared my throat. "Begin tutorial."

Nothing happened.

I said, "Begin piloting tutorial."

Nothing.

"Forward.

"Accelerate.

"Drive.

"Fly!"

Pointing ahead of me, I did my best Patrick Stewart impression, and said, "Engage."

The Throne responded, inching forward slower than cold molasses. In fact, an entire flock of geese passed by, honking rudely.

Frustrated, I grabbed the armrests and shook them, then leaned forward and yelled, "Go!"

The chair rushed forward suddenly, sending me back into the cushions. Then the Throne reacted, immediately halting and reversing.

I realized that my weight propelled the thing, just like my old floatboard.

Leaning forward a little at a time, the Throne moved at my command, building up speed until I whizzed past the flying-V of geese. "Honk, honk!" I yelled at the birds, laughing.

Now soaring hundreds of feet in the air above my high school, held back by a seat belt attached to a chair attached to absolutely nothing, I was so scared, so terrified, that I laughed.

I was so high, going so fast. There were no adults, no supervision, no bullies… no nothing. Like utter chaos. But at the same time, I was in control.

When I leaned hard left, the Throne intuitively responded with a tight barrel roll. The wind roared in my ears and froze my exposed arms and face while my heart pounded at my rib cage above my somersaulting stomach. But I wasn't afraid; I was exhilarated. I could do this.

And now I finally understood what the word 'exhilarated' meant. Whatever this Throne thing was, I was *good* at flying it.

Now if I could just figure out why Grandad built it. And why he gave it to me.

Chapter 3

Flying was an absolute rush, to say the least, and I had to concentrate on the task of piloting, to get a handle on my emotions and maintain control. Carefully, I leaned back to slow the Throne to a halt hundreds of feet above my high school.

"Begin cloaking tutorial," the soothing voice coming from the floating Throne said.

"Cloaking? This thing has cloaking?" I asked, wondering if the interface could really answer or was just repeating prerecorded snippets.

"The first cloaking option is projection."

"Projection?" Before I finished the word, the Throne vanished.

Well, not vanished, I was still sitting on it, I just couldn't see it anymore. But looking around, behind, between my legs... the Throne was invisible. I was just a body, sitting in the middle of the clear night sky.

"Cool, but I can still see *me*. How can I be cloaked?"

In response, the Throne's calm feminine voice said, "Second cloaking option. Light warp."

"Light warp?"

The Throne reappeared.

"Visible light spectrum now warped," the voice intoned.

I waited for something to happen. Nothing. The wind whistled and tugged at my hair and clothes. Behind me I could hear those geese again, honking periodically, getting closer and closer until the soft thwapping of their beating wings growing louder.

With a honk and a thud, a bird crashed into the back of the Throne, the impact strong enough to shove the flying chair. I spun to see the poor thing falter for about ten feet before finding another gust to sail on. But ahead, the next goose in the V was coming straight at me.

The bird couldn't see me, its beak headed right for my chest. As fast as it was going, what kind of damage could that beak do to me? I was about to be the first person killed by a fly-by beaking a thousand feet in the air. Holding my breath, I flinched, leaning back, and the Throne reversed, accelerating backward and pulling me out of the beak's range.

"Visible light spectrum?" I repeated, realizing the Throne and I were invisible. I pictured the light bending around me in a force field like a bubble.

"Affirmative. Visible light spectrum warping in Cloak mode."

I rubbed together my hands. The air was cold hundreds of feet up.

"How do I fly down?" I asked, hoping to get back to warmer air.

"Compress your posture."

I slouched in my seat, like avoiding being called on in class. The Throne descended like a swift elevator. After I sat back

16

up, the Throne stopped to hover just above the roofline of Jefferson High School. From here I could see the gym—where I never showered because I thought the other guys would see I hadn't hit puberty yet—and the cafeteria where the smart kids stopped sitting with me when they saw my grades, and the library where I hid just about every day after that.

I didn't want to think about going back to school this week. "Get us out of here."

"Request to engage autopilot."

"Yeah, go for it. Autopilot, engage!"

The Throne took off, flying higher and higher, accelerating as it skimmed hilltops and dipped into valleys, like the world's most intense roller coaster.

We'd gone miles across the inky black night, now a good twenty minute drive away from home. Wind stung my eyes and deafened my ears, tears flowing back from one to the other. I opened my mouth to speak a command, but air filled my lungs like balloons, rushing in too fast to allow a breath.

But it was *amazing*. Nothing existed but me, this Throne, and the sky. And I. Was. FLYING.

After adjusting to the high speeds, I could breathe again and whooped in elation, every once in a while shrieking at a sudden turn or a quick drop leaving me momentarily weightless. It sometimes felt like I was tumbling out of the Throne, testing the fit and strength of the seatbelt.

It accelerated, the whole Throne shaking as it sped up. The exhilaration in my chest changed to a cold, jumpy feeling. With another turn, a twist, and a drop, the Throne felt out of control, and my excitement changed to fear. I definitely peed a little.

I wanted to shout to stop, slow down, switch off autopilot,

but I choked just trying to inhale. So, I shut my eyes tight and gripped the armrests.

The Throne stopped abruptly, then said in a calm tone, "Begin shape-shifting tutorial."

We were above a rock quarry, like a stadium chiseled several stories into the ground, a lake in the center instead of a playing field.

The tutorial continued, "Shape-shifting. The Throne is programmed with twenty basic shapes. Please exit the Throne to begin tutorial."

Unsure how to exit, I sank in the throne to descend, but the Throne remained hovering about ten feet above the highest cliff in the quarry.

I had to figure it out, like a puzzle Grandad designed to lead me to him.

"Disengage autopilot?" I said, still slouched.

I plummeted, my stomach climbed up my throat until the Throne thudded onto granite. Taking my first step on solid ground, my knees were wobbly like Jell-O.

The calm voice of Throne said, "Autopilot disengaged; begin basic shapes tutorial."

Orange light glowed from within the Throne. The gridlined seams of the smaller cubes reappeared, sliding around like a tile puzzle until the Throne wasn't an antique chair anymore. It was a motorcycle.

"Cool!" I blurted out.

Then the motorcycle glowed with the orange gridlines again and became a small car. Then it shifted into a van. Then a hang glider, followed by a small helicopter. Like flipping through tv channels, the Throne glowed orange and morphed smoothly from one object to the next: go-cart, motorscooter, and even a horse!

The chestnut horse, much taller than me, was so real, its mane drifting in the wind, even smelling of hay and manure. I reached out to touch its velvety nose as the gridlines formed on its coat.

"Error, back away," the voice warned in raised nasal tones. "Back away. No contact while shifting! Emergency safety shutdown."

I withdrew my hand as the glowing lines transformed the horse back into the original hovering cube.

"Engage shape-shifting tutorial again," I commanded, but the cube stayed silent, bobbing slightly as it hovered a foot above the rock. My chest tightened as my voice went up. "Re-engage shape-shifting tutorial. Re-engage basic shapes tutorial. Basic shapes tutorial, Throne, engage!"

The Throne didn't react. At the moment it was just a five by five by five foot block, hovering, mocking me. My cheeks flared with heat as I yelled, "Disengage autopilot! Do what I say!"

I shoved the cube, but it had no give. Punched it, but it was heavy and solid, like punching a wall. I hit it again and again with balled up fists.

"Listen to me!" I yelled, and that lump in my throat came back. I picked up rocks and chucked them at the cube, throwing them harder and harder with all my might until I fell to the ground out of breath, somewhere between wanting to keep punching and needing to curl up to cry.

"Engaging emotional measures. Comforting protocol."

My eyes closed, and I felt the warmth from the Thrones's orange light activating. Something rested on my shoulder, something soft, and warm. I opened my eyes to see the Throne was now a teddy bear. A big one, as tall as an adult.

Without thinking, I wrapped my arms around the bear, hugging it tight. Fuzzy, but warm, like when Mom would cover me in bedsheets fresh out of the dryer. The bear responded by putting an arm on my back and rubbing. I held onto the furry body, eyes still closed but now tears escaping. Dad would have called me every name in the book for acting like such a baby, but I didn't care.

"Tutorials will continue tomorrow," was the last thing I heard before I drifted off to sleep, and either in a dream or reality, the soothing feminine voice called me, "Kiddo."

* * *

BANG! BANG! BANG!

I woke to pounding at my bedroom door.

"I'm up!" I shouted back, before covering my head with a pillow. *Wait, how'd I get back to my room?*

"And don't go back to sleep!" Mom called out. "You can't hide in your room forever!"

It was already Sunday morning, and I realized my parents thought I'd stayed in my room since they left for the funeral yesterday. I didn't remember flying the Throne home, or getting back into my bedroom, or anything after hugging the teddy bear.

At the thought of the Throne, I ran to the window to check to see if the shipping container was there. It was, folded back into its original shape. There was no sign anything had changed.

DING-DONG!

The doorbell chimed. I didn't see any cars in the driveway, but I couldn't see past the shipping container. Who'd be here on a Sunday morning?

Mom called me, using my full name so I knew I was in trouble. Running to the living room still in my jeans from yesterday, I wiped the sleep from my eyes. I stopped at the sight of three adults in black suits looking over Mom's shoulder from our front doorstep.

Sweetly but through clenched teeth, Mom asked, "Do you know why these nice people are here to see you?"

Chapter 4

The three adults on our doorstep were led by a guy whose face looked sour even behind sunglasses, as if disappointment were a Latino guy in a suit.

"We're here about the science program you applied for," he said with a gravelly voice and a fake smile. Not as if he was up to something, but like grinning made him uncomfortable. This guy was clearly more at home frowning.

When Mom looked back at me, the leader of the suits tipped his sunglasses and winked. "Didn't you apply through your school?" he asked.

Now, I don't like lying, but chances are I would have *hated* getting caught taking top-secret technology on a joyride, so I went along with it.

"Oh, yeah," I said. "I signed up for that a while ago. I forgot."

"Well," the man continued, "we are here because you've been accepted with a full scholarship, and the program will begin immediately!"

Mom whipped her head back to the suits. She said carefully, "I'm not sure about this, about the timing of this. We've had a recent loss in our family, and haven't really had a chance to—"

"Of course," the man interrupted. He removed his sunglasses to reveal serious brown eyes, worn and sad in a permanent squint. "We all knew…him. A great man, an amazing scientist. It was a beautiful service. You have our deepest condolences."

I didn't buy it; this guy was lying. Not about his condolences, but he either didn't know Grandad at all, or he knew a lot more than he was leading on.

"Thank you," Mom said, before directing a sharp look at me and adding, "And thanks for coming to the funeral."

They all shuffled awkwardly into the living room when Mom stepped aside, smiling politely. We lived in a blue-collar part of South Carolina, and our side of town was, well, white. I couldn't remember seeing anyone in our house before who wasn't.

The Latino man stood rubbing his hands together. The two with him were a dour-faced white lady and a tight-lipped Indian man. The solemn woman had close cropped silver hair and a steep nose. Without speaking, she condescended, sitting up properly in the loveseat, hands folded in her lap. The Indian guy squeezed in next to her, their elbows rubbing and pants riding up their legs. Both were uncomfortable in their suits.

Not the Latino guy, though. He looked like he was born in a suit.

"I'm Luis Escondido," he said. "And these are my coworkers, Dr. Bird," he gestured to the woman with the hawkish nose, "and Mr. Verma." He indicated the Indian man. "We work in the Research and Development Department at Powers, Limited."

"The phone company?" Mom asked with her Southern lilt I hated but shared.

I rolled my eyes. Everyone knew Powers, Limited. They were a company rich enough to make someone disappear, and my grandfather was totally the kind of guy who would find out something that would get him into trouble.

Dr. Bird answered in a terse voice, chewing her consonants, "Telecommunications, yes, but also alternative energies, space exploration, bio-engineering, and defense contracts."

"Plus micro-technologies," I mumbled to myself, remembering an article I'd read. Everyone turned to me. Embarrassed, my skin got hot and my eyes went to my lap. I prepared to get yelled at for interrupting.

"He's right," Escondido said, nodding. "We've recently moved into micro-technologies."

Dr. Bird continued reciting her memorized pitch. "Powers, Limited also participates in a semi-annual science research program. We assemble a team of scientists, all visionaries in their fields, and we pair them with college or high school interns."

Maybe this *didn't* have anything to do with Grandad or the Throne. But I couldn't remember applying for any science program.

There was a jingle of keys at the front door, and Dad walked in, stomping his boots off. He'd gone into work this morning for extra hours.

All of the suits got to their feet, and Dad froze when he noticed the strangers in our living room. For a second, he flashed a disappointed look, and I was sure I'd be in trouble after everyone left. Mom caught Dad up on the program, which Escondido may or may not have been lying about. I could tell from the way Dad's nostrils flared he wasn't happy.

Escondido continued, "This program is for American defense contracts. Not weapons. Camouflage. Stealth technologies."

My stomach about jumped into my throat. This *was* about the Throne. Did these guys work with Grandad?

Dr. Bird made eye contact with me, then turned away, her collar shifting to reveal a black line on her neck, a tattoo peeking up from inside her suit. The other guy, Mr. Verma, just smiled a tight-lipped smile and nodded along with everything Escondido said.

"What's cost?" Dad cut in with his thick Southern accent that made him sound just plain dumb. Mom rolled her eyes like always when he brought up money.

"I'm glad you asked," Escondido said. "We're prepared to offer your son a full scholarship, including a stipend for meals."

"How much time it's gonna be?" Dad asked.

Mom said, "They want him to start *immediately.*"

"It would be a three-week program," Escondido rushed to explain. "Only because we're close to deadline. Normally, we'd spend six weeks leading up to..."

The suits on the loveseat shifted and eyed each other before looking back to Escondido, who continued, "...the program's finale."

Whatever this 'finale' was, it made them all nervous, eyes darting around the room and fidgeting. Mr. Verma's jaw clenched as he swallowed.

"This is what, after school? Weekends?" Dad asked.

"Powers, Limited is a respected company on the cutting edge of science and technology. Schools jump at the chance to have one of their own work with us. We usually get permission for students to miss school. Dr. Bird doubles as team doctor and as a tutor, and has teaching certification for most states in the

US." The woman nodded.

Escondido continued, "The program would be three weeks straight, seven days a week, eight to ten hour days, culminating in the three day…finale. Just a field test. In fact, we refer to it as 'the game.' The Military Camouflage Challenge, or MC Two. We would need to start tomorrow morning, but he'll be home in time for dinner every night."

Dad had more questions. "Well, if he ain't going to school for three weeks, there any sports, or physical education? He good at science and math, but we believe in a complete education."

"The program will be very physical," Dr. Bird interjected. She opened her mouth to say more, then thought better of it. Whatever made Escondido uneasy about the 'finale,' Dr. Bird seemed twice as scared.

Mom looked to Dad, saying something without talking. When she spoke, it was to Escondido. "We appreciate it, and we're so proud of our son…"

She was about to say no, I could tell. This was Mom's way of letting people down easy. Dad interrupted, "This don't have nothing to do with the shipping container in our driveway, does it?"

My heart jumped again. "What?" escaped my lips.

"Stay out of this, son," Dad said, flashing angry green eyes like my own.

"It does, sir," Luis Escondido said, his lilting voice making light to diffuse the situation. "But that equipment was meant to be delivered elsewhere. We apologize for the mix-up and will get the conex box off of your property immediately."

"Well, that mix-up crushed a good amount of gravel's got to be replaced," Dad said. Mom rolled her eyes again.

"Absolutely, sir."

"We just think that this may be," Mom steered the conversation back, "a little too soon considering what this family has just been through."

"Could be the perfect thing," Dad countered. "To keep his mind busy on other stuff, and give us some space in our... grief."

We all looked back and forth between Mom and Dad like a tennis game. This was turning into a fight. Fast. The suits didn't know what to say, but thankfully didn't say anything.

"Well, we have a lot to talk over," Mom said as she stood. The suits stood as well.

"Of course," Escondido replied. "Here's my card. Please give me a call, text, or email to let me know what you decide. Unfortunately, time is of the essence, so the quicker we could get an answer—"

Dad cut him off again, "We let you know when we decide."

"Well," Escondido said as the suits shuffled out. "You have our deepest condolences. Goodbye."

Mom closed the door behind them and immediately got into it with Dad. "Starting tomorrow, Frank? Are you serious?"

Dad railed back and the fight was on, so I headed to my room to listen to music and try to fix my floatboard for the hundredth time.

It was no use. The magnets I'd attached to make the thing hover had broken off. Mostly I wound up staring out the window at the shipping container. Maybe this is what Grandad used to do, recruit kids for Powers, Limited. But then why didn't he recruit me? Why wasn't I an intern under Grandad?

Mom called from the living room, this time not using my full name. I could tell from her voice she'd lost the fight. I was going to join this science program, and work with these suits on the Throne. Maybe Grandad faked his death and made contact with the outside world through Escondido, his team, and the Throne.

They were my only way to finding Grandad.

II

Part Two

New School

Chapter 5

A t six a.m. the next morning, just like any other school day, Mom knocked on my bedroom door. Only it wasn't a school day for me, and I was dressed and ready to go by the time she peeked her head in.

"Wait, you're awake," she said.

"Yes," I replied.

"And you're dressed."

"Yes. Are these questions?"

She put a hand on her hip. "From kindergarten to freshman year, I've had to drag your butt out of bed every morning for school."

I shrugged, "So?"

"'So?' So what's the big secret about the science project?" She folded her arms and leaned on the doorframe, awaiting an answer.

My heart skipped and I tried to keep my eyes from growing to the size of saucers. My big secret was I believe this was my chance to find Grandad, to jump into some world of espionage and rescue him, but no one could know.

"It's not a prison sentence like high school." Recovering

by throwing some teenage attitude at her, I shoved past her through the door.

Mom blocked my path out the door and said, "Hey, little mister. This is a big deal. It's going to look good on a resume someday. But it's going to be a lot of work. And there may be times when you get angry, or sad, or lonely. If you need time for yourself, you tell Mr. Escondido, and you take time for yourself. Don't push yourself too hard. Remember we love you, whether you are in this program or not."

I tried to wriggle past her, but she stopped me again, saying, "And no pressure. If you don't qualify, then you can just head back to school like normal. No matter what, you'll still be my hero."

I had to try my luck while she was having her Lifetime made-for-TV-movie moment. "No sports?"

"We'll see."

That phrase never meant anything good. If I didn't qualify, I'd be forced to play something and she'd see I was nobody's hero. I hated it when Mom called me that. I wasn't brave enough to stand up to bullies or even go to Grandad's funeral. Not exactly hero material.

Just then, a scraping noise screamed from outside. A big diesel truck was dragging the shipping container onto its trailer. The giant box skidded across our mostly-dirt driveway spitting sparks past a second truck filled with fresh gravel. The red shipping container containing the Throne pulled away, revealing Luis Escondido, still in a black suit, leaning against a plain white van. If he didn't look so unhappy, he'd look boss.

But as he saw me approach, Escondido rushed to get off the phone, saying hurriedly, in a high-pitched, panicky voice, "Well, I guess we'll find a final team member, then. Thank you."

Fumbling to put away his phone, he forced a smile under his sunglasses as he opened a door to the van. "Good morning. Are you ready for your first day, Captain?"

I wanted to ask about his secret phone call and the final team member, but it was just another big government secret that had to do with this science program. Despite Escondido's giving me that silly nickname, it still felt like I was in trouble for playing with the Throne. And I was still caught between arguing parents. Plus, I didn't know if there even was a science program, or if this was all just a cover for something…else.

Inside the van were three rows of seats. Escondido drove with the shotgun seat empty. Mr. Verma sat alone in the middle row of the otherwise empty back of the van. With his fluffy eyebrows turned up in a happy salutation, the Indian man had shed the uncomfortable-looking suit, wearing torn jeans and a vintage pro wrestling t-shirt. Sitting in the way back with the casual doctor's focus on me, I felt hyper-aware of my lame high school dress code outfit, a red collared shirt and khakis.

"'Sup, bro," he said with a lazy mumbling drawl. I'm not sure what I expected him to sound like, but it definitely wasn't a California surfer dude.

"Hi, Mr. Verma."

"It's Harpreet, dude," he said.

He was so relaxed. After the encounter in our living room, I'd thought these guys were like serious agents with government secrets. Harpreet, putting his earbuds in and drumming on the back of the driver's seat, was no agent.

I asked, "Where's the lady from yesterday? The teacher?"

"Bird," answered Escondido. He steered the van off the

highway into an empty plaza. "And she's a medical doctor who just happens to be team tutor. Bird and our navigator are finishing up their last day of school before the game."

"Oh, are they at the aquarium today?" Harpreet asked loudly, over his own music.

"Wait, the last day of school? It's September," I said.

"They'll go on hiatus until game competition—*if* we make it to game competition."

The van pulled into an empty mechanic's garage, and I wondered what kind of science program they were running out of this empty building. I saw only concrete and what looked like a couple of oxygen tanks. We parked, and Escondido and Harpreet got out. Escondido told me to stay in the van in his deep, serious voice, like there would be no argument.

The two adults circled the van with the tanks, pulling hoses that spurted silver stuff. It was like being in a gas station car wash, only instead of water and suds, a silver sludge sprayed onto the windows, and then brushes spread the goop.

After a few minutes of brushing and splashing noises, the two men got back in and put on their seat belts. For some reason, it smelled like a carnival. Harpreet played a phone game as Escondido put the van in gear. Nobody felt it necessary to explain the silver goop, the sweet carnival smell, or the abandoned garage to me. More secrets.

Escondido said like a tired old bus driver. "OK, next stop, Atlanta Aquarium."

"Atlanta? That's like hours away," I said as we started forward.

With the windshield covered in the thick silver liquid, I couldn't see where we were driving, but the concrete wall of the garage was just a few feet ahead. I braced for impact as we drove ahead…only we didn't hit anything.

Instead of impact against the wall, I had a smushy feeling: a wave, like getting the willies or jelly legs after riding on the Throne. As if all my muscles strained really quickly at once, and then relaxed.

No one else in the car reacted, though. I shook it off. Maybe I just imagined something weird. Maybe we hadn't driven through a wall. Or was there some secret passage leading to a laboratory? Before I could ask, Escondido put the van in park and then the doors opened, letting in a whole lot more light than was just in the garage.

A passenger climbed into the front door, someone new, and the sight of them seized my breath. Warm brown eyes under striking brows weighed and judged me. Thoroughly.

My chest fluttered and my hands went clammy, and I was dying to know what they thought of me. The new passenger had one of those faces that could be fourteen or twenty-four—pale skin, high cheekbones, jutting chin, and a tuft of black hair with a purple streak in it.

They also could have been a man or a woman. Tall, but wide-shouldered, they were wearing silver earrings and jewelry, as well as an all-black ensemble, jeans and a loose sweater. Kind of Goth, kind of emo. I would say she was attractive—she was absolutely gorgeous—but I wasn't totally sure whether she was a she.

And I wasn't sure what it meant if I found a *he* attractive.

I'd been holding my breath until the van door slid open. There was the carnival smell from earlier again. Cotton candy! The silvery goop smelled like cotton candy.

In a button-up white shirt that made her look like the old

lady who took care of Tweety and Sylvester, Dr. Bird got in next to Harpreet, sitting primly upright beside his slouch.

"Chase," she said, "may I introduce another team member? This is Mx. Hunt, team navigator and my best student. This is Chase Hawkins, team intern and captain."

It sounded like she had just called them 'Mix' Hunt? I wasn't sure what that meant. I supposed my official title was intern, and I guessed calling the low man the boss was a dig, but Hunt didn't seem impressed. The team navigator didn't turn to look at me or shake hands, but through the sun visor mirror, Hunt flashed those brown eyes, maybe partly green. I still felt like I was being judged.

"How'd the final go?" Escondido asked. Hunt shrugged while getting out a laptop.

"Exceptional!" Dr. Bird offered.

"Well, that's one test down." Harpreet asked me, "What about you, Champ? Think you'll qualify for the game?"

"Don't call him 'Champ,' Harpreet," Escondido warned.

"Don't treat him like a child," Dr. Bird added.

"Don't talk about him like he's not sitting right in front of you," I cut in. Hunt looked at me through the mirror with what might have been a smile. Embarrassed, I kept talking. "What is this science program anyway? What's this game?"

Dr. Bird answered in her usual choppy delivery, "The DARPA Military Camouflage Challenge."

"High tech hide and seek, bro," Harpreet answered, making rock-and-roll devil forks with his hand. To my surprise, Dr. Bird rolled her eyes and laughed.

Hide and Seek? They recruited me for a top secret game of hide and seek? None of it made sense. Why would DARPA, the Department of Defense's R and D Department, sponsor a game of hide and seek? And this team wasn't made up of soldiers or spies, they were all…*nice*, teasing each other and chatting. Like the geek clique at school, who only hung out because they were all in the same classes. And nobody was explaining how we got to Atlanta. I had so many questions.

"Where are we?" I asked. "You said they were at the Atlanta Aquarium. Was there some secret passage in that mechanic's garage?"

Escondido put the van in reverse, looked to Hunt's laptop, and he said, "Would someone explain?"

"I don't really know how it works," Dr. Bird said, shrugging.

"We wrinkle space through a stargate, bro," Harpreet said, still on his phone.

"What's a stargate?" I asked.

"Come on!" Harpreet said. "Kurt Russell? James Spader? It's a classic!"

"What does that have to do with a secret passage in a garage?" I asked.

Harpreet, disappointed I hadn't seen whatever movie it was, returned to his phone, saying, "Wrinkling space. We teleport with the help of spacial lubricant."

I waited for him to explain more. He didn't.

"Oh," I managed. Maybe they were going to keep their secrets through jargon.

"Ready when you are, sir," Hunt with the purple hair said to Escondido, presenting the laptop. On the monitor, I saw a parking garage with one wall coated in silvery goop, just like the outside of the van. And that's when I saw the goopy van in the garage on the monitor. It was the security feed, live.

Everyone buckled their seatbelts calmly as I pawed for mine and tried not to soil my britches.

"Wait. What are you doing?" I asked. There was nothing behind us but the concrete wall.

Escondido took his foot off the brake and the van moved backward. Again, I grasped the handhold closest to me, shut my eyes, and prayed to Einstein's ghost. But impact never happened. Only that weird smushy feeling again.

When I opened my eyes, it was even brighter in the van. The goop covering the windows and windshield glowed, lit from behind.

"Come along, Captain," Escondido said dramatically, to reveal the outside. Navigator Hunt didn't care, though, and was already out of the van, too cool for school.

Light poured in, showing we were no longer in the garage. We were in a barn, an honest-to-God, hay-on-the-floor barn. Sunlight poured in through the gaps between the two-by-six boards that made up the walls. The wall behind us was covered in the same goop as the van.

How far had we traveled? We must have somehow gone to Atlanta and then to here.

I'd never been in a barn before. I sneezed, the air thick with hay, fur, and the smell of ammonia as I followed the team over to a series of lockers—new, freshly painted grey, metal lockers that clearly didn't belong on the dusty floor of a barn. Each of the team members opened one of the lockers and withdrew a white lab coat, goggles, knee-pads, and various safety equipment.

Escondido handed me a helmet, gloves, and wool-lined jacket to put over my school uniform, saying, "Here you go, Captain."

"Why do you keep calling me that?"

No answer.

The outfitted team headed to the barn door, and I followed, asking, "Hey, what gives? We just 'folded space' to teleport here?"

"There's going to be a lot of cutting-edge technology you'll be exposed to, Captain," Dr. Bird said.

"Seriously, why do y'all keep calling me captain? I thought I was the int…" I trailed off as the barn door slid open to flat fields of corn stretching to the horizon. Like the lockers in the barn, there were computers and electrical equipment that didn't belong on the clearing in front of a big old farmhouse. I stopped and asked, "Wait, where are we?"

"Iowa," Hunt answered.

"Iowa? Like, all-the-way-out-in-the-Midwest, Iowa?" This science program, a game of hide and seek run by DARPA, was taking place on a farm in the Midwest?

"Yes," said Escondido, leading Hunt and Dr. Bird to the tables in front of the barn while Harpreet unlocked a large black storage bin. Escondido continued, "And we're behind on your training. Please put on your helmet, Captain."

"Why do you keep calling me that? I thought I was an intern?" I asked again.

"Because you're the team captain, sir," Escondido said. "Captain SteelCut insisted on it."

"Captain SteelCut?"

"Yeah, Captain SteelCut," said Dr. Bird. "The king of hide and seek. Your grandfather."

Chapter 6

"*All* of you knew Grandad?" The lump in my throat came back.

In the bright Iowa sun, standing in a circle around a table of laptops and cords and antennas and microphones, the team nodded. The whole team was in on the secret, or at least fine with keeping their relationship with Grandad from the rest of my family, and probably from the authorities.

Escondido seemed to hesitate for a moment, then put on his extra-serious face and said, "All of our conversations from here on out are classified."

Dr. Bird said, "SteelCut rescued me from a dead-end job."

"Years ago, he recruited me out of the military," said Escondido.

"That dude totally believed in me when no one else did," Harpreet added, tugging at his Ultimate Warrior tee.

"*He'd* never give up on anybody," said Hunt, who seemed to address the team. What did that mean? Did the team give up on somebody?

"And in three weeks," Escondido continued, "if you qualify, you will take his place in the finale—the DARPA Military Camouflage Challenge, the MC Two. That means we only have three weeks to get you ready."

My mind reeled to make sense of all of this information while confronting the fact the MC Two was a legit government operation. It was so legit, it started with a physical, poking and prodding by a doctor in a lab coat. Even in the dusty barn, I felt like an astronaut.

In awkward silence, Dr. Bird examined me, taking my temperature, heart rate, pulse, breathing rate, etc. Every so often I'd get a glimpse of the tattoo under her collar, greenish-blue like the tail end of a snake. She almost caught me staring as she was typing my vital signs into a tablet.

Harpreet walked over and set up green standing curtains for privacy. We were surrounded by the privacy screens by the time Dr. Bird said, "OK, Captain, please remove all of your clothes."

My stomach twisted. I was what Mom called a "late-bloomer." Sure, my voice had changed, but puberty hadn't hit me...*everywhere*, yet. Dr. Bird must've noticed my hesitation and said, "All of it. We don't have all day. Nothing I haven't seen before."

Her words less than comforting, I was properly embarrassed to learn the context of the "turn and cough" reference. The doctor continued to prod my body while typing on her tablet as I stood there hairless and cold, feeling small. I focused on finding out about Grandad, or SteelCut as they called him. "You said Grandad saved you from a dead end job?"

"Yep," she answered simply. I waited for her to continue, but she did not.

"To work for Powers, Limited as a part of this DARPA competition?"

"Yep."

41

This lady was a tough nut to crack. No questions got me any further. As I dressed, Dr. Bird attached a battery pack to the belt on my khakis, and slapped stickers on my chest, neck, and wrist, before helping me into a fighter pilot jacket and helmet.

Back at the clearing between the barn and the cornfields, the team had assembled the clean, grey plastic folding tables into a square, covered it in laptops, and flanked it with black plastic bins.

Escondido removed a cube as big as a bread box from one of the bins. It was gridlined, sectioned into smaller cubes, just like the Throne. He felt its weight in his hands as he said, "Doctor?"

The hawkish woman smiled wryly and clapped her hands. Escondido tossed her the cube, which Dr. Bird caught like a basketball. She tossed it in her hands, back and forth, with surprising skill, saying, "Today, we start with a basic shapes tutorial."

"I've already done that one," I said. "And the piloting tutorial. Stopped at the shape-shifting one."

Dr. Bird and Escondido exchanged a worried glance. Harpreet, on the other hand, laughed and said, "I told you the Throne was on the move."

I still wasn't sure if I was in trouble for my joyride with the Throne. I prepared myself to sit in a chair in front of a big desk and answer numerous questions that would make me feel small and queasy.

But no one was mad. They didn't even use the word "disappointed." In fact, they all laughed, except Escondido, who sternly said, "Do not access this technology without the team again. It's dangerous."

Glancing up from a computer, Harpreet stopped laughing to ask with sudden realization, "Wait, is he even old enough to drive?"

Eyes went to me, but thankfully Escondido answered, "Good to know you read the file, Harpreet. He doesn't need a license. The Throne is not street-legal, and has more safety features than any manufactured car."

"The old intern could drive," Harpreet said as he returned to his computer terminal.

Did the old intern wear stupid wrestling shirts? I thought to myself.

"I can get my learner's permit soon," I said like an idiot.

Thank goodness Dr. Bird called me over for lessons. Hunt and Harpreet stayed at computer terminals while Escondido got on his phone again. Was this another secretive call about a final team member?

Dr. Bird ran the handheld cube through basic shapes, the same as the night of Grandad's funeral. But instead of tutorials spoken by that calm voice, Dr. Bird and I sat in rocking chairs on the farmhouse's dusty wooden porch and talked, the little cube shifting through the lessons between us.

"Each of the basic shapes is a vehicle which you operate like the device it resembles," Dr. Bird said.

"What devices did Grandad... er, SteelCut, usually use?"

"Captain, you'll have to learn what works for you. Maybe a motorcycle, hang glider, or mini-helicopter."

I looked with wonder at the silver device, like a Rubik's Cube the size of a basketball. "Mini-helicopter? Dope."

"'Dope' indeed." Dr. Bird had one of those teacher voices that always sounded nerdy when pronouncing slang, as if kid's words were a different language. She was so sincere, though,

I couldn't imagine her involved in any conspiracies to hide Granddad.

"You know what else is 'dope,' Captain? *Advanced* shapes."

The cube, currently a motorcycle the size of a golden retriever, morphed into a bush, a dark evergreen. As the wind picked up, blowing dust around, the bush swayed and each individual needle played in the air. Without meaning to, I whispered, "Whoa."

Feeling the bunches of ball-bearing-sized berries and the sharp needles, I pinched against the very real sting. "Ow, it's—"

"A juniper bush!" Dr. Bird completed my thought. "I programmed this one. Took an entire day to explain the texture of the needles."

"Dope," I said again, amazed at how natural the plant felt.

Pocketing his phone as he stepped onto the farmhouse porch, Escondido interjected, "Wait until you start programming it yourself."

There was a fake enthusiasm in his voice, making me wonder whether the call he'd just made had anything to do with me or the other team member. He said, "You two seem to be getting along well over here. How about a field test?"

"A field test?" Dr. Bird's grin fell and gave way to angry worry. "We haven't even covered the operating system! Or the Lack! Or the safety features! We can't just skip ahead!"

Escondido's hand went up to stop Dr. Bird as he nodded at Harpreet toward the remaining plastic bin. Opening it, Harpreet removed a shiny black drone, plastic and square with four helicopter blades on it, a bigger version of the ones from the toy store. I swallowed hard. Was that thing that would be seeking me? As Harpreet placed it on a table and inspected each engine, the little emotionless killer robot stared at me.

Escondido held up three fingers, speaking loud enough for everyone to hear. "Three weeks, people." His secret phone calls were rushing Dr. Bird's process.

"Now, the purpose of this field test," said Dr. Bird, "is to acquaint you with employing shapes during a session with an active Seeker."

"But what about SteelCut? What shapes did he use to evade-"

Escondido cut in. "Captain, you will need to run, hide, and use this cube to disguise yourself from that." He pointed at the drone, hovering a few feet above the table. The wind from the drone's engines flapped Harpreet's wrestling t-shirt as he controlled it remotely by laptop.

"Louder!" Escondido commanded. The Ultimate Warrior fan hit a button, and the whirring of the drone's four engines grew louder. Escondido raised his voice to continue, "We'll give you a head start. There are two silver posts half a mile away."

The little toothpicks sticking up above cornfields glinted.

Escondido shouted, "The goal is to touch a post and return to the barn without getting tagged by the drone."

At that, the drone shot a paintball at Dr. Bird, bursting on her shoulder, a blue splatter on her white lab coat.

"Unnecessary, Harpreet!" Dr. Bird flashed an angry look.

"And begin," said Escondido, arms folded with his weight on his right leg.

"Two minutes remaining," An even-toned voice said within my pilot helmet, loud and jarring. My shoulders tensed.

It was so distracting, the giant drone, the voice in my helmet, Dr. Bird's protests, Escondido's secrets… I had to find out what they knew about Grandad! I asked again, "But what would SteelCut-"

"Captain," Escondido, face sour, whispered, "you should be running."

Chapter 7

As I froze in fear, a million thoughts ran through my head. The team members manning their stations watched me expectantly. Hunt nodded toward the shiny poles at the edge of the cornfield.

So I ran.

Forcing aside questions about Grandad, the team, and what they had to do with each other, I played along. About three-quarters of the way to one of the silver posts, I slid into the cornfield to fiddle with the cube. Grabbing a cornstalk, I brushed it up against the cube and said, "Shift into two of these, seven foot tall." The little version of the Throne was so intuitive, I soon had a panel wall that looked like corn.

Once the drone's whirring was audible, I hid behind the stalks, crouched with my hands on the cool, dark dirt. As the drone flew overhead, I repositioned the cube to stay covered, but the drone sensed the movement.

A paintball splatted my shoulder before I knew it was fired. The impact gave me a pinch through the leather pilot's jacket, through the wool lining. Good thing I had a helmet on.

"Captain, you're out," said the voice through the speaker in the helmet. Even through the hiss of the speaker, there was something familiar about their voice.

"Good first try," Escondido yelled from next to the barn. "Come back and let's go again."

I sulked back to the bar with the drone following me, whirring overhead like it was proud of itself.

Hunt and Harpreet were still on their respective laptops. Escondido and Dr. Bird were waiting for me, arms crossed, parental disappointment on their faces.

"You didn't use any shapes!" Bird said.

Escondido asked, "Do you want another shot right away, or should we talk about what went wrong?"

Weird. Adults usually just told me what to do; few of them ever asked what I wanted, especially when it came to teaching.

"Another shot," I mumbled.

"Alright, let's run it again!" Escondido said to the entire team. Dr. Bird visibly disagreed, giving the Latin man a scowl, but didn't say anything. That's when I realized how serious this was.

Teachers would always rather tell a kid what to do: what to say, how to act, and what to learn. If these adults were willing to let me try and fail until I learned something *my way*, they must be pretty desperate. They needed me.

Maybe I could use that leverage to find out about Grandad.

* * *

The rest of the day flew by. I got out making the cube into corn stalks again; I tried four walls of corn like a screen, but the top of my helmet was visible. After making the cube into a rock, I hid under it, but the only rock in the entire cornfield stuck out. When I hid inside a rusted out old truck, the drone could hear my breathing echo.

But when I made the cube into an umbrella the color of dirt and hid beneath that, the drone hovered overhead, scanning the area, taking its time whirring right above me, and then it passed me by. Holy snap, it worked! Once it got quiet, I took off, running through the corn field as the leaves and ears scratched at my hands, jacket, and helmet.

Then I was there; I'd made it to the silver post. In a rush of adrenaline, I slapped its aluminum surface.

BOOM.

The post shook as a tinny rumble echoed across the farm.

My heart stopped. I slowed my breathing to listen for the whirring, and cupped my hands around my eyes to scan the horizon. And then, there it was. Across the fields of corn, the little black drone, a skeletal square flying above the crops, headed right for me.

I broke into a sprint, closed dirt-colored umbrella in hand. My mind raced faster than my feet could. Sticking with what worked, I dropped to the ground hiding beneath the umbrella.

That's when I saw it—my trail. The line of broken cornstalks behind me, the tracks through the cornfields leading right to me. I had to get out of there.

I sprinted for the dirt road between the fields. The drone followed, well behind, but gaining. Across the road, past the rusted truck, and back into the corn I ran, but not before picking something up first.

Once I was breaking corn stalks into another trail, I opened the umbrella then threw what I'd grabbed from the truck: the tread of an old tire. The circle of rotten rubber bounced ahead several feet, bounding through crops ahead of me. I dropped to a knee under the umbrella as the whir of the drone came up behind me. The 'Seeker' took its time above me before moving on to follow the tire's trail.

Shifting my weight from a kneel to a runner's crouch, I counted to three then launched forward.

I'm no athlete, but I never ran harder, pumping my arms, umbrella in hand, driving the earth behind me with piston legs. With all my energy, I ran for the barn, my breath burning in my lungs. Over the sounds of my footsteps, the swish of the corn silk, and the booming of my heartbeat, I heard the whirr.

I couldn't tell how far the drone was, and I didn't care. This was my chance. The barn was less than a football field away.

Once out of the corn and on the clearing, I opened my umbrella again. Covering my back and head, it caught in the air and slowed me down. The whirr was right on me, the barn closer and closer. I heard the THP THP THP sound of the drone firing and then the tapping of the paintballs against the umbrella.

On I ran.

I let go of the umbrella and it paused, stuck in the air behind me. The drone unleashed more paintballs as I slapped the wooden wall of the barn. When my palm bounced off the splintery surface, the last paintball hit me in the back.

"Safe!" I yelled instinctively.

Harpreet and Dr. Bird cheered and patted my shoulder, shaking other's hands. Even Hunt was clapping. Everyone except for Escondido.

Shifting his weight to his right leg and folding his arms, he said, "Your shoe." Then, without another word, he walked back into the barn.

I pulled my shoe off to see, and sure enough, there was a splotch of runny blue paint. Must have dripped off the umbrella.

The calm voice of Hunt echoed, coming at me from a few feet away, then an instant later within my helmet. "Captain, you're out."

Hunt's voice. It was the same one from the shipping container the night of the funeral! The Throne's delivery to my house; Hunt was behind it. To give me a head start maybe. And maybe Hunt had other secrets they kept from Escondido. Or secrets about Grandad.

That night, after "goop-gating" home, instead of reading or going to bed, I organized. There were still clues. Maybe no interrogations or eavesdropping, but some information about Grandad. I wrote down everything I could remember.

In an old notebook, each team member got a page with their name up top. Then, I wrote, "Knew Grandad."

On Hunt's page, I added, "The voice of the training modules," and underneath that, "Trying to help," but erased it.

Seven pages in all, including "Final Teammate" and "persons of interest list" which included the Powers, Limited CEO Todd Fowler and "the last intern." Then I listed the team together.

Powers, Limited team:
  Luis Escondido
  Dr. Bird
  Harpreet Verma
  Navigator Hunt
  Intern Chase Hawkins

?

All the pages pretty much empty was pretty depressing written out. But the team needed me to get better, and I needed to know where to start looking for Grandad. So I made plans on where to hide in the corn. The MC Two *had* to have something to do with Grandad's disappearance. If I got good enough to qualify for the MC Two, I could investigate the playing field for clues. Who knows, maybe Grandad was so good at hiding, he was still there!

* * *

The next day, I was ready for the farm with so many ideas—use the truck more, hide on the barn roof, more fake trails through the corn. But when we stepped out of the goopy van, we weren't in the barn. We were in another empty garage with a gooped-up wall reeking of cotton candy.

"Is the stargate broken?" I asked Harpreet as we made our way to a new set of lockers.

Wearing a different Ultimate Warrior t-shirt today, Harpreet answered in a hushed tone, "Naw, bro."

"Where are we?" I asked.

Dr. Bird answered solemnly, "Syria."

If we were training in an Iowa cornfield and a war-torn country, where would they hold the MC Two? My plan to search the game's arena was falling apart.

Chapter 8

"What the f..." I came real close to cussing, but stopped myself. *"Fudge* are we doing in *Syria?"* I whispered the country's name.

The team shushed me, not like we were in danger, but like we had to be respectful. Like in church.

"Why are we in Syria?" I asked Hunt as the team approached another set of lockers to suit up.

"Training," was all Hunt said.

I asked Dr. Bird as she covered me in electrodes. She answered, "You have to prepare for any environment. And you need to learn to play the game carefully and safely."

Escondido butted in, voice stern. "The rules are the same as the cornfield. Here, the posts are three floors up and three floors down. Stay inside the building. Stay away from caved-in floors or sheer drops. It's dangerous."

"Then why are we here?" I asked again. A training session of hide and seek in a war-torn country felt...disrespectful. Like playing hopscotch on the sidewalk next to a funeral.

"Because the competition arena can be anywhere," pointed out Dr. Bird.

"The playing field's not always in the same place?" I asked.

"No," Dr. Bird answered. "A random number generator picks the location of each game."

"Goldarnit," I swore under my breath. Between a corn farm in Iowa and a Syrian war zone, the game really could be *anywhere*. Anywhere but the site of Grandad's disappearance. Or of any clues.

Maybe fourteen stories high, the parking garage was partly demolished, the jagged walls opening to a cloudy grey sky. All other buildings in the area were similarly damaged, blown clean like concrete skeletons. I'd never been this high up without a safety rail or seatbelt; I felt like I'd be blown clear off with a gust of wind.

The familiar laptops, tables, and bins from the farm were somehow comforting, just as out-of-place in this drab parking deck. Again, the scientists set up the drone, gave me the minicube, and told me to hide, but not without a few more safety warnings.

Once the session started, I changed the minicube into an umbrella again, this time mottled grey, but the drone tracked my footprints. THP. The ceiling was too low for Dr. Bird's miniature helicopter shape. THP. And all attempts disguised as a chunk of broken concrete failed. THP.

I was tagged fourteen times. Brutal. And nobody said anything between sessions—no advice, no review of lessons learned, not even a "Good Luck." Nobody would look at me, noses buried in their work.

When we were leaving, the team let me help goop up the van for the first time. I should have been excited to learn about the new tech—it was teleportation for crying out loud!–but I couldn't bring myself to talk to or even look at my teammates.

Following Harpreet and Dr. Bird, I brushed the sweet carnival-smelling goop on the van while Escondido hosed the wall with a fresh layer, and Hunt stalked around with a laptop.

Eventually, we filed back into the van. Harpreet occasionally sighed or furrowed his eyebrows, but even though the rest of them were less obvious, the whole team was frustrated. Disappointed. Me, too. At the end of the day, my only new clue was I wouldn't be playing in the same arena where Grandad disappeared.

* * *

The next day, excited for a new location and a fresh start, I planned to ask where Grandad would hide here, and then steer that conversation into where everyone saw him last. I was ready.

My heart dropped as we "goop-gated" to the same garage in Syria.

"We did this one yesterday," I said.

"But we didn't make progress," Dr. Bird mumbled, her eyes trained on Escondido. She had a different vibe than usual, almost pouty. Mumbling wasn't like her.

We suited up reverently, the metallic timber of the opening and closing lockers the only sound. Sticking to my plan, I took a breath then said as casually as possible, "What do you think Grandad would have said about this arena?"

"Sometimes," Escondido said, closing his locker, "you've just got to shut your yap and do your job."

Yeah, Grandad would have said that.

The only way I would be able to ask more about Grandad's disappearance was to earn the team's trust, which meant qualifying for the game. That started with beating the seeker in Syria.

Suddenly Dr. Bird spoke up, sluggishness evaporated, like she'd had a lid on and finally bubbled over. "It's a disservice to the Captain, forcing him into live field tests without more training!"

Escondido didn't seem to hear her, walking out to the computer terminals without responding. Begging for time for tutorials, Dr. Bird made her case to Harpreet and Hunt, but the team manned their individual stations on headsets, each at laptops in front of the wall deemed "base."

Dr. Bird was still begging for more time when I took off with the minicube to hide. Why was Dr. Bird so afraid for my safety? Did it have anything to do with whatever happened to Grandad?

Feet pounding pavement, kicking up clouds of dust, I ran, heading upstairs directly for the silver post. Three flights up, I slid behind a pillar and waited.

That dang whirr approached, now my least favorite sound. The drone had flown outside of the building and up each floor. No fair.

Disguising the minicube as a reflective sheet, I showed the drone more grey concrete and clouds, and the whirr passed by. The drone hadn't seen me. With the sheet of mirror under my arm like a surfboard, I sprinted to the pole.

This time, I lightly touched it before heading for the staircase. The whirring came up from behind me, I cut left as a paintball whizzed past my ear.

Panicking, I commanded the sheet of mirror to magnetize.

The rectangle, repelling the rebar within the building's concrete, settled into a hover at a hip-level. I ran and leapt onto this new floatboard and surfed through the air.

Leaning into a banking turn, I dodged a barrage of paintballs. Successfully avoiding the line of fire, I was now headed through a hole in a wall and out of the building!

My heart stopped as the floatboard tipped down and out the building, diving straight for the rubble-strewn ground thirteen floors down. Yelling, I commanded the minicube to shift into rope.

Honestly, I didn't know if it would work, I only knew at that moment, falling out of a building, I wished I had something to hold on to. The board glowed orange and changed. I grabbed a handful of rope looped at one end around exposed rebar and slid down like firemen on a pole, the friction hot through my gloves.

And then, in one motion, my body stopped falling down and jerked forward, swinging then tumbling onto the concrete in front of the team. Rolling, I pushed off the ground into a sprint, colliding with the wall "base" as the whirring returned.

"Yes!" Dr. Bird whispered before composing herself and deferring to Escondido.

He stood, shifted his weight, and chided, "We told you to stay inside the building."

I made excuses as I sucked in air. "It wasn't my fault! I was flying, and then I was falling, and-"

"But," he interrupted me, "you succeeded in evading the drone."

I couldn't believe my ears. A compliment? From Escondido, the human Eeyore? I put up my hand for a high five, but he left me hanging.

"We need to advance training," he said sourly.

Dr. Bird gasped. Without a moment to enjoy my victory, I collapsed to the dusty concrete, gulping breaths. "Advance my training how?"

Leading the team back to the lockers, Escondido said, "First, silence the drone. Also, seek the Throne's heat signature from now on. And move onto timed sessions."

Dr. Bird explained, "Instead of playing tag with the drone, you'll be playing hide and seek."

Harpreet added, "For like, hours at a time, dude."

"And upgrade the equipment," Escondido continued. "Let's go to the office." We got back in the van even though it was before lunch.

After gooping it silently, I got in, buckled up, and asked, "Does this mean we're done for the day?"

"Nope," Dr. Bird said as the van drove through the goopy wall. Then she opened the van door to harsh fluorescent lights someplace bright, white, and…musical.

The funky bassline of 90's hip-hop blasted from speakers across open office space. High ceilings buzzed with traffic of drones, walls taken up by art the size of tennis courts surrounded a crazy floor plan of mismatched desks, and arcade games populated by twenty-somethings, mostly in VR headsets with trendy and colorful haircuts. Where had I seen this place before?

The far wall sported the familiar Powers, Limited logo in 3D letters a good thirty feet tall. A smile spread across my face with the odd elation of experiencing something after seeing it on TV, in commercials, in magazines, and online. It was surreal.

Beyond daydreaming for years of working here as an

inventor, Powers, Limited seemed like a cool place to work. Everyone there was pretty young, younger than my parents. Would it be easy to get a job here one day since I was technically an intern?

The team shuffled single-file down the hallway to a door labeled "R & D," where Escondido typed on the doorknob keypad while placing his palm on the door, which scanned his hand like a copy machine. He said his name to some invisible microphone somewhere, and the door opened automatically. If being low-key kidnapped hadn't been so annoying, the security would have been impressive.

Checking around for eavesdroppers, Escondido said quietly, "Captain, it's not that we don't trust you, but at this level of security clearance, I have to tell you: Who or what you see in this room is classified. You must tell no one about anything or anyone you see in here."

'Who'? 'Anyone'? This wasn't just secret technologies, he was talking about a *person*. A person whose existence was top-secret. He must be talking about Grandad! Politely as I could, I slid past the rest of the team to get through and see the old man.

What I saw on the other side of the door froze me mid-step.

Chapter 9

After elbowing to get through the top secret door first, my jaw dropped. We'd gone from the open-air office hallway into a much bigger room. Bigger than big. Bigger than an aircraft hangar. Vast. So vast, it felt like we were outside. The ceiling looked to be a hundred feet up, the room a half a mile long.

The floor was like some bizarre yard sale. Scattered about the concrete were thousands of all kinds of random objects: a standalone basketball goal, a thirty foot tall rocket, a couch, a tank, a two-story house, a dumpster, several cars, and an oak tree complete with treehouse. All dwarfed by the size of the hangar. Like toys dumped onto the floor. Facing the enormous room were stand-up desks on wheels with widescreen monitors displaying a chasing line like a heart rate, a definite step up from laptops on folding tables.

Taken aback by the vastness, I momentarily forgot about seeing Grandad and said out loud, "What *is* this place?"

"The training center," a voice answered, calm and even, an inhuman facsimile of Hunt's voice emanating from the computer bank.

"Where is he, then?" I asked, almost jubilant after taking it all in.

"Where is who?" Dr. Bird answered.

"What is it y'all call him? Captain SteelCut!"

The team, halfway down the metal stairs to the hangar floor, paused. Nervous eyes went to Escondido.

Licking his lips and wrinkling his forehead, Escondido said carefully. "Captain. SteelCut, your grandfather...passed away. He... You don't believe he's alive, do you?"

It was Hunt who answered. "You're the one getting dramatic with the security clearance, keeping quiet about 'anyone who he might see.'"

My cheeks burned with embarrassment. I hated when everyone knew something I didn't. It made me feel like a little kid.

Escondido crossed his arms, but his eyes changed from serious to sad. "I was in the game. I was there when your...I was there when your grandfather died. He fell into the Lack, the source of radiation that powers the Throne from within-"

Harpreet interrupted, "That's not what the Lack is."

"Whatever it is," Escondido raised his voice to continue, "it's over eight hundred degrees, and he fell into it."

It couldn't be true. I swallowed hard against the lump in my throat. Escondido couldn't have seen what he thought he did. I refused to believe it. My eyes grew hot, but I blinked back the tears. Grandad must have found a way out of it Escondido didn't see. Nobody had any faith in Grandad; that was the problem. Nobody believed in him except me.

"Wait," I said, making sense of the clues. "Who's the final team member then?"

"What final team member?" Harpreet asked

Escondido stuttered in answer, but I interrupted, "In your secret conversations on the phone? You're keeping it from the team."

All eyes went to the Latin man, who stood off balance, clearing his throat. "There's no secret."

"What's he talking about?" asked Harpreet.

"I…this is my first year. The paperwork…" Escondido looked down, defeated, and shrugged. "I filed the team paperwork wrong. I just copied it from last year, and in order to compete, we need a final team member. I'm sorry."

It wasn't good enough. "Why'd you file paperwork before I qualified?" I asked.

"There are no qualifiers," Harpreet said. "Luis made them up, bro, in case we had to go with the old intern."

"'The old intern?'" I asked. Then it hit me and boiled my blood. There was a "Plan B" this whole time. And they lied about it.

Harpreet answered, arms crossed, "Escondido hated her. Got her kicked off the team."

Escondido objected, "Harpreet, please. Captain, we considered our first sessions as qualifiers, of sorts."

Dr. Bird added, "To make sure you'd be safe flying the Throne."

"To make sure I wasn't too stupid?" I asked, my face hot, struggling to keep my eyes on Escondido.

His eyebrows tilted, and he shrugged, saying in a broken voice, "I'm doing my best."

The wool of my bomber jacket collar was hot and wet on my neck. All eyes were on me, and, afraid that I wouldn't be able to hold Escondido's intense stare, I snatched the minicube from Bird, said a command, and warped light.

I ran onto the hangar floor. Of course, I didn't know where I was going, but I didn't care. My sneakers squeaked on the clean, sealed concrete floor. I pushed my legs as fast as they could go, until I couldn't tell whether I was out of breath or starting to cry.

I turned at a gas station pump and found a couch to bury my face in. I screamed into the pillows.

I was angry at Escondido for doubting Grandad.

Angry at myself for misunderstanding.

Angry at everybody for giving up the search.

Just angry. Just plain angry.

I don't know how long I was on the couch. Nobody from the team came to talk to me. Mom or Dad would have, if this was at home. But chances are Mom and Dad's arguing would probably be what had gotten me mad in the first place. This was different. The team just left me alone.

Then I got a text from a new number. It was Hunt, asking if I was okay. *How'd they get my number?* I thought. My skin went warm again from the attention, but different this time. I texted back, "I'm fine," ending any more conversion. I didn't want anyone's pity.

Eventually, I composed myself and washed my face at a drinking fountain before returning. By then, I'd gotten turned around, and it took me a good half an hour to find my way back.

When I finally found the workstations, everyone was busy and not paying attention to my return. Except Dr. Bird, who was rocking slightly back and forth while looking at me expectantly. Ecstatic for the time to run through some tutorials, her choppy way of speaking just sped up. "Your umbrella trick utilizes projection mode." The minicube shifted into a shield. Dr. Bird grabbed it, and the minicube disappeared entirely, as did Dr. Bird behind it. "The minicube projects what's behind, in essence making it invisible."

Her hawkish face slid up out of nowhere, just a disembodied floating head above where the top of the shield had been. "But just step to the side…"

Dr. Bird nodded at me to move. I walked around, and the shield's image flattened out until I could see her holding a shield matching the office wall.

"The Throne can warp light around you."

Again, Dr. Bird disappeared. I circled where she was just standing, but this time there was no trace of her or her shield.

"Toss me a paintball," said Dr. Bird from nowhere. I grabbed one from the drone's repair table and tossed it to where Dr. Bird once stood. It vanished.

"I've done the light warp tutorial," I said. Standing around desks was boring enough without going over the same lessons.

"Well, did you know warping light in the desert, in ticker-tape parades, precipitation, smoke, or fog will give away your position? When the air around you is visible, the warped light field is going to look like a big marble, or a crystal ball. Keep in the clear, and you'll stay invisible." The paintball reappeared, flying in an arc back to me. I dropped it, and Dr. Bird laughed, visible again.

While she was explaining how to use light warp, the rest of the team was busy at their work spaces. Nobody was paying attention to our conversation, so I figured I had an opportunity to grill Dr. Bird.

"Seems like a big drawback," I said before carefully broaching the subject. "How come you and SteelCut never came up with a way to fix the crystal ball problem?"

"The crystal ball problem is always there with light-warping tech," Dr. Bird said. "That's why the Throne also uses projection."

"Makes sense." I kept going. "Was Grand-SteelCut always so good at only being found when he wanted to be?"

"Absolutely! He was an elite contestant, right up to the point he…" She trailed off. Was she stopping herself before saying too much, or getting choked up?

"Right up to the point he *what*?" I pressed.

Dr. Bird stuttered as she changed the subject. "There are… there are limits to any form of camouflage. After all, one is never *truly* invisible."

I wasn't going to learn any secrets from Dr. Bird, but then again, I couldn't see her being in on any big secret. Although, if Dr. Bird thought Grandad was dead, then she meant that he was hiding right up to the point when he died. That would mean that Grandad disappeared *during* the last game!

My imagination ran wild with the implications. Kidnapped by another team? Killed and the government covered it up to protect the game?

Just then, the double doors at the far end of the hangar flew open. A short man in the middle of a crowd of murmuring people hurried in. They stopped between a Christmas tree, a mud hut, and a bouncy house. The person in the middle of the mob, a short man with close-cut brown hair and beard, spoke to his entourage, crowding to listen while keeping up.

It was that signature beard, disheveled brown with blonde on the edges, that gave him away. The group of twenty or so people crowded around him scurried off, back through the double doors to do his bidding. That was the kind of power you had when you were thirty-five-year-old super-genius billionaire Todd Fowler, CEO of Powers, Limited. And he was walking over to us.

I could feel the team stiffen, stand straighter. Everyone but Hunt, who leaned in and whispered with a smirk, "That's the last member of your team."

Chapter 10

Wearing his signature blue hoodie over a white button-up shirt, jeans, and red Doc Martens, the unassuming man shuffled over, hands in his pockets. I'd only seen Todd Fowler on video, when he was onstage, accepting awards, shaking hands with world leaders and making speeches. But now he was walking toward us, and each of my teammates held their breath. He got shorter and shorter as he approached, the team getting more nervous. And with good reason, he owned the building, funded the team, and signed their checks. He'd been Grandad's boss, too.

"Mr. Fowler," Escondido's voice wavered and he cleared his throat. His usual commanding confidence melted. "We weren't expecting you."

"Well, when I heard our new captain was in the building, I had to introduce myself."

His eyes fell on me. Uncertain of what to do, I reached out to shake his hand. I'd never met a billionaire before, and here he was—Nobel Prize winner, Time Magazine's Person of the Year several times over, and author of my favorite book, 'If It's Meant to Be, It's Up to Me.'

My hand was clammy and trembling as I reached out to shake his. I couldn't hold eye contact, looking down as I shook his petite, black hand...an African-American's hand. An African-American *child's* hand.

But Todd Fowler wasn't an African-American child.

This imposter, whoever they were, noticed me noticing their hand, and withdrew it quickly. They said perfectly in Todd Fowler's voice, "I thought that girl was supposed to replace Captain SteelCut. The intern?"

"There were...discipline problems," Dr. Bird answered.

"Wait," I said, collecting my thoughts, trying to figure out who this person was before they could get info about the Throne's tech.

The imposter CEO talked over me. "All testing demonstrated she was quite capable."

"Hey," I tried to interject again. This time Escondido motioned for me to be quiet.

"At the end of the day, sir, it's a team," Escondido stated.

"I thought that, at the end of the day, it was a competition?" the pretender asked.

I'd had enough of this. Whoever this person was, they were lying to the team. I shouted and pointed an accusing finger, "You're not Todd Fowler!"

Escondido and Harpreet backed away. Bird gasped. Only Hunt wasn't surprised, picking and looking at purple strands of hair.

"Thank goodness y'all got at least one brain between you." Smiling, the fake Fowler grabbed his ears and pulled off the Todd Fowler head like it was a hat, revealing a young Black girl, maybe a year younger than me. And she was pissed.

"So." She said in her own voice, in an accent almost

Southern, but worlds different from my family's drawl. She craned her neck any which way as she said accusingly, making the beads on the ends of her pigtails bounce. "How come y'all stealing my spot? Why isn't there some attorney somewhere hauling y'all off to court 'til my training starts?"

I hadn't even thought of using the minicube to impersonate anyone, but to impersonate Todd Fowler in his own corporate headquarters? That took guts.

"The standing agreement was to make the team intern the captain for one competition if SteelCut should...perish," Escondido answered.

"Yeah! And I've been sitting at home eating pizza rolls, reading last Spring's Ball guide, waiting for a phone call! I'm the team intern!"

"You *were*," Escondido corrected her.

"Now he is," Dr. Bird said, pointing me out.

"Him?" The girl, still dressed as the CEO, put down the minicube and said, "He gets the Throne when he turns eighteen anyway. How come you made him captain when he ain't got no experience, and y'all don't have but two weeks?"

"He's demonstrated amazing instincts," Dr. Bird pointed out.

"Of course he has," the girl said. "He's grandbaby SteelCut!"

My fists clenched when she said it. "Don't call me that," I muttered.

"Why aren't you enrolled in college somewhere?" Dr. Bird asked.

The girl ignored her question. "So let me guess," she said as she paced around the workstations, head high, hands behind her back. "Things ain't progressing fast enough, Dr. Bird is frustrated she can't run tutorials, Escondido is pushing everyone to move too fast, and Diamonds here is one failure away from abandoning the boy and calling me up?"

"To be honest, Harla, I think he's almost there," said Hunt in their calm tone again. "But I still think we need you on the team."

Harla stared down Hunt (who she had called Diamonds?), her face silently reading them the riot act. Finally, she said, "Well thank you, Diamonds. Nice to hear I'm some kind of second choice."

"I didn't say you were a second choice. The reality is Chase is captain. But I think we need you on the team. On his team."

Harla, shorter than me but not by much, patted her head between two pigtails as she said. "You know, next competition I'm putting together my own team."

"What about *this* competition?" Hunt, or Diamonds, stood. I'd never seen Diamonds look someone in the eyes like that. The two stared each other down, surrounded by a hot air balloon, a bookshelf, a playground slide, and the rest of the team.

But Harla and Diamonds glared at one another like they were in a room by themselves.

"*This* competition?" Harla responded, suddenly not caring. "I guess I don't have a team for this competition."

Escondido tried to regain control of the situation. "We don't need any other team members for this competition."

"Excuse me?" Dr. Bird asked.

"What?" Harpreet exclaimed. "Didn't we have a heartfelt moment when you admitted you screwed it up and kept it from us?"

"We have our team," insisted Escondido.

"None of y'all knows how to drive the Throne better than

me," Harla said to the team.

Escondido said, "SteelCut did."

Harla stepped to Escondido, a good foot shorter, but staring knives into him. "And where's he now?"

That quieted everyone. And again, I felt like the only person in the room who wasn't in on the big secret.

"So where *is* he?" I asked.

Everyone's attention fell to me except Hunt's, which stayed on Harla.

I reasserted, "Where's he now?"

"He passed on," Escondido's voice rasped.

"But you didn't show him?" Harla asked matter-of-factly. Her eyes bounced around the team as her tone changed, commanding, but energetic. "Well, someone pull up the gameplay footage from the last competition. What do we have to watch it on here? We could just use the Throne for a monitor."

Nobody answered, nobody moved.

"Does this mean you're on the team?" Diamonds, or Hunt, or whatever their name was, asked Harla.

"No it doesn't!" Escondido pleaded, lacking his authoritative voice.

Harla wheeled to face him, "I imagine you're getting phone calls from the secretary's office asking for your team roster for the Fall Ball Guide. Sorry, Diamonds, we were rudely interrupted. I'm not joining any team without working with the captain first. And Chay-Z, you should have been shown this a long time ago."

Under her breath, Harla whispered something. Across the hangar floor, the Throne levitated, shined orange, and folded open into a large screen. Hurrying over to a nearby couch on the hangar floor, she dragged it by the arm to face the screen. She laid down, legs over the back of the couch, and patted the empty couch cushion. "Everyone, have a seat. Chay-Z, take off that ridiculous fighter pilot gear. Work's done for the day. It's time you watched the last time we saw your grandfather."

My heart jumped.

She looked to Escondido, busy grabbing folding chairs. "Can we make the intern fetch us popcorn?"

"No," Escondido said.

Chapter 11

The video feed showed a desert, a dirt road cutting through a dried-up lake bed. The road took an abrupt turn as the landscape terrain fell away to a canyon, a sheer rocky cliff face.

All too suddenly, a blur of shapes tumbled onto the sandy road—a motorcycle, followed by a flying log, and what looked like a camouflaged Optimus Prime. Out of the boondoggle of dust and machinery, the motorcycle drove off the cliff and morphed into a hang-glider, the projectile log took a ninety-degree turn down the rock face, and Optimus Prime skidded to a halt before getting splattered with orange paint.

The three blurry objects were being pursued by a robotic arm, like the kind that builds cars, only with an all-terrain vehicle base. Wheeling onto the screen, it stopped at the cliff's edge, shooting spurts of orange. Next to the arm, Optimus Prime stood at the precipice, aimed its arm down into the canyon and fired some gun or cannon. The video ended.

I wasn't sure what I had just seen. Was Grandad somewhere in that jumble? Did he die falling into the canyon? Plus, did I just see that log climb down that cliff?

Harla skipped back and paused the footage mid-chaos. The sun-bleached log was in the foreground, parallel to the landscape, with tiny appendages I hadn't noticed before. It was running on metal legs. What looked like Optimus Prime was a fifteen-foot camouflage mech suit with a pilot in its chest.

And there, in the middle of it all, riding a motorcycle and wearing a silver cowboy hat, was Grandad. He'd never looked so cool before. Always so nerdy, like me—cowlicked hair, glasses, pale from spending too much time in a lab. But there he was, between the mech suit and the log, riding a chopper into a canyon.

Finding out he had so many secrets was infuriating. Why not tell his family he rode a motorcycle? I would have ridden with him.

But it wasn't just the motorcycle, it was all of it: the competition, the Throne, the team. I could keep secrets! I was his only grandkid. Why would he hide these things from me?

"You deserve to know the truth," Harla said. "That's the last any of us saw him, except Luis. That's Escondido driving the stick bug. He saw SteelCut burned in the Lack. That's the truth."

"Can you back it up?" I asked, my voice cracking.

The video rewound until the robotic stick bug and Grandad's motorcycle jumped backwards back onto the cliff's edge.

"There!"

A blurred tableau of the three competitors stayed paused. At that frame, all pilots were visible, including the pilot within Optimus Prime's chest and the person in the robotic bug.

"That's you, Mr. Escondido?" I asked, pointing at the brown

thing, half cricket, half mantis.

"Yeah, that's me."

On the monitor, I pointed at the window on the underside of the insectoid vehicle, and asked, "Right there?"

"Yeah," said Escondido, his face in a flinch.

"And you ran straight down the cliff-face?"

"Yeah," he replied.

"Straight down? You didn't turn?" I pressed.

"Yes," he shifted weight to his right leg, "straight down."

"Then you didn't see Grandad fall into the Lack," I said, crossing my arms. "Your own vehicle blocked your view."

The team let out some soft gasps as all eyes slid to Escondido.

"He-he was falling into the canyon," he stuttered, "And when I got to the canyon floor, the Throne crash landed."

Harla confirmed quietly, "There was no body."

Glistening light collected in Escondido's eyes. His voice dropped to a whisper, and he sounded afraid of his own words, "He was falling, and then the hang glider was falling, and then that awful crashing sound."

"The Throne was overheated," interjected Harpreet. "It affects the time she takes to shift. Stalled out midair."

Escondido continued, facing the monitor, "There was just his helmet, that stupid chrome cowboy hat, hitting the ground. No body." He gathered some strength back in his voice as he said to me, "He burned up. That's what happened. That's the truth."

I was shaking, holding my ground best I could. My hands hurt from how tight I held my fists. My body felt empty, hollow, just like my head while I tried to come up with something else to tell them, to prove Grandad had to be alive.

Maybe Harpreet would come up with something nobody

thought of, something about the workings of the Lack, but he said nothing.

Then I saw the look in Diamonds' eyes. Pity. It was too much, and I had to look away.

"Whitebread, walk with me." Harla headed into the hangar floor. There was nothing to do but follow.

Still in sight of the team on the couch but out of ear's reach, she slumped into a swingset and I joined her, absentmindedly kicking our feet. We dangled for a moment, between a Zamboni and a two-story house.

After a long day of impersonating one of the richest men alive, she sounded tired. And pissed. "There's a lot of secret-keeping in this competition, Wonderbread. You got to get over it. Your granddaddy hated secrets, but that's the life. And he was good as hell at it. Good at all this—designing the Throne, leading the team, playing the game. And he always talked about how good you'd be at it one day."

"But I'm not," I said. "We're behind on training because I'm too stupid."

"Shut up," she said sternly. "You ain't stupid. Don't say that. It's an excuse to give up."

Grandad used to say that, too.

"It's just new, right?" Harla said. "And the team is new at training a captain rather than following one. You going to get good at this. Real good. I should know; I'm going to be good as hell at this, too. You got my spot. I'm supposed to be Captain, and everyone knows it. But I'm not, and you are. And I ain't gon sit around and let you feel sorry for yourself when you have an opportunity I don't."

Still mad, I felt better knowing she was mad, too. Even if she was kind of mad at me.

"Who *are* you?" I asked the girl with angry dark eyes and pigtails, still dressed like Todd Fowler. "Like, what do you do on the team?"

"What, they don't even talk about me 'round here? I'm Harla Gamble. You can call me Miss or Miss Gamble. Ace at standardized tests, hella strong hand-eye coordination, and math whiz. Intern for two competitions, and the only one besides SteelCut to pilot the Throne. And I like hot chocolate with almond milk and vegan marshmallows."

At her last sentence, I was confused, but shook her hand. I smiled as our eyes met, and felt a different kind of embarrassed.

Without thinking, I blurted, "I've never heard a math whiz talk like you before."

"Like me how?" Her dark eyes narrowed under an angry brow. "Black?"

"What?" I froze. "No."

"Listen, mayonnaise-face," she said in low, quiet tones, taking her time with her words. "We both say y'all and ain't. And I ain't heard you saying anything that's actually smarter than me."

"Okay, okay," I said, burning in embarrassment. I had to change the subject and went for common ground, like an olive branch of friendship. "I like hot chocolate, too."

Mouth pulled to the side in confusion, Harla looked at me like I had three heads. She shouted over to the team, "Y'all telling me interns don't even go on coffee runs no more? I ran my butt off getting y'all coffee twice a day when I was intern. But now this tow-headed kid has the same last name as SteelCut, he exempt? No way."

Escondido folded his arms and soured while the rest of the

team chuckled, but I didn't think Harla was making a joke.

She addressed me again. "Go get everyone's coffee orders. The machine is down the hall on the left of the red bean bags."

I did. I got everyone's coffee orders, and then went into the office of whispering, phone-typing, young professionals, and entered the orders into a futuristic beverage machine. Making two trayfuls of hot drinks for the team, one by one, I realized I believed my team.

Grandad was out there, I knew it. But the team—*my* team—wasn't in on it. There were no more secrets behind every conversation. And with Harla here, it would be easier to speak my mind.

I just had to figure out how to rescue someone from the Lack. I was smiling by the time I returned with the second tray full of coffees. By then, the screenshot of Grandad was gone. All the scientists and Harla were at their terminals. I even saw "Miss Gamble" freshly scrawled on one of the lockers in sharpie.

There was a sense of accomplishment in handing out the coffees. I'd gotten everyone's very specific order right. And for the first time, I felt I'd helped out my team.

"Now," Harla said after blowing the steam off and sipping the hot chocolate, "how far along is the training?"

"Moving way too fast," squawked Dr. Bird.

"Bro's on full stealth, whisper quiet," said Harpreet.

"Orion," Harla corrected before asking, "And how's Chay-Z doing?"

Instead of answering, everyone bobbed their head, part nodding and part shrugging.

Harla cracked her knuckles and smiled. "Well, can I see him in action?"

III

Part Three

Training Montage

Chapter 12

Escondido took back command of the team. "OK, game-speed equipment. Get out the big one, Orion. And the Throne, too." He went to his workstation to cover the day's schedule as Dr. Bird reapplied the electrodes on my body, and Harpreet climbed onto a nearby forklift and zipped over to the red shipping container, the one from our driveway. He reversed away from the shipping container, and the forklift was holding up the Throne. The *real* one. Harpreet zipped in and out of the shipping container again, his forklift now withdrawing a new drone, this one the size of Mom and Dad's bed. This hadn't been in the shipping container before.

Four wings, each taller than me, had engines taller than Escondido at the corners. It was sleek, black, and terrifying. I swallowed hard as the forklift lowered the Seeker drone, feeling sweat develop on my upper lip and temples.

I paused suiting up, and Dr. Bird's hand fell on my shoulder. "Don't worry. It's just a game of hide and seek."

Standing, weight on his right leg, Escondido didn't look up from a screen to say, "We're going to increase the difficulty."

"Increase the difficulty?" I yelled.

Dr. Bird answered by pleading with Escondido. "He doesn't have the knowledge to pilot during faster gameplay!"

"From now on," Escondido continued, "if the drone gets paint on you *or* your equipment, session over."

I wasn't sure what Escondido meant by 'my equipment.' If my jacket or helmet got hit with paint, of course I would be out.

Hunt whispered without eye contact, "Your Throne."

That was the first time anyone had called the Throne *mine*.

"So, if you abandon it and use it as a diversion, if it gets tagged, you're out," Dr. Bird explained.

My eyes went wide. I felt so stupid. At any time, during any session, I could have left the minicube anywhere, made it resemble me, and used that diversion to win. So obvious. If it were a snake it would have bit me.

Maybe I *did* need some of Dr. Bird's training modules.

* * *

Hiding behind a dumpster, I stood so I could see the drone in the reflection of an RV's rearview mirror as I caught my breath. The drone, or "Orion" as Harla called it, shot and splattered paint on the RV.

Time to move. I was trying out what I'd learned from Dr. Bird, and I disguised the Throne to mimic me. Orion flew after the fake me while I ran the other way.

Fake me was following my orders to the letter, running across the entire hangar, leading Orion to follow behind, banking around the rocket, ducking under the oil rig, then landing while shifting into something big and steel. Emitting a shower of sparks, a bank vault screeched to a halt, immediately fitting in with all of the other random objects on the training center floor.

I hid in a camping tent for a spell after the screeching ended when I heard Hunt's voice in my headset. "You're out, Captain. Session over."

Removing my helmet, I walked over to a dining room table dripping paint and morphing back into a cube. I asked, "How did Orion know the table wasn't real?"

"Heat signature," said Harpreet.

Escondido folded his arms and scolded, "Never separate from the Throne during the sessions, or during competition."

"Actually," Harla corrected him, "it's no big thing as long as you keep some of the gear on you."

"No," Escondido asserted. He pointed his finger for emphasis as he told me, "If the gear gets tagged, you're out, whether the gear is on or off."

"Actually," Harla said again, "according to the rules, as long as you keep at least one-fifth of your machine on your person, you and that machine part are considered the contestant, while anything else can be considered discarded gear. I'm telling you, I've had nothing better to do for the past few weeks except study the rules and eat Totino's pizza rolls."

"Is she right?" Escondido asked the team.

"She's totally right," Harpreet answered.

"Which means…" Harla said as if she was continuing making one long point, "This session's still on."

She looked right at me as a paintball busted against the back of my head, like a sharp pinch, then cold.

"Ow." Stumbling forward a little from force, and a little just from being startled, I couldn't help but make a face from the pain.

Harla laughed. *"Now* you're out."

* * *

That night, staring at my notebook that was brimming with new information, it was obvious the best lead on Grandad was learning more about the mysterious orange radiation that powered the Throne, the Lack. I also didn't rule out the possibility Grandad "goop-gated" at the last second to safety without Escondido knowing. Either way, both "the Lack expert" and "knows more about goop-gate than anyone" were written on Harpreet's page. I updated the team roster with Harla's name, stewing over how she made me look like an idiot in front of the team.

Powers, Limited team:
  Luis Escondido
  Dr. Bird
  Harpreet Verma
  Navigator Hunt
  Intern Chase Hawkins
  Miss Harla Gamble

* * *

The next day, before the first session, Escondido wanted to reconfigure the work stations to "reflect the set-up of the mission control room."

"It's time to get organized." Still scowling with arms folded, Escondido spoke with a sense of anticipation.

Bird measured and marked an outline of the mission control room in blue tape on the white floor. At the front of the 'room,' a minicube was set up as a screen showing gameplay. Escondido referenced the schematics on a workstation, pointing up near the screen and saying, "Navigator up front."

Diamonds and Harpreet moved a table to where Escondido pointed, situating two laptops and more monitors in front of the comfy chair before Diamonds popped a squat. Knowing I was to be captain of the team, I remarked on the number of computers they set up in front of Diamonds. "Navigator's pretty important, huh?"

Their eyes met mine in a way I hadn't seen: determined, proud. They gave a curt nod. Diamonds was the navigator, every bit.

"Yeah," Escondido said, "the navigator acts as mission control's eyes."

"Wait," Harla butted in. "Y'all telling me there ain't been no role call? Y'all tripping. What kind of busted team is this supposed to be, anyhow? I'm Miss Harla Gamble, call me Miss, and I'll be a supporting team member because Escondido ain't given me a real title yet."

Then Escondido said, "I'm the team coordinator and director at mission control."

"Yo, I'm Harpreet Verma, resident quantum mechanic."

Dr. Bird corrected him, "Equipment manager."

"I am a quantum mechanic," Harpreet jokingly corrected

back, rolling his eyes. "Just so happens I also dabble as an equipment manager!"

"Team doctor and trainer," Dr. Bird stated while setting up her workstation with more monitors than anyone else.

Harla laughed, adding, "This is probably the first year you have to worry more about the health of the team members in mission control than the one in the field."

"That's super ageist," Harpreet pointed out.

"I'm just saying we have a new, young captain and a bunch of…" Harla struggled for a word.

"Old people?" Harpreet said. "Ageism, bro."

I couldn't tell if the team was mad at Harla or not.

"Come on, Dr. Bird-" Harla started.

"To imply a young person in the field is at less health risk than a team of senior persons, yourself included, *is* ageist."

"Yeah, we're not the ones who are going out there tangling with the General and his giant robot, dude," Harpreet said, laughing. My head swiveled at the phrase "giant robot."

"Who's the General?" I asked in a commanding captain voice but feeling like the one left out of the joke.

"He was driving the Battlesuit in the footage we watched yesterday," replied Escondido.

"Camouflage Optimus Prime? What's so bad about him?" I asked.

Everyone peered around the table at each other, hoping someone else would answer.

Dr. Bird swallowed and looked to the other teammates as she answered, "We'll get into competitor profiles soon enough. Captain Holter has a pattern of play we classify as… aggressive."

"And, he's gon hate you," Harla said, sipping her hot chocolate.

"Why?"

"Because," Harpreet said, "before SteelCut started playing, the General and the other soldier dudes were running the game. But after he joined, SteelCut kept winning, and the General kept coming in second."

"Plus, Holter's just a hater," Harla added.

"AHEM." Dr. Bird cleared her throat to stop the talking. "We will get to the competitor profiles later in our training."

That shut everyone up pretty quickly. Competitor profiles was evidently a subject the team took seriously.

"Thank you, education coordinator," Escondido said, before helping Harpreet rearrange some tables.

"What exactly is a navigator?" I asked Diamonds. "Aren't I the pilot?"

Diamonds said calmly and quietly, "The navigator lets you know where things are on the playing field."

"Like what, hiding spots?"

They rattled off a list without inflection, "Hiding spots, food, fresh water, other contestants, natural predators, shelter from weather disasters, lava flows, and of course, the Seeker. This competition isn't going to be easy."

"You're the captain *and* contestant," Harla butted in. "There technically isn't a pilot. Remember, you're going against other captains of other teams, and they're not going to use technology like the Throne."

"What will they use?"

"We will cover that later," Dr. Bird said loudly.

Harla said quickly, as Escondido tried to silence her by repeating her name, "Light-bending, lots of advanced camo, at least one shapeshifter, a genetically modified animal clone will be in there, and somebody gon use mind control."

"MISS HARLA!" Escondido finally raised his voice.

My mouth fell open. I didn't know what to say. I didn't even know where to start, so I dumbly repeated the last thing I heard. "Mind control?"

"We'll cover it later!" Dr. Bird and Escondido said at the same time.

"Yeah, more time learning what you can from your team, and less time freaking out about stuff you can't control," Harla said, tipping back her drink to finish. "Like you can't control General Holter squishing you like a bug, but you *can* control how much soy milk goes into my hot chocolate."

I tried to take advantage of the subject while Escondido and the team were busy reconfiguring the practice. "I could learn more about the Lack…"

"You should go on another coffee run," Harla said. "Then talk to Diamonds about hiding spots."

My eyes grew wide for a second, and I did my best to keep them from flashing over to them. Talk to Diamonds? I imagined my voice cracking, or saying the wrong thing, calling her a him, or the other way around. I could feel a little head rush imagining their critical green eyes staring into me.

"Captain's gotten enough coffee today." Escondido used his leader voice, loud enough for everyone to hear, as he begrudgingly admitted, "Miss Harla's right, some time between Captain and navigator could help out the team. Meanwhile, Miss Harla can help us put the finishing touches on Mission Control, just as soon as she apologizes."

Everyone turned to Harla.

"Oh!" She said it like she remembered something frivolous, like remembering to switch a lamp off. "I'm sorry, Harpreet. I was being ageist without realizing it. Which isn't an excuse. So thanks for pointing it out."

* * *

I realized Diamonds and I had never talked before. I mean, we had spoken in passing, when the group spoke, but never just the two of us. As captain, I should be able to talk with anyone on the team. However, when we went for a walk around the hangar, I stuttered, nervous about how to start a conversation.

"So, Mr...Miss...Ms. Diamonds."

"You can just call me Diamonds," they said without looking up. "Or Hunt. Hunt's my last name."

"Your Christian name is Diamonds Hunt?" I asked.

"No, Captain, 'Diamonds' is the name I chose."

Stuttering and trying to talk to cover up, I said, "Of course. Of course it is. A chosen name. OK. I was wondering if I could ask you about your theories on hiding spots, like, in general? Like how Grandad might have picked his hiding spots?"

Discerning eyes searched the hanger, from a bank vault to a ten foot tall buoy. Diamonds said softly, almost not even to me, but rather to the hangar, "He didn't."

"He didn't?"

"SteelCut didn't pick hiding spots when I was his navigator."

"Who did?"

"Me," they said, making a left past a picnic table set with plastic food.

The idea of Grandad leaving the task of finding hiding spots to a kid stopped my feet. I had to jog to catch back up, "Ms.

Hunt."

"Please don't call me 'Ms.' Hunt." They stopped in front of an old barbershop chair to face me, not to admonish me, but to state a fact. "You can call me Diamonds, or Hunt. I use 'they' pronouns." Walking again, Diamonds returned to a conversational tone. "I can see what makes good hiding spots…"

Cheeks blood-rushed, I was so embarrassed; they had corrected me once already not to call them 'Ms.,' and still I went and said it again. My stomach clenched, my skin was all cold and slick as I was rearing to fess up an apology, but instead, Diamonds walked ahead, pretty much ignoring my slip-up.

How on Earth Diamonds didn't get upset with me, I haven't a clue. According to Dad, and pretty much every other guy I knew, being called a girl was just about the biggest insult you can throw at a guy, outside of calling him gay. Now, I knew I wasn't my dad or any of the high school bros, but I couldn't imagine being as cool about it as Diamonds.

I felt a weird sense of relief, but not an entirely good one. Like a weight had been lifted off my shoulders but put onto Diamonds'. A weight they took on constantly.

Continuing, they waved at the two-story house as we passed it. "There's a hot water heater in the basement. Insulation would mask the Throne's heat signature."

They pointed out a clawfoot tub and said, "Fill that with hot water, and you'd be able to stay submerged for several hours. Orion doesn't know a tub full of water will even out to room temperature. You don't have to outlast Orion, Captain, just Escondido."

They gestured up to the edge of the ceiling, "Your umbrella

trick will work best in distant corners behind the heaters and A/C vents. You could even use your flying surfboard trick with the Throne in projection mode."

"In Syria, I magnetized the Throne to make the surfboard float. But there was metal in the floor to repel," I said.

"Talk to Harla about it. If the Throne can fly, your surfboard should be able to. And the *best* hiding spot," they said, stopping at the Cold-War era rocket, the tallest thing on the eclectic hangar floor. Without looking up at the towering projectile like I automatically did, they continued, "Would be to fire up the rocket, and fuel it with the energy of the Throne's connection to the Lack."

"I guess I don't understand what the Lack is."

"Me neither, really. All I know is that it powers the Throne, holds it together. You should ask Harpeet about it. Harpreet loves to talk about the Lack."

"Harpreet hasn't talked about the Lack so far, though," I said.

"Well, I don't talk too much, Captain. But here we are," Diamonds said, the beginning of a smirk turning the edge of their lips. Knots formed in my guts, and for a moment I couldn't take my eyes off that smile, but I regained control and steered the conversation back.

"So, what do I do when I fire up the rocket?"

"Keep the power low enough so it won't lift off," they said. "Hide in the exhaust."

"In the exhaust?" I blurted.

"In the fire and smoke blasting out of the missile's engine."

"Hide in the fire under the giant rocket?" My voice cracked.

They answered evenly, "Yes. You should try it out the next session. It will hide the Throne's heat signature."

I furrowed my brow, whispering, "I bet it will."

Chapter 13

When it was time to start the next session, my hands were shaking as I zipped up my jacket. I took deep breaths, trying not to appear scared, thankful I was wearing the ridiculous fighter pilot helmet to obscure my face. I couldn't believe I was going through with Diamonds' missile idea.

As Escondido yelled to hide, I took my time walking up to the base of the giant spacecraft, the Throne hovering behind me. The rocket stood impressively above the rest of the training center, three stories high; the engine at the base was taller than me by a bit. A few feet away, I could hear Escondido cursing aloud to hurry. But what I had to do wouldn't take long.

Just like Diamonds said to, I changed a part of the Throne into a touchscreen operating the rocket. I then converted the remainder into a fireproof cube around me. It grew hot in the space; it was only big enough to sit. The walls pushed against my arms, the ceiling loomed, touching my hair. My limbs screamed to move freely. Then I remembered some of Harla's wisdom, and converted the interior of the heat capsule to projection mode.

There I was, sitting cross-legged underneath a rocket designed to break Earth's gravity to blast into space. I made the fireproof walls of the Throne double-thick (just to be sure) before I commanded the rocket to engage thrusters at a mere five percent. Then, just as Diamonds had instructed, I received a low fuel warning, and commanded the outer edge of the Throne to expand, exposing its orange gridlines. As those gridlines expanded, the rocket engine was supposed to use the energy and radiation of the Lack, whatever that was.

It was evidently working, because I got bored sitting there. Luckily, I had Wi-Fi, so I watched old sci-fi movies on my phone. Two films into the Jurassic Park series, my knees had grown stiff and my neck hurt. My body was anxious to stretch. I checked the time; I'd been hidden for five hours. I cut the rocket engine, engaged the coolant system, and turned off the dinosaurs.

As I walked out from under the missile's cone bottom, I was met with applause from the scientists, and a paintball in the helmet from Orion. Escondido had that sour expression on his face with his arms crossed, but everyone else was joyous. Harla let out loud whoops which Dr. Bird hilariously copied. Even Diamonds smiled, and of course I felt myself blush, so I stayed in the helmet.

* * *

Since the team had eaten lunch while I was engulfed in flames, I ate a PB and J on the random boat in the middle of the training center while everyone else packed up for the day.

"Permission to come aboard, Chay-Z," Harla said from the hangar floor. Even making a boat analogy, she wouldn't call me captain.

She climbed up and we dangled out feet off the stern.

"Here's the deal, corn pone," she dead panned, dropping her voice to a serious whisper. I wondered who she didn't want listening in. "If you still think SteelCut's out there somewhere, alive…"

She scooted so close our hips were touching, and I could feel the heat coming off of her. She smelled like flowery body wash and cotton candy, and I forced myself not to think about how nice her skin and eyes were. It made me shift uncomfortably. Then she hit me with the bomb: "I think he's alive, too."

Wait, what? I ignored any flustering feelings I had from being so close to Harla, and dug for answers. "But when we watched the feed from gameplay, you said—"

"I said what I had to in order to get on the team. I want to know what exactly happened out there to SteelCut. Just 'cause I dog on Luis doesn't mean I'm not telling him what he needs to hear. Chay-Z, I don't know you. But I doubt that you *need* the game, the R & D program, and this team, as much as the rest of us do. I need this. My college applications look great on paper, but then I interview for scholarships…"

Harla exhaled into a slump and her eyes unfocused, like staring at something too depressing to look at. "I end up playing myself. Say the wrong thing, talk the wrong way. But if I got something like an award from DARPA? Signed by the Secretary of Defense? Even if it *is* classified, it's my ticket to a free ride anywhere. I don't need you to play the game, Chay-Z. Until I get a team of my own, I need you to win."

We sat there, legs dangling off the boat. She had spoken from the heart, and I think we were both surprised by how much Harla needed this team.

"So, what do we do about Grandad?"

"Ain't no 'we.' I about dogged everyone on the team and got myself uninvited to my own coming out party. *You*. You got to keep asking questions. Harpreet's always trying to keep the Throne from overheating." She lowered her voice before continuing. "What if the overheating is just Lack trying to stabilize?"

"Well, then it would act differently. It would give off less energy," I replied.

"Exactly. We've never seen it stabilized because Harpreet *keeps* it unstable to power the Throne. I think if we let it overheat, we can actually get inside the Lack."

I was surprised. "Inside the Lack? What's inside the Lack?"

"Right now, I think it's your Grandaddy."

The idea hit me like a ton of bricks. Then it got my mind working.

"So. I'll just overheat the Throne then. Let's do it right now." I started getting up, but Harla grabbed me by the arm.

"No, fool! I got kicked off the team for asking too many questions. The Throne, which *I* was supposed to pilot this game, mysteriously appeared at *your* doorstep. Someone, or something, sent it there, trying to keep me off the team." She kicked her feet at the air for a second, and I took a bite of my sandwich even though I felt sick to my stomach. I had just started to trust the team.

Harla broke the silence, suddenly scrunching her face up with curiosity, "What's that you did in Syria with the mirror?"

"The mirror? Oh, the floatboard? It's based on an old

invention of mine."

She stopped me, "Slow up, Wonderbread. Didn't ask your life story. What'd you do, ionize it?"

"I magnetized it."

Irritated, she said, "That's what I said. How'd you propel it forward?"

"I jumped on it."

She thought for a moment, before saying, "If we add a basic exhaust fan to that shape, you can use it in actual gameplay. Plus, it will help hide the Throne's heat signature."

I was confused. "I thought we wanted the Throne to overheat?"

"Only when *we* want it to. During gameplay."

Thinking about deceiving the team made me feel like my sandwich would come back up. "I don't think the team knows anything. About Grandad. I'll learn what I can about the Lack, but I don't think anyone on the team is lying."

Harla waited to answer so long I thought I'd turn purple. Why did I care so much about what she thought about me?

"I hope you're not as dumb as you look, Chay-Z," she said, shaking her head. I *guess* that was a compliment? "Now, call the Throne over here."

Bristling at her dumb comment, I said slyly, "How do you know it's not here, just in stealth mode?"

"Because I know, corn pone. Call it over."

Harla knew how to handle the Throne better than Harpreet, which seemed odd. After all, he graduated from college, had a PhD, and even helped Grandad build the thing, but this girl knew more about this advanced piece of technology at fifteen years old. Plus, she had a way of talking that made feel like a little kid getting chewed out. And she might just be the only one I can trust to help find the truth.

* * *

"Captain, we need to talk about how you're winning," Escondido said at the end of the day as we loaded into the van. "Moving forward, we're going to train under full competition rules. You won't be able to fly or hover over thirty feet in the air."

"Maybe we could run up-and-go drills," Dr. Bird suggested to Escondido as we gooped up the van for traveling.

"I think we should run full simulations, with Gamble and I out on the field with the Captain and a handful of drones," Escondido said, almost as a question to Harla.

Dr. Bird added, "He needs to get his body used to the stress levels associated with live gameplay."

Harla put away the goop hose. "So, we gon' pretend like we got all the time in the world? We gon' hafta do all of it."

Escondido said as we got back in the van, "OK. We'll run a new training structure covering all bases starting tomorrow."

He stopped the van. We all got out and Harpreet hosed off the van, rinsing off the silver sludge reeking of sugary cotton candy.

"I'll meet you guys at the hangar tomorrow," Escondido said.

"Why?" Harla asked. "Where will you be?"

"Digging up a bug," Escondido answered.

I waited for him to explain, but he didn't. I expected someone to ask another question, but everyone acted like they understood. We got back in the van, and Escondido drove.

"Captain, this is your team," Escondido explained. "Time is short, and we have a lot to do, but should you decide to pause training to investigate your grandfather's death, then we will. If you ever want to pause to just talk, with any of us—in private or as a team—we will follow your lead. OK?"

My face getting hot, I felt myself getting mad, except when I spoke, I felt like crying and my throat tightened. "OK."

The van pulled over in front of my house. Out the driver's window, Escondido said to me. "Good night, Captain. Eat, and get some rest."

Still buzzing from the emotions of the day I knew it would take me forever to get to sleep, so I read and reread the rules Dr. Bird had printed out from this year's Fall MC² Guidebook.

Chapter 14

The next day we started without Escondido. I warmed up with Dr. Bird—jumping jacks, push-ups, yoga, sprints, and meditation. I drilled the Throne's shapes tutorials with Harpreet. I ran up-and-go drills with Harla, going from hiding spot to hiding spot, always on the move.

While I was switching spots, the hangar doors burst open and in crawled the world's biggest stick bug. I mean it, this thing's thorax was twenty feet long, at least a meter around. Its eight spindly legs must have been ten foot each. Its body was a mottled grey, white, and brown, just like some sun-bleached log. And as it crawled through the doors and up the hangar walls, I could see it was…pregnant? A little bubble stuck out from the belly of the over-sized insect. The whole sight made my skin crawl.

But that bubble was no baby. It was a cockpit. And this was no insect, it was a vehicle…driven by someone in full pilot's gear. The pilot got out of the stick bug's round belly and took off his helmet, revealing Escondido. The sight gave me the heebie jeebies.

As if he were walking out of any normal vehicle, Escondido

said, "Today we will incorporate the final piece of equipment you will use during the competition." He held out his fist and opened it to reveal a colorful gadget, the size of a pill.

"A jelly bean?"

"No, it's not a jelly bean," he said. "It's a comm system."

Harla interjected, "It's an over party! Over!"

Diamonds smiled while Harpreet and Dr. Bird oohed at Harla's outburst, leaving me out of whatever the joke was. In fact, I was pretty happy when Escondido squashed everybody's fun, declaring, "NO over parties. This comm system will keep you connected to mission control throughout the game. You and Diamonds should get used to working together to find hiding spots and track competitors."

I pinched the little jelly bean out of Escondido's palm and went to pop it in my mouth.

"No, don't"!" Escondido screamed.

"I'm kidding," I said, giggling at getting Escondido to lose his cool. I inserted the thing into my ear.

Harla laughed, "He got you pretty good, sir. Over." Then she laughed harder.

Grimacing and rolling his eyes, Escondido was putting on an act of annoyance rather than his former impatient aggravation. I think he liked having Harla around.

"Hello, hello. Testing one two testing," I said, guessing what people said when they tested out microphones.

"This is Diamonds, over."

Whatever this 'over' joke was, it wasn't ending anytime soon. Fine. I knew radio jargon, too. "Kiddo One to Diamonds, Kiddo One to Diamonds, read you loud and clear, over."

For the session, Harla used the minicube, shifting it into a cushy recliner. From seven new bins, Harpreet pulled lightweight drones, each the size of a coffee table. Once set up and spread out on the floor, the drones disappeared. Light warping. Finally, out came Orion.

With the ten of us, the hangar felt real small. Too small for eleven flying machines. Harla sat in her minicube disguised as a recliner, cushy red with duct-tape holding one of the arms together, hovering at eye level. Escondido strapped into his stick bug.

I was sweating a little as Dr. Bird announced the start of the session. Immediately, Harla and the old recliner vanished. Escondido drove his stick bug over to an empty spot on the floor. Each of the stick bug's legs folded in, and the bubble holding the pilot vanished. I surfed the floatboard up to the corner of the hangar ceiling, switched to the umbrella like Diamonds said to, and waited for the digital clock on the wall to countdown the release of Orion.

The clock digits reached 00:00, and Orion lifted off. From this height I had a great view of the entire playing field. I could even see little warps in light of some of the hidden drones.

Suddenly, the umbrella shook and collapsed. Something—someone—had control of the Throne.

I fell. Fast.

Hurtling toward the ground, the umbrella's contorted light bent and folded until the emergency system kicked in, converting back to the Throne, diving and scooping me out of midair, barely stopping me from becoming a hangar floor pancake.

"Rats!" Harla yelled and laughed. Of course that's how Harla would play!

Now that I was vulnerable and out in the open, Orion spun around to pursue me. I piloted the Throne through evasive maneuvers, barrel-rolling as Orion spat paint bullets after me. Luckily, some of those bullets splattered midair, leaving floating splashes of color, and a couple of the light-bending drones were out. In my earpiece, the team cheered, but I still had Orion on my tail. There was only so much airspace in the big room, so I banked a U-turn to fly back up the length of the hangar.

I was panicking, repeating "What do I do, what do I do," under my breath.

Another barrel roll to avoid Orion, and I heard, "You need a quick change. Something that will puzzle him."

Of course! Diamonds was in my earpiece!

"Why didn't you say anything earlier?!" I asked.

"You didn't ask, Captain."

"A quick-change? To what?" I yelled. I was running out of places to go. Orion was now at the center of the room, thirty feet in the air, rotating to follow me with a stream of paintballs.

I dove down to the dumpster, landing into a run. Only I didn't run past the dumpster. I sent half of the Throne, disguised as me. I stayed behind the dumpster, switched the remainder of the Throne back into the light-bending floatboard, but remained crouched. Ahead of me, the Throne disguised as me darted from the dumpster, around a Greek statue, and into the front door of the two-story house. I was rather impressed the fake me was so nimble on his, or my, or its, feet. A trail of paintball splatters followed the fake me up to the doorstep.

Orion descended, hovering, guns still fixed on the house's front door. It shot several times through front windows, trying to thread the needle through the glass panes to hit its target within. Even through the front door, Orion continued the assault of paintballs, changing the house's glass windows into a burst of blue confetti.

Then, the shooting stopped. Orion froze, mid-air, no longer firing, no longer descending, guns no longer aimed into the house.

Orion's head, the round center of the drone, shifted. Its dual gun barrels split and swiveled to aim in opposite directions. A series of paintballs, four, to be exact, fired in quick succession. Each paint bullet whizzed through the air, then stopped abruptly, now a hovering splatter. Orion had just gotten four smaller drones that then appeared.

I took the opportunity to climb into the dumpster.

"Who's left?" I whispered to Diamonds.

"One drone, Escondido, and Harly."

"'Harly'?" I asked out loud, surprised at the nickname.

"Captain! Orion heard you!" Diamonds said in my earpiece, but it was too late. I'd spoken too loud. A couple of paint bullets pinged off the side of the dumpster. Orion was coming for me, and I was trapped like a bug in molasses.

"Get out of there, Captain!"

"What's the nearest metal object?" I asked Diamonds.

"What?"

"Nearest metal object, something heavy."

"The rocket is northeast of you."

A sliver of light poured into the dumpster as the lid cracked open, grasped by Orion's claw arm. As Orion lifted and the stripe of light widened, I set the Throne to magnetize, pointed it northeast, and turned the magnet on to full blast. The dumpster squealed and jerked, and I tumbled within. The cover slammed shut as the big tin box lurched into motion.

The dumpster sped across the hangar floor and crashed into the rocket, the momentum popping open the hinged lid, sending the Throne and myself into the air. The Throne's emergency protocol went into effect again, shifting into the old chair to save me, but I had other ideas.

"Floatboard!" I commanded, somehow landing on my feet atop the flying board.

A string of paintballs whizzed past, hitting the crashed dumpster and rocket. Orion was right on me. I banked around the two-story house, hoping the remainder of the Throne hadn't been paint-balled.

Pushing the floatboard to accelerate, I took aim at Orion. The drone was still firing paintballs into my wake as the floatboard sped on, cutting the air, closing the distance, and flying right into the seeker drone.

I leapt off.

Hunks of black plastic and rotors flew every which way as Orion and the floatboard collided.

Explosion.

I hadn't expected an explosion, and I'd certainly never been this close to one. I could feel heat wash over me; the impact of it like a punch in my gut. As I flew back, the remainder of the Throne crashed out of the front door of the house, already transformed from a duplicate me into a smaller antique chair. I slammed into the seat as it scooped me up and away from the blast.

The splattered floatboard and the drone collapsed into a mangled heap on the ground, smoldering. The session was over.

I raised my arms in victory, expecting a surge of cheers and clapping from the sideline of scientists, but they were silent. After a flash of orange gridlines, the floatboard was a minicube once more, half of the Throne, unharmed from the explosion. Escondido and Harla got out of their respective vehicles, stunned looks on their faces. In fact, everyone's mouth hung open, eyes wide.

"What is it?" I asked as I awkwardly lowered my arms.

"That was our only Seeker," Escondido answered. "You weren't supposed to tamper with it."

I'm pretty sure Harla and Diamonds were smiling.

Harpreet attacked Orion's remains with a fire extinguisher, and Escondido got on his phone immediately. Harla and Diamonds tried not to laugh and failed.

Dr. Bird tried to continue nonchalantly, "Moving on. It's time for game theory, so have a seat, please."

The sprinkler system in the hanger engaged, showering us in cold water, while the fire alarm whooped with a siren and strobe light.

Chapter 15

Once the fire alarm was reset and the team dried off, Dr. Bird set us back to discussing game theory.

"Game theory, like zero-sum games and mutually assured destruction?" I asked, trying to think of any time I'd heard the phrase.

"You're too smart for your own good sometimes, Captain. We need to talk about the game. The Military Camouflage Challenge. The MC Two. Its history—"

Harla interjected, "The Em-Cee Two? Nobody calls it that."

"Everyone calls it the MC Two," said Escondido.

"I just call it that because that's what you called it, sir," Dr. Bird said to him.

"Everyone calls it that." Escondido furrowed his eyebrows, then asked, "Why, what do you call it?"

"It's the MC *Squared*, fool!" Harla laughed and pointed at the serious man.

Escondido thought about it for a moment, arms crossed, that sour expression on his face, then let out a low rumble. His shoulders started to bounce. I'd never seen him do this. Escondido was…laughing. The whole team joined in.

"Y'all fools at NASA called it the MC Two?" Harla hooted, barely able to breathe.

Escondido could only shrug as he laughed.

"Can we get back to the lesson?" asked Dr. Bird, doing her best to keep a straight face. "The MC *Squared* is more than just hide and seek. It's a strategy-based tradition with a rich history. And to play the game to the fullest of your potential, you'll need to understand that history—"

Escondido jumped in, "Politics."

"Players," added Harla.

"History," Diamonds muttered out loud, but not to anyone in particular.

"Yo, Bird already said history," said Harla.

But Diamonds didn't seem embarrassed. Instead, they looked at me with a twinkle in their eye and said, "Very important."

"So today," Dr. Bird continued, "we're going to begin with the history of…" Dr. Bird's eyes darted to Escondido, then back to me. "The history of your grandfather in the game."

The lump in my throat came back. Not that it ever went away, not completely, but I had gone long enough without thinking about Grandad I'd forgotten about the lump.

It crawled up to the back of my mouth. I tried to swallow it down, but it didn't budge. I concentrated on the lesson to distract myself from that cold quivering feeling of sadness, that thing that lived inside me now.

"To protect the player's identity," Bird continued, "we use handles or nicknames. Your grandfather went by SteelCut. And Captain SteelCut was the most successful contestant in the game's history."

"For decades, your father reigned as champion," Escondido

paused to let that number sink in. "Twenty-four games. The second-most games won is Captain Holter winning four games. The second-longest winning streak was Captain Primo with three."

"*Twenty-four* games?" I was flabbergasted. "He won against nine other players, twenty-four competitions in a row?"

"SteelCut was the k ing of hide and seek," said Dr. Bird. "Today, we're going to cover technology and capabilities. Steel-Cut preferred vehicles over apparel, telepathy, or organics. He started with the electric thin screen car, which depended on technology similar to the Throne's projection mode, and revolutionized cooling systems.

"Next came the thinscreen buggy, followed by the thinscreen tank, all of which ran on batteries. The shifter tank was next, the first nuclear-powered vehicle. Then came the nuclear thinscreen shield. Then, for the following eight years, SteelCut alternated between shifter vehicles and thinscreen shields, but was always held back by one problem."

Everyone's attention drifted over to Harpreet, who smiled and shrugged, "Not enough power, dude."

Dr. Bird nodded. "Until SteelCut and Harpreet stumbled upon the Lack and learned to harness its energy. Using power from the Lack, your grandfather won three years ago without using a vehicle for the first time ever."

"What did he use instead of a vehicle?"

"A device known as The Parasol," Dr. Bird replied.

"Like an umbrella?" I asked.

"Exactly like an umbrella. He used thinscreen technology, powered by the Lack, which allowed projector mode and basic light warping. He almost lost that year, but he didn't, and for the next five games, his vehicle incorporated both thinscreen technology and shape-shifting."

"The Throne," I said as I realized it.

"Yes! Named because SteelCut was the king."

"And also to clown on Captain Holter," added Harla. "Turns out, American generals got a problem with kings."

Dr. Bird continued, "And utilizing the Throne, SteelCut won four more games in a row."

"Five," I corrected. "You just said he rode the Throne for five games."

Everyone looked around the room, at each other, at the ground, anywhere but at me. "What?" I asked.

Escondido finally answered. "He…didn't win his last competition."

I knew what Escondido was going to say; he was going to say because Grandad died. The lump in my throat grew bigger, and my face was getting hot. Then Harla's voice peeped in, and it calmed me, "Escondido won that game. He's reigning champion."

"And you're not playing this year?" I asked him.

"I've got my team," Escondido said firmly.

"And that's the history of SteelCut in the MC Squared," Dr. Bird concluded. "Any questions?"

My heart jumped as I immediately saw my opportunity, finally, to talk to Harpreet. I tried to sound calm as I asked, "I guess I just want to learn more about the Lack."

Again, all eyes drifted to Harpreet, who nodded knowingly like he'd been expecting such a request since the day I walked into the hangar.

* * *

I walked with Dr. Harpreet Verma, who did more of a shuffle in his worn old sneakers and yet another vintage pro wrestling tee, until we came to a park bench on the hangar floor.

"What can I do for you, Cap?" He checked his phone before pocketing it again.

"I need to learn about the Lack."

"The Lack, yeah. Clean, abundant, pain-in-my-ass energy source, dangerous as all get out. Let's see…about three decades ago, your peepaw and I—"

"My peepaw?" I asked.

"Or whatever you Southerners call grandfathers. What'd you call him?" Harpreet asked.

"Grandad."

He shrugged. "Weird. Anyway, your peepaw and I were working on a perpetual motion machine, you know, just for fun. I figured a tiny fission reactor could do the job. Your peepaw was going to use little particle dudes suspended in an ionic vacuum.

"Well, we weren't getting it done, and we were pretty down on ourselves. Long nights at the lab, probably got a little sloppy, and, well, blah, blah, blah, there was this tiny nuclear meltdown."

The horror must have shown on my face, but Harpreet continued the story, "In order to chill the damage, your quick-thinking peepaw contained the meltdown in his ionic vacuum. We tried to dispose of the whole mess within a quantum energy field. Then with a magnetic field. Then a gravitational one. But instead, by the end of the whole thing, we accidentally created, or discovered, the Lack.

"The Lack is a quantum vacuum. Not only does it lack matter, but there is no recordable energy within. No radiation.

It doesn't conduct sound or light. It *lacked* anything. We can't measure gravity, or even space, within this glowing orange quantum field, containing an ionic vacuum, containing a fission meltdown."

I stared at him. "So what is it, then?"

"Well, we don't know, bro. The only way to define it is by classifying what it isn't. What it lacks."

"And it gives off energy?"

Harpreet tried to explain, "It sat dormant in the lab for years. Several labs, really. It was in this box, glowing orange, as we moved from one game to the next, from one lab to another. Until one day, we had a problem with the thinscreen shield, and when it ran out of power, it started siphoning off energy from the glowing orange box. We spent the next several months stabilizing the fields until the Parasol was field-ready."

I took a moment to try to sort through this in my head. "So if Grandad fell into the Lack, you think it vaporized him?"

"I honestly don't know, dude. When the Throne morphs into a smaller object, like the floatboard, all those little cube dudes have to go somewhere. I like to think the Lack is some sort of dimensional rift, and ol' Peepaw SteelCut is still out there, wandering the multiverse."

Wow. Of all the possible things I'd figured happened to Grandad, multi-dimensional transport wasn't one of them. For some reason, it made me feel better knowing Grandad could be out there somewhere, quantum-leaping through existence.

"Thanks for talking to me. You're real smart. I've never heard anyone so smart that talked like you."

"That's kind of a real crappy thing to say," Harpreet stopped chuckling. "Dude, that's bias. And it sucks to hear someone say you don't sound smart.

I deflated, "I'm sorry, Harp-"

"And you said something like that to Harla, too. That thinking is straight racist. Inherent social bias. And yeah, we all got metric tons of them, and some people think dudes like you with accents sound dumb, but when people are biased against you and your accent, they laugh it off. I saw them laugh it off when SteelCut talked like a hick but won every game. When people get biased against someone like me or Harla, we lose jobs or don't get into schools."

I was so embarrassed. How could I have said something so stupid? So racist? I didn't mean it to be, but that was part of Harpreet's point. I stuttered, grasping for some kind of apology that didn't make me look or feel worse.

I think Harpreet took pity on me, taking a deep breath, then talking to me frankly, "Bro, you got to watch out, biases are totally impossible to see. They warp your thoughts around them, so you can't see them, just like a bend in light. Other dudes can see them. In fact, you got to depend on other dudes to point them out to you. Then, we just got to listen.

"As a kid from the middle of nowhere with that accent you got, there's gonna be a lot of people who are going to think you're dumb. It'll happen when you meet the other captain dudes at the Ball. You have to use it to your advantage, bro. Or they'll eat you alive. Maybe literally."

He didn't *literally* mean "literally," did he?

IV

Part Four

The Ball

Chapter 16

The Ball became the next big thing to talk about, no matter how much Escondido and Dr. Bird stressed the importance of sessions.

Harla talked about what people would be wearing.

Diamonds wondered in what city it would be held.

Harpreet mused which of the captains would be the first to threaten to hurt me.

It was another conversation where I didn't have anything to say. I just laughed at everyone's jokes, nodded, and tried to listen. Once I noticed how many conversations were about telling me what to prepare for, warning me who was most dangerous, I barely spoke at all. I just wanted to get to it—get to the game, and get to the player who saw Grandad last. The General.

That last week at the office, sessions were grueling against Harla and Escondido, who was reigning champion for good reason. I actually found myself looking forward to the game theory lessons from Dr. Bird, and I've never looked forward to a class in my life.

One day, Harla acted as Seeker, and I was found three times

before noon. Splitting off with Dr. Bird for game theory, we talked about the history of DARPA, the government agency that ran the MC Squared. Meanwhile, I didn't notice Harla and Diamonds had walked off together.

After I'd shared with Harla what I learned from Harpreet about the Lack, I had hoped she abandoned her mistrust of the rest of the team. Unfortunately, Harla found out how the Throne must have found me.

During lunch, I ate alone on the hangar floor, a habit left over from the school lunchroom. When I headed back to the team, I heard a voice whispering, begging.

I was surprised to turn the corner to find the voice belonged to Diamonds.

"Then quit the team, or don't, I don't care! Learn to like Escondido, or at least get along with him if you want to stay on the team, but I didn't do anything!"

Harla's glare went from burning holes into the red-faced navigator to me. I instinctively ducked to hide.

"Oh, no you don't corn-pone! This isn't about you, Chay-Z!"

My ears were on fire, and my stomach jumped somersaults when Diamonds' teary eyes looked up to mine, angry, hurt and ashamed. I couldn't bear to look at them, at either of them, and I rushed past to get back to the computer terminals.

"That's right, fool!" Harla yelled. "This is between me and D about who they decided to give my inheritance to!"

That part confused me. Were they arguing about me? But I wasn't sure if I was something they were arguing over, or if I was something in the way of their friendship.

However the conversation went, Hunt and Harla rejoined us after the break, after having cleaned up and calmed down. I had the feeling the argument wasn't over, but the two of them were too good at their jobs to let it affect them. As I came to find out, though, Harla *was* affected.

That afternoon, as Escondido and I were the last ones in the game, he shifted to the offensive and got ahold of the Throne by the chair leg with his stick bug's mantis-like arm, throwing me in the line of Harla's paintball fire. I managed to regain control without crashing and splattering on the hangar floor, but I was out.

Only, Escondido and Harla kept playing.

Normally whenever I'd gotten out, the session was over. But today, Escondido and Harla didn't stop. They kept on for *hours*. Again, I had that feeling things were happening out of my control, without my input.

The team watched for a while, at least the exciting parts, but not when Escondido found hiding spots as Harla lost her temper seeking. Eventually, everyone went back to business, attending to the Throne or studying. When Harla would flip a car or kick loose a fire hydrant, everyone would look up for a second before going back to what we were doing.

Dr. Bird and I were in the middle of a second game theory lecture when Harla gave up at the end of our scheduled workday.

They left the hangar in shambles. Like a war zone, smoking rubble everywhere. The second floor of the house was demolished, the dumpster flipped over, the rocket had launched and blown a hole in the hangar ceiling.

Escondido and Harla calmly got out of their vehicles, which were dented, bent, smoking, and leaking lubricant and fuel. Escondido was bleeding above his eyes. Harla had a busted lip.

"Wow, you two leave everything on the playing field, huh?"

Dr. Bird asked, chuckling uncomfortably. Both the players, still catching their breaths, said nothing as they walked into the garage, shed their gear, and got in the van.

I couldn't tell whether Escondido and Harla were mad at each other or just exhausted from the session, but neither said anything the whole way home.

As I went to get out, Dr. Bird stopped me. "Captain, have you been reviewing the Throne's manual?"

I nodded yes.

"Then it's time for some more interesting study material." The serious woman smirked a bit as she handed me an official-looking manila envelope, covered in diagonal red stripes with the words "Top Secret Classified DARPA" stamped on it.

Once safely home alone in my room, I opened the envelope, breaking three official seals to do so. A slim booklet printed on glossy paper slid out. It reminded me of an instruction manual for an appliance. Words splashed over an American flag on the cover read, "MILITARY CAMOUFLAGE CHALLENGE BALL."

Inside listed the ten teams, each of their sponsoring companies, their camouflage technology, and a blurb about the team's captain.

Powers, Limited's page displayed a photo of the Throne, a list of all of the challenges Grandad won, and a question mark in place of the current captain's photo and blurb.

Flipping through the rest of the contestants, I was surprised to see that, page after page, each captain had a secret identity protected by similar question marks. Only General Holter showed his face.

Holter's eyes stared forward with a dark dead stare, like some bird of prey. His thick jaw clenched, his lips tightened firmly, but somehow he seemed at ease. His dull green uniform was as decorated as a Christmas tree at a mall. His skin was tan as a penny, like a thick hide or armor, each wrinkle a scar from some battle he'd won at great cost. His blurb was even more intimidating.

"Two-star General Esau W. Holter of the United States Marine Corps, US military advisor to the United Nations, and former advisor to the President, believes the purity of the game has been lost, and anticipates restoring the military exercise to its former glory, devoid of civilians, private-sector technology, and most of all, children. Operating Battlesuit 9.4x sponsored by the Department of Defense."

I gulped hard and remembered the gameplay footage from the last MC Squared. Desert Camo Optimus Prime. And he'd be coming after me.

Flipping the page, I tried reading about the next contestant, Captain Mars, with his question mark for a profile pic, but my mind kept wandering back to Desert Camo Optimus Prime. The wrinkly tan sheer of General Holter looking out the windshield chest of the huge Transformer, taking aim with wrist guns, hands converting into cannons, and missiles coming up from his shoulders. He fired. BLAM!

My eyes popped open as I gulped for breath. I was drenched in sweat down to my sheets. I'd drifted off to sleep, but now, it was morning and the van was in the driveway. The Military Camouflage Challenge Ball Guide file was still open to the list of participants.

Fall MC² Competitors:
  (new competitor)/Powers, Limited
  Captain Mars/Trillions Solutions

119

(new competitor)/NASA
Captain Mist/Mayhew, International
Captain The Warrior/LAPD
Captain Stab Whisper/Shadow Systems
Captain Shinobi/Einstein Society
Captain Kamaeleo/Shanglebranch
Captain Furcifer/BTU
General Esau Holter/Department of Defense

Chapter 17

That morning marked the last full day of training, two short days before the MC Squared, so I tried to be nice to Mom. Three days away would be tough on her. I took my time eating breakfast with her, letting the team wait in the van. She asked about plans for the day, and even though I kept it vague, she was so interested in everything I had to say, anything I took the time to say to her. She smiled when I talked. My teammates smiled at me all the time, but when she smiled at me that morning, it made me feel warm. I hugged her extra tight, and thanked her for the hot breakfast.

* * *

The "goop-gate" didn't take us to the office. Instead, we landed in yet another garage, although this one wasn't empty. A wall-sized screen had pictures of different people, with a long list for a caption. I recognized the program pic of Holter, but none of the others.

"I wasn't sure if you had the chance to peruse the contents of the envelope you received yesterday," said Dr. Bird.

"The General," Diamonds said.

Without realizing, I'd drifted over to his photograph, mesmerized. Hearing Diamonds' voice, I snapped out of it.

Ten photos in all. Most were blurry surveillance snapshots of pale guys with military haircuts. Past the photos were two rectangles the same size, each with a question mark inside. Past the rectangles was my school picture, the one where I was frozen dumb-looking, mid blink.

"These are all of the contestants of the fall MC Squared," Dr. Bird explained. "We won't be releasing your photo, Captain."

"These photos weren't in the program," Harla said.

Escondido said carefully, "These pictures were obtained from…outside sources."

"Technically, it breaks no rules," Dr. Bird said.

Harla butted in, "It's not *not* cheating, though."

I wondered what other teams were doing. Maybe even research on me; that technically broke no rules. I knew better than to say something.

The list below Holter's picture showed his preferred equipment as the vehicle BattleSuit 9.4x plus apparel and that he was a highly aggressive player.

The other six white guys pictured were all classified as aggressive players with codenames like "Kamaeleo" and "Spectrum." They used equipment and apparel with nonsense names like "Scatter Swarm" and "Fracture Shield," sponsored by companies I'd never heard of — Shadow Systems and Mayhew International. One contestant, Spectrum, who used the Scatter Swarm, was sponsored by NASA.

"That's my old team," Escondido said as I read about team

NASA. "I don't know what the Scatter Swarm is, but if it's anything like my old stick bug, it'll be a vehicle with classic camouflage technology to mask its tracks, noise, heat signature, or smell."

The Seeker would be tracking my *smell*? I was suddenly aware of how long three days was going to be, in the field, away from a bathroom.

Among the nondescript white guys was a young girl, even younger than me, with Asian features and her hair in a bob. She wore a frilly pale yellow dress, and a pair of antennae stuck out the top of her headband. "Captain Mars" worked for Trillions Solutions, Inc. She used telepathy apparel and was a neutral aggressor. I swallowed hard.

The first question mark contestant was from the Boston Technological University. "They're crazy about clones. It'll be clone technology," Harla chimed in.

The other question mark represented the Einstein Society, a think tank of geniuses. "They sometimes rotate one of their members into the game, but there's no telling what they'll do," Dr. Bird said. "But they'll be dramatic about unveiling it at the Ball. And it'll be something we probably haven't thought of."

That ended up being the topic for the rest of day: reviewing prospective competitors. Quizzing on technologies and techniques. Repetition of names with their sponsors. And always talk of the Ball.

"Unfortunately, the Ball is mandatory," explained Dr. Bird, "and not only is it something you have to do, it's something you have to do alone."

"When I'm captain," Harla said, "I ain't going to mingle with no General, a telepath, and the six stooges all by myself!"

123

"Unfortunately," Dr. Bird said again through a fake smile complete with furrowed brow, "the Ball is mandatory."

"I'll be in your ear," Diamonds reassured me.

"Much like in the competition," Dr. Bird continued, "the Ball is technically anonymous. So you can hide your face. You'll be allowed to wear a helmet, should you so choose."

Dr. Bird gestured to the photos of Captain Mars and General Esau Holter, both choosing to show their identity on the playing field.

"Ha!" teased Harla. "You got to wear that stupid helmet in public!"

Not only did Harla's opinions and insults really tick me off, but I was doubly ticked off I even cared what Harla thought.

"Stupid?" Escondido said, honestly stunned. "It's a fighter pilot helmet!"

That got Harla howling. I felt my face get hot, and my ears burned. A hand landed on my arm. It was Diamonds calming me down.

Suddenly, Harpreet chimed in with a thought. "Wear the minicube, dude."

"And show up as Todd Fowler?" Harla tittered. "Can you imagine little man as Todd Fowler!"

"It's easy to joke when you're not out there," I muttered to myself, sick and tired of everyone making light of everything.

"Captain—" Escondido started.

Not another lecture or scrap of advice. I could not stand one more time someone talking to me to their heart's content while my only job was to sit there and process it without an original thought between my ears.

Talking to everyone for the first time in I-didn't-know-how-long, I said, "No! Stop calling me that; I'm sick of it. You're

124

not out there. It's so easy to talk and joke about things when you're safe in mission control, and all of these things, all of this training is easy to do in a hangar against Orion, but what about when we're on the field? And I'm alone? For three whole days?"

Escondido didn't look at me. That sour, disappointed face grimaced at something in the hangar, maybe a burn mark on the wall.

"We'll all be on the comms, sir," said Diamonds.

"But not in the field. Not in danger like me."

"It *could* take even longer for the Seeker to get everyone," said Harla, shrugging and tilting her giant black and red afro. "It just *usually* goes about three days."

My nostrils flared as I said through clenched teeth, "That's supposed to make me feel better?"

"Calm, dude, there's tons of emergency measures to keep you safe," said Harpreet.

"The game is designed to be non-lethal," offered Dr. Bird.

"But all y'all think it killed Grandad!"

"You think you're the only one who lost him?" Harla's voice rang out. She stood with her hands clenched, fuming. "You think I wouldn't kill to have your spot? Just to have your problems?"

"Enough." Escondido put a stop to the argument before it escalated. "We need to concentrate on the Ball and keeping Captai...keeping Chase safe."

Everyone got very quiet, moping as they removed their lab coats. I was still pissed at Harla. She always went out of her way to embarrass me in front of the team. Always teasing. She was just angry I'd been made Captain instead of her. Just jealous SteelCut was my Grandad.

I immediately felt shame when I thought of Grandad, bringing him into this. Now I was angry at Harla, the team, and myself. And they were the only ones who could keep me safe during the game.

I didn't say a word while getting out of my flight suit at the lockers, gooping up, or piling into the van. I just stewed, thinking about it all

When the van drove through the goop-gate from the Powers, Limited office to the garage by my house, I knew I had to speak up or tears would gush out. I was mad, pissed, and hopeless this thing I'd spent all this time on wasn't getting me any closer to finding Grandad.

And what if they were right? What if he was dead?

"I'm quitting the program," I said.

The van filled with a wave of reactions.

"No!" Dr. Bird protested.

"Now, Captain, this is—" Escondido started.

"You damn fool!" Harla laid in to me. I immediately felt my temper ignite, inhaling sharply through my flaring nostrils while my ears burned red hot.

With a warning glance, Diamonds stopped me from saying another word. They sighed, holding eye contact with me, and then said quietly, "Captain, can I talk to you? Alone?"

I felt more in trouble having to talk to Diamonds about this than anyone else, like when the quietest guy in the martial arts movie steps up to fight last, and you just know he'll be the toughest.

We stepped out of the goopy van, the garage air thick with the oily cotton candy smell. The muted headlights through the goop provided little light, but I could see Diamonds from their pale skin. I stood not two feet away from them, dying, waiting for them to say something. For a moment, I thought they moved toward me, the beginning of a run, breaking out in a sprint toward me, rushing. I blinked hard, wondering what would make me think that. I chalked it up to nervousness about the Ball.

After about forever, Diamonds spoke, dropping the even tone that was such a mainstay of their voice, whispering in their upper register, "Don't be a brat, Captain."

I was shocked and tried to cover it by feigning hurt. "Excuse me?"

"Excuse yourself," they said in high, hushed tones. This wasn't like them. This was different. This tongue-lashing was fast, passionate, and unrelenting, "You can't quit on us. You signed up for it. You took the Throne on a joyride and acted all sweet and innocent when the team showed up at your front door. You agreed to join, got your parents to agree. And now, now that we're *so* close, you say you quit? You can't! Without you, there's no team."

"What about Harla?"

"What about her? Everything's decided, Chase! The forms are filed. You're the team captain for this year. If we sit out, it puts us behind on intel and tech, if we can even convince them to restart the program after that. So, stop being a spoiled brat. Suck it up."

I couldn't look at them and ran my hands over the valves of the spacial lubricant tanks. Diamonds ducked to make eye contact with me, their eyes fierce, their voice quavering, "Your granddad? He recruited me after I got kicked out of a science school for the gifted. Chances are I couldn't get accepted into any sort of academy even if I tried."

I didn't know what to say for a second, then asked quietly,

"What did you get expelled for?"

"I didn't get expelled. I was asked not to come back. Because of 'remedial social skills.'"

"Because you're trans?"

"Because I'm quiet! Introvert to a painful extent. And I'm not trans, I'm enby."

"What's en-bee?" I asked. I had never heard this term before.

"Non-binary."

"So you don't have like, a..." I didn't want to have to say the word.

"What's between my legs is none of your business!" Diamonds barked at me. "Would you want your...penis to be a topic for team discussion?"

My stomach tensed. Dr. Bird was the only one on the team who for sure knew my...prepubescent secret. But what if she said something? She and Harpreet seemed like friends, they might have talked about stuff like that.

Diamonds continued, going back to their calm, even voice, "As long as I'm on the team, I get to study with Dr. Bird in the off-season, getting enough credits to transfer into college. If the team sits out a game, maybe we lose funding, there'll be no R&D department, no team. And I'll go to a recommended schooling facility equipped to handle 'special behavioral cases' like mine."

I didn't know what to say. Suddenly, I realized there were four other team members with their own reasons to be on the team, and I just threatened to fire them all.

"At some point in time, you're going to have to stop hiding from everything and find your reason for being in this game. And it's OK if it's just to help out your team. But it can't be because you're sad about losing SteelCut."

Once they brought him up, knowing we were speaking in private, I had to know if they were keeping something secret. "When I asked you what you thought happened to him, to Grandad, over the comms you said you couldn't talk about it. Why?"

Light glinted off the tears in their eyes. They whispered, "Because Escondido blames himself. And I'm still sad about losing SteelCut, too."

They went back to the van, and I followed, neither of us saying anything further. But we didn't have to. In the van, Harpreet was panicking about going back to his parent's lab. Everyone quieted as a knowing nod passed between Diamonds and Escondido. Nobody said another word as we drove home the last time before the Ball.

Chapter 18

"So this session will be the closest situation to gameplay yet," Dr. Bird said the morning of the Ball, as I hid yet again in the hot water heater in the now-one-story house on the hangar floor. "Remember, Escondido and the PhasmatodeaX, the insect vehicle, won last year. That means the Seeker in this MC Squared will be DARPA's attempt to recreate that technology. It may not be a stick bug, but rather something that uses all of the same technology. Or, it may just be a stick bug."

I imagined a stick bug ten times the size of Escondido's, as big as Godzilla. I swallowed hard and checked my cheeks for sweat. Luckily, Diamonds wasn't still upset with me for quitting last night and spoke up, "Last game was played in desert conditions, and the year before was the Arctic, so I think this will be a built-up area, a bigger population fingerprint. They generally don't do cities. The habitat of a remote indigenous people would be my guess."

Picturing the Kaiju stick bug walking through the canopy in the Amazon, trees coming a third of the way up its thorax, crushing huts under insectoid feet, I imagined the sudden pain and death that would come under its giant foot.

"Who's going to be piloting it?" I asked.

"Who's going to be piloting what?" Dr. Bird asked back.

"The stick bug."

"Oh, no one." Dr. Bird pulled up schematics of Escondido's old stealth vehicle, saying, "The Seeker is controlled by a computer. Self-driving, like Orion."

"The Seeker is going to be a stick bug robot AI?"

"The Seeker is going to have limitations just like any contestant. Compared to the Throne, the PhasmatodeaX is slow, in motion and camouflage. It also can't fly or shapeshift."

"Unless dude gets upgraded," Harpreet said.

"How do you think I'll do?" I asked.

"*We*, Captain," Diamonds corrected me, "We are a team."

I couldn't help but smile at them as I asked, "How do you think *we*'ll do?"

"I think we'll come in third or fourth."

Wow, they put it bluntly. My smile faded.

They assured me, "There's nothing wrong with coming in third or fourth, Captain."

"Bird said my Grandad won dozens in a row and lost his last game. How'd he do in his first game?"

"He came in tenth place," Diamonds deadpanned.

"Tenth?!"

"Yeah," answered Harpreet, "SteelCut was pissed. Fowler called him into a meeting the next day, and then fired the whole team. SteelCut hand-picked them from then on. Demanded complete control of hiring. Started the Internship program to recruit young dudes, students, before education ruined them."

I couldn't help but laugh. Grandad always said that. 'You

learned how to learn as a kid, and then education ruins you.' Through the speaker, I heard Diamonds laugh, too, in their quiet, demure way.

Then they said in a serious tone, "I'll talk to you about your grandfather, Captain, but I don't think he's coming back."

It shocked me Diamonds would bring it up now, during a session. And then I realized who wasn't on the comm set. Escondido, the Seeker, was on the playing field. That's how come Diamonds spoke so freely.

"You think he got burned up in the Lack?"

"Difficult to say, Captain. Burnt instantly, transported into space, crushed to a microscopic level, simultaneously melted and boiled…but whatever happened to SteelCut, the truth is, he's not coming back."

And the monster of sadness was back, gripping me tightly by the throat. I was glad no one could see me, but based on my heart rate and breathing, Dr. Bird probably could tell I was on the verge of tears. Diamonds stayed quiet on the other end of the line.

The hot water heater wound up being a great hiding spot, and I sat there for the rest of the day without being caught.

* * *

That night, I stopped by home and changed into my black jacket, a white button-up shirt with one of Dad's only ties—yellow with blue whales, and grey pants with my church shoes.

Escondido pulled me aside before getting in the van. "The only reason I took this job is because I disagreed with SteelCut on one big point."

"What's that?" I asked.

"I didn't think kids had any business in the game."

"Wait. *That's* why you took this job?" I was shocked.

"To prove myself wrong. I thought it was too unsafe. I was certain a child wouldn't survive. So I volunteered, knowing if I pushed you enough, kept you out of your comfort zone, you'd learn to adapt. To keep you safe out there. Plus, I had Harpreet install a dozen more safety features. Because you were just so awful when we started training."

"OK, where are you going with this?" I said.

"When I was piloting, in the Marines, I had a—"

"Wait, you were in the *Marines*?"

"I am a Marine," Escondido replied, in a tone leaving no room for doubt or argument.

"Oh, you're so much cooler now."

"What does that mean?" Escondido asked, sounding a bit paranoid. When he saw me cracking a smile, he shifted. He didn't relax, just adjusted his posture. "Anyway," he continued, "I had a good luck charm I had on all my flights except one. The one I crashed."

"You were in a plane crash?"

"A jet crash. That's how I lost my leg." Escondido lifted the one leg of his black pants to reveal a matte black prosthetic leg.

"YOU ONLY HAVE ONE LEG?"

"Do you have zero awareness, Captain? You know what? Forget it. Here. I wanted to loan you these. For luck."

He handed over a jewelry box, bigger than the one in Mom's nightstand. Under the hinged lid, stuck on a square of plastic cotton, shined a golden pin, a pair of golden wings behind a globe and anchor.

The pin felt important, heavy with a responsibility Escondido bore. It wasn't tough to imagine him as a soldier, as a Marine. But was Escondido stepping down as an MC Two Captain and loaning me this pin because he felt guilty Grandad had died? Shaking the thought from my head, correcting myself that Grandad had gone missing, I felt that sadness in my throat along with the heavy gold wings in my palm.

Thankfully, Escondido got back in the van without saying a word.

I put on a brave face to hide being scared senseless about this Ball.

And the game.

And meeting General Holter.

Plus I never knew Escondido was a Marine. I was impressed.

Chapter 19

I had previously thought I worked with a bunch of grown-up professionals. Mature people. Role models, even. But when they caught a sight of me dressed up, they turned into idiots. Diamonds and Harla screeched, tousling my hair and pinching my cheeks, while everyone else catcalled, whistled, pulled at my tie knot, or brushed dirt off my shoulder. I could tell I was beet red.

Once everyone settled down, Harpreet, in a t-shirt designed for some movie or video game called "The Black Cauldron," talked about our arrival. "Here's the lowdown, bro-town. The plan is an entrance that'll outdo the Einstein Society."

"We've received directions from Todd Fowler himself," Dr. Bird said, adjusting my neck tie. "He said to make sure you make a big splash when you get there."

Harpreet continued, "I'm thinking we paint your face, tie a bunch of colorful tassels to your elbows and knees, and you rush in just go, like, totally wild." He looked around at our blank faces. "What? Ultimate Warrior?"

Dr. Bird said, "We have to take advantage of every opportunity to gain an edge. Your game handle and your entrance—pure psychological warfare. Remember, nobody knows the identity of our team captain."

Harla said, "Fools probably think it's Escondido after he jumped ship to Powers, Limited."

"Other rumors include Todd Fowler himself," said Dr. Bird.

"So the reveal that the team captain is a kid is a big one," pointed out Escondido.

"Who'd think Powers, Limited would go all out on some kid?" laughed Harla.

"Have you decided on your handle yet, Captain?"

I stuttered for a moment. Honestly, I hadn't thought of it. I figured they'd either just call me by my name, or a nickname would naturally occur.

Changing the subject, I asked, "I can leave after I've met each captain, right?"

"Right," Dr. Bird reassured me. "And you have a few minutes now to think about your handle."

"Specifically, six minutes." Diamonds said, eyes glued to a laptop. "And now we have a direct video feed of the Ball."

They showed the laptop screen to the rest of the van. The feed displayed a grand ballroom with high ceilings, crystal chandeliers, and shiny marble floors filled with dozens of people milling about, most in tuxedos and gowns, and several in military uniform. Here and there, a person was wearing a motorcycle helmet.

The other captains.

It all was so stuffy and boring except in the corner of the ballroom past a couple of columns, in a big cage, was what looked like...but couldn't be...a dragon.

Filling up most of a cage the size of my bedroom, a long tail curled on the floor outside the bars. It was bigger than a bison but difficult to see through the grainy feed, so I couldn't tell its color.

Before I could ask the scientists what the deal was with the dragon, and why no one was talking about the dragon, there was movement on screen. Descending into the shot, slowly, hovering midair, was our team's Seeker drone with a pair of mounted tanks.

"Orion!" I said.

"Naw, bro, a total rebuild," Harpreet responded. "He flies, but he isn't field-ready yet. That little dude will be at 100% in time to train for the Spring Game."

"*She*'ll be ready. Her name is Artemis," Harla corrected.

On the screen, Artemis went to work. *She* floated over to the nearest wall, near the intricate crown molding, between huge portraits. Presenting two spouts, the drone sprayed the wall with goop.

I smiled with understanding. Harla placed the minicube in my lap. She'd already shown me how to control the surface of the minicube as a helmet by blinking.

"Alright, Captain, what do you want the minicube to be?"

"I don't know. What do you think?"

"Well," she replied, "the Fowler idea isn't trash, but you ain't tall enough, and you ain't got the hoodie or Docs. Maybe like a cartoon caricature of him? Something funny-looking?"

Escondido butted in, "Harla, no! This is all about mind games. He needs to intimidate. The helmet covers the eyes and masks emotion. It gives captains an edge."

I pointed on the screen at a uniformed man I recognized walking around the ballroom floor. "What about him?"

"General Holter is different," Escondido said with either reverence or fear, I wasn't sure. "When you're in the military your whole adult life, the mask that hides emotion is your face."

"Is every captain trying to intimidate people?" I asked.

"Most likely."

"In that case, call me Captain Kiddo."

I whispered a couple of words into the minicube, and it morphed at my command. I slid it over my head. Everyone looked at me like I had an ear growing out my nose.

"Are you sure about this, Captain Kiddo?" Escondido asked me, obviously thrown for a loop.

"This ain't exactly…intimidating, Chay-Z," Harla said.

"It might just be genius," Dr. Bird pointed out. "His size or age *can't* intimidate anyone. An unhealthy disregard for self could prove an advantage. This could make them think he's unhinged."

"Maybe they'll underestimate him?" Harpreet asked hopefully.

"What do you think, Diamonds?" I asked, my voice reverberating through the minicube helmet.

"Captain," they answered with a wry smirk, "I think I just received the updated participant roster, you cool cat."

Fall MC² Competitors
  Captain Kiddo/Powers, Limited
  Colonel Esau Holter/Department of Defense
  Captain Mars/Trillions Solutions
  Captain Spectrum/NASA
  Captain Mist/Mayhew, International
  Captain The Warrior/LAPD
  Captain Stab Whisper/Shadow Systems
  Captain Shinobi/ Einstein Society

Captain Kamaeleo/Shanglebranch
Captain Furcifer/BTU

Escondido floored it, and the goopy van sped off before screeching to a spinning halt. Outside, I heard the string quartet abruptly stop. Someone screamed. One person dropped a glass that shattered on the marble floor.

The van door opened, and I stepped out, adjusting my tie and shooting the cuffs of my shirt. From the shoulders up, I wore an oversized orange cat head. With big, disinterested amber eyes, a pink nose, and a white goatee.

An overhead PA system crackled, then a familiar voice came up. It was Diamonds, speaking evenly, "Participants, sponsors, and most esteemed guests, Powers, Limited is pleased to introduce to you, Captain Kiddo, pilot of the Throne."

There were gasps and a smattering of clapping. The dragon, obviously disturbed by the ruckus caused by the van, hissed and spat, sending guests backing away. One scaly eye caught mine for a moment, wild and angry, and my blood froze.

Chapter 20

Behind me, the van lurched into motion and reversed back into the goopy wall. But instead of crashing, the van and the splotch on the wall merged, like the vehicle had driven straight down into a deep muddy lake. I didn't want to show my reaction seeing the van goop-gate from the outside for the first time, so I blinked the commands Harla had taught me, and my cat helmet yawned.

The ballroom was bigger than it seemed on the laptop. Big, quiet, intimidating and ornate. It wasn't a tenth the size of the hangar, but all of the matching gold-on-white furniture, the string quartet, the jewelry, and champagne flutes, as well as the dozens of strangers, made it much scarier.

Plus the cage with a dragon in it in the corner.

Once the party settled back into motion, I couldn't see the dragon from this side of the room, thankfully. I was afraid I wouldn't be able to keep my eyes off the beast—or, rather, the clone.

"There are hors d'oeuvres at your two o'clock, fifty feet away," Diamonds said in my ear.

"Thanks," I whispered as I made my way there, looking

around the room nonchalantly. No one could see me sweating through my cat helmet. I threw some fried shrimp into my fanged mouth. They fell into the helmet, hit me in the nose, and eventually slid into my mouth. They were good, and it was too bad I had to avoid dipping sauces.

"Captain Kiddo," a masculine voice growled from behind me. A guy in a sleek black tux, his face covered by a motorcycle helmet with a black visor, leaned in as he said, "Just make sure you stay away from the Scatter Swarm on the playing field. Just play the game and stay away from everyone else."

He bumped into my shoulder as he walked by, a move I'd expect from one of the bros from my high school.

"Was that Spectrum?" I asked Diamonds.

Harla answered, "I think the Scatter Swarm is a nano-robotic camouflaging apparel. And yeah, that's Captain Spectrum."

I got another shrimp and found the bar to get a cola.

"How you going to drink that soda, genius?" Harla asked.

"Harla, if you're not going to be helpful, I'm muting your comms," Escondido's stern voice said.

"Captain," said Diamonds, "You can connect multiple straws and run them into your helmet through the cat mouth."

So, standing beside the bar, I pinched a series of small drink straws together. The line of adults getting drinks stared at my cat head, while I craned my neck to see the very top of the dragon's cage.

A man in full military uniform got his drink and marched over with purpose.

"I love it when the enemies bring green soldiers to the battlefield," he growled. Esau Holter, two-star general in the US armed forces, wearing the same decorated uniform as he

141

had in his MC Squared guidebook pic. "You see, son, what most people call luck, I call preparation."

"Captain Holter, right?" I said, knowing from outside my helmet, my cat head appeared to be mewing at the officer.

"Please, call me General Holter. Captain...Kiddo, was it?" He took a long sip of his drink, his grey eyes shooting daggers through my cat eyes. Holter said threateningly, "Well, we'll find out tomorrow how unlucky a player Escondido and his team are forcing onto the battlefield."

He enunciated 'battlefield' in a way that made me picture the bloodiest of scenes. Instead of bumping me as he walked away, he simply looked somewhere else in the ballroom and marched over, acting as if I didn't exist. This guy was good at the intimidation game.

Taking a breath to relax, I made my way through the crowd, keeping my eye toward the one corner, seeing if I could get a glimpse of the dragon. Not knowing if I wanted to catch a peek or not, I felt compelled to. I bumped into the chest of another guy in a tuxedo and motorcycle helmet sloshing and spilling his martini which he wouldn't be able to drink through his closed visor anyway.

Harla said like a child excited for Christmas morning, "Oh, Oh, Oh...is that 'Angry guy'? The guy with the martini, he was the one got hella angry last year, right?"

Escondido sighed with disappointment, "What are you doing, Harla?"

"It's the Angry Guy, right?"

"Yes," Dr. Bird, Escondido, and Harpreet said in frustrated harmony.

"K, Chay-Z. Listen to me. You ain't savage enough for this. So I'm going to tell you what to say and you repeat after me,

OK?"

"OK, but…" And then before I had time to argue, the guy was all over me, neck veins bulging between a tight tuxedo and his black helmet, martini splashing.

"Hey, twerp," he said, reminding me too much of school bullies.

I accidentally chuckled. I really didn't think I'd ever be called a twerp by an adult. This guy was ridiculous.

"Answer like a cat," Harla said.

"Meow," I replied deadpan to the angry guy, before making the cathead yawn, then licking my wrist. Harla laughed hysterically in my earpiece.

"You might as well quit now, you stupid cat. The Warrior is going to win it all."

I repeated each of Harla's insults, trying to match her joke delivery. "'The Warrior'? You call yourself 'The Warrior?' Is your first name 'The'? You know your name as a competitor is 'Captain The Warrior'? Can I just call you 'Captain The'? If we get to be good friends, can I call you 'Thuh'?"

The Warrior's neck flushed bright red, slick with sweat. He was shaking beneath his helmet, giving him a bobble-head effect.

"You're dead meat, cat!" The Warrior gushed.

"I think you mean dead cat meat."

"Dead cat meat…whatever, kid, you're dead."

"Meow."

For a second I thought he was going to hit me, but instead he stormed off like a toddler. I called out after him, "It was nice meeting you, Mr. Captain The Warrior! Cool name! See you tomorrow!"

After that, a couple more doofuses in motorcycle helmets

and monkey suits did their best to talk down to me, but none of it was creative at all as far as bullying went. Besides, I felt myself pulled to somewhere else in the room.

The cage.

I wanted to both run away and and at the same time approach the thing, the monster bigger than the team van. Drawn to it, I made my way across the ballroom to check out the dragon.

Chapter 21

"Is that…" Hunt's voice trailed off.

Harla's picked up, "A clone. Mostly chameleon."

"But chameleons don't change color for camouflage…"

Dr. Bird read aloud, "BTU is proud to unveil Captain Furcifer, a genetically superior clone spliced together from nature's most efficient camouflage. The cuttlefish, the peacock flounder, several cephalopods, and countless spiders were mixed with the base DNA chain of a genetically superior chameleon."

"Where'd you read that from," I asked. "Fantastic Beasts?"

Diamonds made a fake retching sound.

"They updated the guide," Dr. Bird said.

"Why's that dude the size of a Chevy, then?" said Harpreet.

The animal must have recognized me from the goop-gate commotion, because as I approached, it kept an eye on me and crouched. Its scales grew whiter and whiter until it blended perfectly with the wall. Dark gray scales appeared in vertical stripes, mimicking the cage bars. Its prehensile tail wrapped slowly up a cage bar as the chameleon kept one scaly eye on me. My neck hairs stood on end.

"Is someone going to...*ride* it?' I asked.

"No," said Diamonds, the calm evaporated from their voice. "The animal is both the entrant *and* the technology."

I finally understood the "organic" strategy.

"Captain Furcifer," Diamonds confirmed, voice tinged with sadness.

The animal was scared; cages in marble ballrooms weren't natural chameleon habitats. But then again, this was no naturally occurring chameleon. Up close, it looked like a triceratops, a conical head with three horns, only this thunder lizard could change color.

I hadn't considered animals as fellow competitors. In game theory, we had concentrated on footage of SteelCut, always winning. Of course there would be entrants I couldn't have expected.

I went cold, suddenly afraid of whatever the Einstein Society's captain might be. Maybe another animal? Maybe something I'd never think of.

Then I was afraid of all of the competitors' tech. Maybe I'd been underestimating my fellow players.

The dragon's scaly globe eyes kept trained on me as I stood frozen. Suddenly, one of its eyes spasmed to the right, looking past me.

"I think he's cute," came from behind me, a little girl's voice intoned in a sing-song manner. As tall as my shoulder, a little girl stood in a frilly pink dress wearing a Halloween mask of a stereotypical alien: oversized black eyes, no nose, and a big bald dome with green skin. Two antennae poked out the top of her alien head. Under my helmet I cringed from the combination of her bizarre appearance and her high-pitched voice.

"You're a prett-y kitt-y cat," she said. "My kitt-y cat got hit by a car."

"Oh, I'm sorry." I hadn't thought my helmet could trigger any bad feelings.

The girl appeared like she didn't care though, and said with as much emotion as a kid listing the states, "It's OK. Mommy said if I left the back door open, Whiskers would get loose and get hit by the car. It turns out she was right. She also said I'm ver-y curious and make her feel scared sometimes."

The little girl's pale human arms patted the apron front of her floofy skirt as she spoke, and then she skipped toward the chameleon cage, where she pressed her rubber mask against the bars. My skin crawled.

"So…did she let the cat out on purpose?" I asked into the comms, scared of the answer.

"Don't give her another thought," Escondido said. "She's probably not as young as she seems, and that cutesy voice was put-on. She's just trying to get into your head."

"Well, she got into mine," said Harla, "and I'm not even at the Ball. Plus, *sir*, ageism. He said she's 'not as young as she seems…'"

Suddenly, trumpets sounded and the room got quiet. Where had trumpets come from? A team of scientists, adorned head to toe in puffy plastic, gloves, booties, and gas masks rushed around, placing equipment in a circle.

"Who is that? What are they setting up?" I asked.

"It's the Einstein Society. And you're not going to believe this, Captain," Dr. Bird said, "but according to the guidebook, it's a time machine."

Chapter 22

"A time machine?" I asked, wide-eyed.

I'd be terrified if I wasn't so interested. What looked like ankle-high cell-phone towers, about a dozen of them, were all connected with a series of cables. The little pyramids were topped with blinking blue lights.

Once all the towers were connected, the blue lights blinked in unison, and all of the scientists backed away from the circle. The air between the towers strobed, flashing, and the smell of ozone filled up the ballroom. The scientists from the Einstein Society motioned with waving arms to back up all of the Ball attendees a good thirty feet from the circle of lit-up towers. Someone gave a thumbs up, and the lights dimmed until nothing could be seen save for the blue lights topping the pyramids, blinking now faster and faster, counting down as the room continued flashing.

The blue lights changed to red, and the air in the room changed. There was a pressure-change pop in my ears, like when I rode the Throne too high. People gasped and clung to each other in a scared fervor.

A line of electricity appeared, lighting up the ballroom

whitish-blue, jumping from one tower to the next before vanishing. Another bolt connected three towers and reached for a fourth. Suddenly, lightning leapt out among all of the pyramids, like some kind of electric tree. And then, from nowhere in particular, wind. So much wind.

Hairdos, tuxedo tails, and ball gown skirts blew about wildly, and there was now enough lightning to see the room clearly. Ball-goers screamed and dropped glasses as sparks leapt from the circle.

All the lightning bolts converged at the center of the circle, too bright to look at directly, and then went out.

Once the lightning subsided, the flashing blue strobes illuminated a figure standing at the circle's center. The person was clothed in all black, skin obscured except for two fierce eyes.

An honest-to-God ninja. From feudal freaking Japan.

The lights on the towers blinked orange, and the ballroom lights came back up.

Invisible speakers blared, "Ladies and gentlemen, BTU is proud to introduce its team participant as well as technology, Captain Shinobi!"

Within the circle of towers, water vapor danced against the marble. Black soot marred the white tile floor as if someone had lit a campfire. In the middle of the whole kerfuffle, the ninja stood frozen, like a scared deer.

Suddenly, in a blur, his hand whipped out, chucking a small device onto the ground which let out plumes of greenish smoke. Ball-goers covered their mouths and coughed. When the smoke cleared, Captain Shinobi was gone.

"Was that a real ninja?" I asked, excited from the commotion.

The men and women in tuxedos, ball gowns, motorcycle

helmets, and military uniforms searched all around to locate the contestant. Behind columns, statues, above chandeliers and in the corners.

Escondido finally answered, "I think that's a real ninja."

Befuddled, Dr. Bird asked, "Wait. So, they have time travel technology, and they used it to win this camouflage game?"

"That prize money and that fat government contract would fund anything they'd ever want to do," answered Harla. "Just go and ask Todd Fowler."

Harpreet pointed out, "We got technology that can morph into literally anything, dude. And we use it to win this camouflage game."

Diamonds said, "Under the cake table."

I looked about the room, ducked against the bar, sweaty and jumpy and searching for what Diamonds saw.

There. Sticking out from the table's skirt was a small swath of black cloth, maybe a belt or leg wrappings. The white tablecloth fluttered, the black cloth disappeared, and my chest went cold.

Did he see me?

Flying out the other side of the table was a blur, giving off the slightest whisper of a whistle, as it flew across the room before it banked a slight left and chopped a rope holding back a curtain.

With a "SNNNK" sound, a metal snowflake buried into the wall's crown molding. A throwing star. My heart about jumped through my ribcage. Part of me was so excited this guy was real, and so were throwing stars, but the rest of me was scared senseless to be in the same room as him.

The movement of the closing curtain took the room's attention, and everyone looked or pointed, a few brave folks approached the window treatment. Out of the corner of my eye, I caught a black flash and saw the figure ducking behind the dragon…or chameleon.

"Hey, kid!" one gruff voice barked at me.

"What'd you see?!" another hoarse man growled.

I'm pretty sure it was the contestants Kamaeleo and The Warrior.

"Meow I help you?" I asked.

They each tried to look tougher than the other, which didn't work when they spoke at the same time.

"What's going on over here?"

"You see where he went?"

Slowly, I took in each of them with my cat face, then caught my comically long drink straw and sipped cola. I purred. Fuming, they spoke again, simultaneously.

"Nobody makes fun of The Warrior!"

"Captain Kamaeleo always gets his man."

I couldn't help but snicker. "How mad are you that there's an actual chameleon in the game? Much cooler than whatever your technology is."

They stormed off as Harla, sounding very serious and almost apologetic, said, "Chay-Z, I just have to say I was wrong when I said you wasn't savage enough to play mind games."

"That's all the contestants, Captain," Diamonds interjected. "Everybody has arrived."

Escondido said, relieved, "And you've managed to meet all of them except our ancient Asian visitor."

I was about to ask if I could leave and we could go get burgers, but Harla spoke first. "Can we go grab pizza now?"

The dragon's—chameleon's—scaly eye followed me. Its prehensile tail curled around two bars, which slightly bowed together within the reptile's grasp.

Chapter 23

Maybe it was the fact this was my first time in a pizza shop since…well, without Grandad, or if it was that I'd be competing tomorrow against the Army General, the creepy alien girl, a dragon, and an actual ninja. Whatever it was, I had a lot on my mind.

"I'm telling you," Harla was spelling something out to Diamonds, "that ninja dude is great at hiding from low-tech Japanese guards, but won't do nothing against a robo-stick bug."

"I think he's the one to beat," they answered, looking down at their plate of salad.

I pictured the ninja's fiery eyes after his sudden appearance. He wasn't scared, he was angry.

"That chameleon is a ballsy move," pointed out Harpreet as he chewed.

"Come on, the college kids always do clones," answered Harla.

"Yes, but clones the size of dump trucks?" asked Dr. Bird.

"Hyperbole much, Doc? Little dude was wasn't bigger than the van," Harpreet corrected.

My skin crawled thinking about the chameleon's inhuman eyes, with scaly eyelids to the pupil.

"Captains Warrior, Kamaeleo and Stab Whisper," Escondido warned, pointing his pizza crust as he said, "while not memorable in person, are still highly trained soldiers. They will be forces to be reckoned with on the battlefield."

Harla said with her mouth full, "Soldiers ride in companies, in platoons, in regiments. How you think these fools will do solo?"

"General Holter is going to come after me," I said without looking up. Everyone at the table stopped what they were doing and listened. "He wants me out first to send a message. He especially didn't like my kitty face. He's the kind of guy who probably plays better when he's angry."

"I don't hate the kitty face," Harla said.

It wasn't even a real compliment, but I felt an embarrassed bubbling in my gut. I wished I didn't care what Harla Gamble thought of me.

I continued, "The Martian is definitely playing head games with everyone. But I'm the only other kid out there, which makes me a target for her. The chameleon clone, Furcifer, is just a scared animal. He could have all of the natural...or unnatural, advantages, but he's wild, outside his habitat, and will avoid anything he thinks is a predator."

"How do you know it's a 'he'?" Diamonds asked.

"Good point," Escondido said, "Dr. Bird, see what you can dig up on chameleons. Let's identify this thing. Sex, age, life cycle. Anything. And not just chameleons, but everything else they spliced together."

Lowering my voice, I continued, "But Shinobi is the most dangerous."

Everyone shifted in their seats uncomfortably. Dr. Bird finally asked, "Why's that?"

"A highly trained assassin in a foreign setting," I said. "Doesn't know any of the rules. Doesn't even know this is a game. Shinobi knows ancient arts of stealth and murder, and in this case, not much else."

"Technological theatrics should work best," Diamonds said.

"Easy peazy," said Harpreet. "We'll just prioritize pilot safety a little more when the little ninja dude is around."

"And we'll trick the chameleon into thinking you're a predator," said Harla. "Make yourself bigger than it is, show red and black coloring, be aggressive."

At the word, I thought of something, "We should think of how we can use General Fowler's aggression against him."

"Very good, Captain!" said Dr. Bird. She raised her red plastic cup of water to the middle of the table. "I'd like to make a toast, to a great team put together at the last minute, to our Captain Kiddo, who exceeded all expectations of learning SO MUCH in a short amount of time, and lastly, to SteelCut."

Busy fighting back thoughts of Grandad, I'm not sure if I actually said anything when everyone else said in unison, "To SteelCut!"

Then I drank my soda, knowing full well there was a chance it was the last soda of my life.

Tomorrow, I would play the game that took away Grandad.

Chapter 24

Still freckled with chipped paint from all the rocks I'd thrown, the red shipping container drove ahead of the van all the way to the garage. Harpreet banged his head to heavy metal as he steered the big rig hauling the big tin box which held the Throne. A quiet van followed.

Everyone on the team looked good, all dressed alike in uniform, which was generally white button-ups with black suits and ties, probably to match Escondido. Dr. Bird had on a black suit covered by a lab coat. Harpreet's signature t-shirt was one of those printed to look like a tuxedo. Wearing 1950's plastic frame glasses, Harla's black tie and short white button up would have fit in at the launch of the Apollo 11, only with her hair rolled into tight rows making up geometric triangles. She patted her head compulsively.

Diamonds had a long black trench coat over their suit, and a skinny black tie. Their hair was tall and moussed into a bouffant, which brought out the purple streak even more. They even had on eyeliner, and I was afraid I'd blush if I stared too long.

It was dead silent in the van, which felt appropriate. Like

I was some pro athlete focusing before the championship. I just sat forward, elbows on my knees, not really looking at anything while Dr. Bird checked my pulse, heart rate, and blood pressure.

Diamonds broke the silence, speaking evenly without looking up from the laptop, "Two hours to begin. We're getting the coordinates of the playing field now."

Once at the garage, it took forever to coat the entire van, truck, and trailer in spacial lubricant. Between the two vehicles, the smell of cotton candy was so thick I could taste it, wondering how long into the game my gear was going to reek as I suited up in the corner by myself.

"One hour to begin," said Diamonds.

I chewed on my nails until Escondido slapped my hand away. I was picking at a zit on my forehead until Dr. Bird said, "Gross, Captain, don't do that." I nervously tapped my foot until Harla stepped on my toe; though she continued to pat her braids by habit.

Off into the corner by myself, I worked on my breathing. Calming techniques. Meditation. But when I closed my eyes, I saw Desert Camo Optimus Prime taking aim at me.

I started meditation over again, working on breathing before closing my eyes, focusing on the ground beneath my feet. I closed my eyes. Desert Camo Optimus Prime was looking down at me, falling. I was falling...into the Lack.

Holter. Standing at the precipice, Holter saw Grandad riding the motorcycle off the cliff. And shot him. I had to track down Holter during the game and confront him about what happened to Grandad.

With purpose, I suited up, starting with one of Dr. Bird's field medkits. As I drilled captain names, I adhered stickers to monitor my vitals for the duration of the game…in other words, for the next few days. These stickers would be the way the team found out if I died playing the game.

By my locker was a box, wrapped in a bow, about the size and shape of an under-bed storage bin. A tag by the bow read "To: Captain Kiddo. Try this on for size. Love, Your Team." And everyone had signed underneath. Harla's signature had an LOL next to it. Gooping up the van, Harla was threatening to spray Harpreet with the spacial lube, Harpreet pretending to get mad. Everyone was laughing. I couldn't even crack a smile.

Removing the ribbon and opening the box, I saw the gift. So far in training, I'd been wearing an old, worn out bomber jacket and khakis. First off, I was no pilot, so I felt like some wannabe, and the khakis were a part of my idiot school uniform. The gift from the team? A new uniform, the only thing I'd be wearing for the next who-knows-how-long: a brand new brown leather bomber jacket and a fresh pair of khakis.

Great.

No one saw me chuckle a bit as I was pinning Escondido's pilot wings to the uniform that must have been his idea. We had never discussed a uniform change, so I still had my grey camo army boots, matching long-sleeve shirt, and black leather gloves. With a command, the minicube morphed into my cat-head, and I felt like some playable character in StarFox.

We piled back into the lubricated van. "Thirty minutes to begin," said Diamonds.

On the laptop, we watched the gooped up truck as it drove the shipping container through the goop-gate.

Dr. Bird cleared her throat and said, "I meant what I said

at the pizzaria about you being a great student, Captain. So, why aren't you better in school?"

"What?" She wanted to talk about my performance in school? Now?

"Your grades are unsatisfactory. You're smarter than that. Why? Are you trying to impress your friends? Is it uncool to be too smart?"

"I don't know."

"Is it a girl?" Dr. Bird teased.

"No." I felt my cheeks burn and did my best not to look at Diamonds.

"Well, what is it?"

"He's hiding," Diamonds stated matter-of-factly.

"That's not it," I said almost automatically, defensively. But I had the feeling if I thought about it, I'd find out they were right.

"Well?" Dr. Bird redirected the question, "Why have you learned so much better with us than in an academic setting?"

"School is..." I searched for the word as Escondido put the van into drive, then inched forward into the garage wall. Immediately, the sludge covering the windows shone in silver, lit from behind. Escondido parked and opened his door first, revealing this game's location: a sunny subdivision of almost identical two-story houses, all in neat rows with matching yards. I found the word I was looking for. "Boring."

This year's game was in suburbia. Diamonds had been right about a man-made footprint. Cat-headed, I got out of the van and took in the rolling hills of cookie-cutter homes with manicured lawns. The smell of cut grass mingled with cotton candy inside my helmet. The sound of dry autumn leaves made an ever-present white noise.

Big houses on little lots, just like the rich side of the town where I was from, except the trees were different and it was cold for Fall. I didn't know what I was expecting for a playing field, but it wasn't this. The only thing interesting to look at was the series of tractor trailer trucks unloading equipment.

The emptiness of the place was a bit creepy—no happy neighbors walking dogs, no cars sitting in driveways. This subdivision sat empty except for the competitor's teams.

In the sky, about twenty feet up or so, hovered a drone, bigger than Orion. In its belly was a shiny dome, most likely a camera capturing it all. I tilted my feline face upward to give the drone a glance, then yawned with a curl of my cat tongue.

The entire street was bustling with teams arriving and setting up. A beeping noise signaled a forklift backing a cage off a truck. Its tail coiled about the cage bars, the flaps on its neck extended out to look like some lizard-lion hybrid, the chameleon was not enjoying its trip on the forklift. His coloring was at a default bright green, and his scaly eyeball darted around to the trucks, vans, and forklifts populating the street.

From another truck, another forklift backed out another cage, this one housing the ninja, sitting peacefully cross-legged, eyes closed. Although completely still, the black-clad figure gave the impression of a wound up coil, ready to pounce in any direction.

The workers busily buzzing around their vans and trucks gave the ninja's cage a wide berth as the forklift drove ahead to the game's starting positions.

Another forklift joined the chorus of beeping, this one dragging an enormous, fifteen-foot tall robot. The thing was green and brown, colored in splotches, with bulky shoulders, guns (or rather cannons) for hands, and hoof-like feet. Definitely an upgrade from gameplay footage, I still recognized camouflage Optimus Prime.

Its clear chest opened like the lid of a fighter jet, and General Holter, sporting green coveralls and a fighter jet helmet, climbed in, lowered his visor, and strapped his mask across his face. The clear dome in the Battlesuit's chest closed, but I could still see the General within. He stared back at me, and then put up his dukes. In mimicry, the giant robot followed suit, displaying its enormous cannon hands and assuming a fighting stance. The huge transformer threw practice jabs, throwing cannon fists in my direction.

From somewhere behind me, I heard Diamonds say evenly, "Fifteen minutes to begin."

Chapter 25

Getting out of three different unmarked vans, three armored guys stiffly shuffled by, like they couldn't bend their knees or elbows. One looked like a bad Iron Man cosplayer, another was a bad Halo cosplayer, and the third a pretty good Predator cosplayer. All of them walked like they were doing C3PO impressions.

"Captains Stab Whisper, the Warrior, and Kamaeleo?" I asked my team.

Harpreet answered, "I think the dude who looks like a Storm Trooper is Mist."

Dr. Bird added, almost under her breath, "Aggressive. Motorcycle with the Fracture Shield."

"You think he looks like a Storm Trooper?" I said. "I was thinking a Halo soldier."

"I think them three are matching," Harla answered. "They must be so embarrassed they wore the same dress to prom."

An engine revved and a motorcycle jumped out of the back of another truck, swerving to a stop. Like a flat-black street motorbike, a tall shield went from where the windshield should be, almost down to the ground, protecting the cycle's front wheel. I guessed at the technology, "Mist's Fracture Shield?"

"Correct," said Dr. Bird.

"And that's Captain Kamaeleo" Escondido said, moving everyone's focus to a black car pulling up. A contestant in a green and brown ghillie suit bounced out of the door, looking like he was made of pom-poms. The angry guy from the Ball stepped on one of the fabric shreds coming off his feet, tripped, and landed on his face. Harla laughed.

"Miss Harla," Escondido chided. "Don't start grudges against the team."

"Fine," Harla said, unlocking the doors to the red shipping container.

"Ten minutes to begin," said Diamonds, not looking up from surveying the area through binoculars.

"The NASA van is opening," Escondido said with a wavering voice, either nervous or just sad because he missed his former team. The only marked vehicle, the white RV had the spacey NASA logo splashed across its side. The double doors in back swung open, a ramp lowered, and a man clothed head to toe in all white emerged.

"Dude, it's Storm Shadow!" Harpreet laughed until he realized he was the only one to get the reference. Harla rolled her eyes.

"How's that captain going to hide?" I asked about the competitor's bright white getup.

"I don't know, bro, but that's tacky after Labor Day," Harpreet joked as he walked around to the back of the truck. Harpreet and Escondido got into the shipping container and pulled me up. We surrounded the tarp-covered Throne, resting in its neutral cube form for transport.

"Captain," said Escondido, assuming his posture of arms crossed, hand rubbing his face and neck, "do we start as the Throne?"

Dr. Bird suggested, "Maybe the floatboard. You seemed most comfortable on the floatboard."

"What do you think, Harpreet?" I asked.

"Oh, I don't know, bro. Do whatever *you* want to do, dude."

Taking the jelly bean from my jacket, I put it into my ear. "Testing one two three, testing one two three. Captain to Diamonds, Captain to Diamonds, over."

Clear as a bell, Diamonds answered in their calm tone, "Captain, this is Diamonds. I read you loud and clear, over."

"Diamonds," I asked, "is Harla on the comms, over?"

"Miss Harla," Harla corrected. "And during live gameplay, I respond to the handle 'Under,' over."

"Captain to Under, what mode should I start the Throne as, in your opinion, Under, over."

"Under to Captain, Under to Captain, all practice sessions began with the Throne. Stick to the gameplan, over."

"Maybe as the neutral cube," Harpreet said. "After all, the more you morph, the more you're slowing down long-term shift speed."

It made sense, and I heard the guilt in Harpreet's voice, wishing he'd made this point to Grandad. Then Harpreet added with a chuckle, "Over."

I decided to take the cubic Throne out as-is.

* * *

Harla gave me a big hug for good luck, and I got a little flustered when her body pressed to mine. Then, before I could say anything back to her, she followed Dr. Bird and Escondido into the van. Harpreet would drive the red shipping container out of here after placing the Throne.

Diamonds approached me, chewing on their nails, holding out their other hand to shake. I reached out and took their hand, slender and soft, but strong. Firm. They leaned in to whisper. My heart fluttered a bit, and I felt hot in the bomber jacket. In a breathy tone, Diamonds said, "Good luck, sir. Follow the display to your spot in the starting ring. Ten minutes to begin." Then they got into the van.

I turned around to head to the starting positions, when suddenly behind me, standing in the center street, the little girl in the kewpie doll dress and alien mask said in a singing tone, "Good morn-ing, Cap-tain Kit-ty!"

I gasped. She'd snuck up on me so quietly! "Hi, Captain Mars."

"You can call me Mary," she said. I could tell she had a cheesy smile as she spoke, even though I couldn't see through the plastic mask. "Oh, lookie!"

She pointed her childlike hand into the air. Above us, whisper silent, an enormous double-bladed helicopter lowered a giant wooden crate, the size of four of the Throne's shipping containers. Looking up toward the sun, the minicube helmet squinted my cat eyes, dimming the light. Mary stood, hands at her sides, watching the chopper place the crate on a manicured lawn and release its rope. The end of the container, almost the size of the side of a barn, fell open.

Within the shadows of the crate, the sounds of steps boomed and echoed. Its eyes glowed to light an insectoid face. Out of

165

the container, holding on upside down to the crate's roof, a robot stick bug clambered out, its spindly legs clamping on and denting the metal. Flat, dinner-plate eyes of bright white sat on its armored face over individually moving mandibles, like stretching fingers where a chin should have been.

This wasn't Escondido's pregnant log. This stick bug was camouflaged to resemble a wide brown leaf, giant and demonic. Its abdomen and thorax segments were flat, flaring out to points every so often. It had shoulder armor up to its neck and mantis-like front arms. The whole shell, or exoskeleton, of the robot was covered in little spikes and spines, and its thorax even came to a sharpened point. Its cricket head ticked in clockwork spasms until I was sure the glowing eyes could see me, its mandibles in constant hand-wringing motion.

It surveyed each of the teams, then the light faded from its eyes and it powered down.

"Captain?" said Dr. Bird. "You're holding your breath again."

I breathed deeply and tried to relax my shoulders as Harpreet walked my way. He slapped and shook my hand, snapped, then went in for a bro hug, complete with two pats. "Captain, dude, we're all set."

"Thanks, Harpreet."

"Lil bro, remember all of your safety options. I altered the cat helmet so you can open it without taking it off. Just pull the ear."

I did so, and the cat head opened its mouth wide enough to uncover from my mouth to forehead, from cheek to cheek. Like my face was the last piece of me to be eaten by this cat.

"And pull it again, dude."

After another ear tug, the cat maw opened even more, like

the cat was coughing up my head.

His usually too-silly, bouncy demeanor changed to too-serious as he furrowed his brow and cleared his throat to speak.

"There's something I like to say when things get serious or get difficult. 'No talent becomes a legend on their own. Everyone's heart one day beats its final beat. Their lungs breathe their final breath. And if what that person did in their life makes the blood pulse through the body of others and makes them bleed deeper and something larger than life, then their essence, their spirit, will be immortalized by the storytellers, by the loyalty, by the memory of those who honor them, and make the running they did live forever.'"

I found myself clearing my throat, fighting back the monster of sadness, and was about to hug Harpreet for his kind words when he kept going, "You, you, you are the legend makers of Ultimate Warrior. In the back, I see many potential legends."

I interrupted, "Wait, what are you talking about?"

"It's the Ultimate Warrior. The wrestler?"

I rolled my eyes. "Okay, I have to head to the starting positions, Harp."

He looked like he was going to say something else, but instead reached out and pulled at my cat helmet's other ear. The cat's mouth closed around my face. Harpreet nodded and cleared his throat, then he turned to go. Was he crying?

As if he read my thoughts, Harpreet turned, revealing tears streaming down his face. His voice cracked as he shouted, "You are the Ultimate Warrior fans, and the spirit of Ultimate Warrior will run forever!"

He turned to run away back toward the truck. Jogged, really. Diamonds' voice through the comms broke the awkward silence. "Four minutes to begin."

"Under to Captain, go on and get to the starting position. Over."

But I stood frozen, and the eyes of the Robobug glowed again as it sprung to life. Well, it sprang to its starting posting, jumping off four legs straight into the air like a launching rocket. It flew in an arch to land head-down in the yard of a nearby grey house. It seemed silly, like instead of a tree, the yard had a monstrous leaf planted in the ground.

"Captain, you need to get in position," said Escondido.

A circle of ten points around the stick bug lit up, projected from who-knows-where. Ten points for ten players. Starting positions. I found one pointing with a glowing "Kidd0" above it, putting me smack dab between a tree and the grey house. I took my place there, the cube hovering behind me, the minicube still displaying my cat head.

"Three minutes to begin."

The other contestants took their place. I was between Iron Man, who was either Stab Whisper or The Warrior, and the cage holding Furcifer, the giant chameleon. Great. It's just a chameleon, not a killer dragon, I reminded myself. More scared of me than I was of it. It stared at me, bristling, puffing out its neck and cheeks. Hopefully, it was more scared of me. I did my breathing and calming techniques.

"Two minutes to begin."

All the people in the circle faced outward, so I turned around. In front of me, the cube hovered maybe five feet from the grey house, wedged right next to an enormous oak tree.

"Do I have to start facing the house?" I asked, picturing being trapped against the front door of this nice suburban home by a giant man-eating chameleon.

"No," answered Dr. Bird, "it's a common strategy to move either straight up or even across the circle in some instances."

"If I can start this thing as the floatboard, I'm sure I can clear the house," I said. "I think."

"Sixty seconds to begin."

Harla hummed in doubt and said, "I don't think you got the power for both the acceleration and lift to get up over that roof. What you weigh, Chay-Z?"

Dr. Bird answered, "152 pounds."

Across the circle from me, the General's mech suit shifted into motion, crouching. His gun hands moved down to the ground, grasping a small wheel that came out of nowhere. Another two wheels appeared out of his knees, and the cockpit moved forward as the machine kneeled into a three-wheeled vehicle that looked like the lovechild of a fighter jet and a stealth bomber. On wheels. Pointed right at me.

"Thirty seconds to begin."

"Captain," said Escondido, "we need to pick something."

The giant chameleon let out a weird croaking noise, its eye trained on me. It was green to match the lawn, with dark stripes to imitate the bars.

The General's monster three-wheeler revved its engine. Mist revved his motorcycle engine in response. Beside me, Camo Iron Man's jetpack fired up, letting off smoky exhaust.

Panicking, I commanded the cube to morph into the floatboard.

Harla let out a heavy sigh, paused, then said, "Harpreet, we need an acceleration of twenty-two feet per second squared."

"Do we have that kind of power?" Harpreet asked.

Camo Iron Man's jetpack flared a blast of yellow fire, hot enough for me to feel. I jumped and might have screamed a little.

Escondido sounded shook when he said, "I don't know, Harpreet, you're the mechanic. Do we?"

"Fifteen seconds to begin." The calm in Diamonds' voice was starting to get to me.

V

Part Five

The Fall EMC²

Chapter 26

"Three."

"Two."

"One."

All of the blue lights in the circle turned red, just as Diamonds said, "Begin," simultaneously with Dr. Bird reminding me to breathe.

The floatboard and I took off as I leaned back, repeating to myself, "Don't screw this up, don't screw this up," under my breath and careened toward the house. Behind me, the General's engine roared. My back hand reached for my heel as the floatboard pulled up, higher and higher, tipping back as it climbed upwards, coming up to clear the roof.

THUNK.

The nose of the floatboard snagged on the house's gutter.

The board stopped.

I kept going.

My breath caught in my lungs as my body tensed as the world rushed around me

"Captain!" someone shouted in my ear.

I sailed up, past the edge of the roof, over the house. Bracing my body for impact with the tree in the backyard, I averted my eyes and my hands came up in front of me. I prepared to break all my bones.

But then, time stood still.

Actually, time hadn't stood still, but rather *I* stood still…in the air, floating in some kind of wavy cloud. Like the waves heat coming off the asphalt, but concentrated around me, holding me at every angle.

"Emergency measures activated," Diamonds said calmly.

Up floated the Throne, now shaped like the antique chair, scooping me from that quantum airbag or whatever it was. But as soon as my butt hit the seat, the General drove the Battlesuit over the house, crushing a trail of grey siding, black roof shingles, and exposed wood.

In one move, the vehicle popped a wheelie, unfolded a leg forward, and transformed back into the Battlesuit with a cannon hand aimed at me.

BLAM!

A projectile came flying, then opened into a net.

I felt like screaming, or ducking, or curling into a ball, but instead my training took over. I faced upward, and the Throne lifted off, hurtling straight up in the air. My head flew back and hit the wood of the chair, but I leaned out, and stretched up. And up the Throne went. My heart pounded so loudly in my chest, I could barely hear Diamonds' deadpan delivery, "Captain, you have flown out of bounds. Return to the playing field or you will be disqualified."

"Captain, the elevation! The air's too thin up there to breathe!" Dr. Bird yelled.

She sounded very far away. They all did. My body felt far off, too. Like I was floating away…

"Return to playing field in three..."

I meant to listen to them. I meant to turn. But I couldn't move my body. I felt too far away from my body to control it. My eyes drifted closed.

Dr. Bird was yelling again. "He's almost lights out!"

"Two..."

I felt like dozing off, then a falling sensation. I wasn't sure whether I was awake. More yelling. Other voices. All sound was muffled or distant.

"One."

Then I heard something else. Clear and close by. A distinct voice, whispering from right behind me. The old dry rasp of Grandad, hoarsely breathing the word, "Kiddo," into my ear.

My eyes blinked open. I was hurtling toward the ground, falling. No, not falling, being pushed. I realized I was still in the chair, accelerating straight down. I wondered if there was an out of bounds beneath the ground just in case the Throne buried me.

I leaned back with all of my might, pushing against the Throne's high back. My fingers dug into the Throne's arms. I grunted with the strain.

The direction of the Throne changed to an arc as the ground came rushing up to flatten me. The seat of the chair scooped me forward, and suddenly, I was flying parallel with the ground, dragging my toes through the grass for one terrifying moment. Then we were steady, flying ten or so feet above the identical yards in between the similar houses.

I let out a big sigh of relief when a robotic voice called out from behind me.

"You're dead meat, rookie."

I didn't see him until he grabbed a leg of the Throne. It

175

was Stab Whisper or The Warrior, one of the white guys in a motorcycle helmet. In stealth mode, he looked like nothing more than ripples in the air. But I felt his grip on the Throne as he took hold with both hands and swung me toward a nearby house.

Flying right at a window, the Throne spun around, so I crashed chair-first through the glass into the second floor. It was a nice house, furnished, expensive. And for a moment, it felt like I was just in another person's house, maybe spending the night at the rich kid's house. Just normal kid stuff. Then another invisible cosplayer crashed through the wall.

Maybe it was the same white dude in a motorcycle helmet, maybe it was another one. Whoever it was, his suit punched holes in the house like it was tissue paper. His gun hands pointed at me, but I didn't wait around to see them fire. I stood from the chair, ran, and leapt out the window I'd crashed through.

"Floatboard!" I called out, and the Throne's board materialized beneath my feet. I had to get out of there, and I pushed the floatboard to its limits until I was convinced we were in an unpopulated area. Before I caught my breath, I wanted to make sure I was someplace safe. I commanded, "Diamonds, find me a water heater."

They did, and I stood within, catching my breath, sweating, and maybe crying a little. My heartbeat was so loud, I was certain it was audible over the comms. I couldn't hear my team addressing me, uncertain how many times they repeated the word, "Captain" until it registered.

"Chay-Z, snap out of it!" Harla yelled into my ear.

I shook reality back into my head. I managed to breathe out, "I can't do this."

176

"Wrong, Kiddo," Escondido said in his stern tone. "You *are* doing this. You just evaded three aggressive combatants and came in direct defensive contact, all within...two minutes of the game starting."

"This isn't a game!" I said. I wanted to quit.

I could never hope to talk to General Holter. I made a list of everything I could use as a white flag to give myself up. This house had white curtains. I had a white t-shirt on under my bomber jacket. I could always convert the Throne into a white flag on a stick for irony's sake.

But Grandad wouldn't have quit. He'd stick to it. Grin and bear it. Put on a tough face, just for show. Thinking of my tough face, for a split second the glow of the Seeker's eyes flashed in my mind, but I stuffed the thought down.

I don't know how long I sat there. It may have been hours, going back and forth in my head about whether to walk away from the competition, which meant walking away from Grandad forever. Plus letting my whole team down. The unfinished basement, with skeletal wood walls and piles of bricks and lumber scattered about, felt appropriately empty and lonely.

"It's a game if you treat it like one." Dr. Bird had said that at some point in the past three weeks, when I thought training sessions were too much to handle. I thought about what Escondido said, how I'd already engaged with aggressive combatants and lived to talk about it. These were soldiers, pilots, a *general*, for cripe's sake. And they were gunning for me, but they failed. Just like everyone trying to intimidate me at the Ball. Maybe I *could* do this.

"The Seeker's in the area," Diamonds announced out of nowhere.

Chapter 27

My shoulders tightened, my fists clenched, and I felt my nostrils flare. After encountering the other contestants, I'd kept my mind off the real enemy here. Robobug. I pictured it crawling over houses, its eyes searching, its gun barrel insectoid mouth flexing and curling.

"End of the street," Diamonds said. "Scanning the area?"

Escondido thought aloud, "It should be going through vision spectrums, searching for tracks, evidence of warped light, heat signatures."

"It's coming closer," warned Diamonds. "Two houses away."

Escondido asked, "Are we sure the hot water heater will block the Throne's heat output?"

Harpreet chimed in, "Yeah, the insulation'll mask him somewhat. Otherwise, it's normal for a hot water heater to be…hot."

Diamonds whispered, "Oh, it's crawling over your house now."

I heard a distant thumping, like a body hitting the floor two stories up.

"It stopped."

"It stopped?" I squeaked out a whisper. Sweat beaded on my forehead. I tried not to breathe too loud. The cylinder smelled like my sour nervous sweat, the cotton candy comfort of the goopy van long gone.

"It senses something," Escondido pointed out. "I don't trust this hot water heater theory. Captain, can you give me a model number so we can confirm the Throne's heat signature is blocked?"

I looked around in the hot water heater, but there were no markings inside of it.

"What's it doing now?" Harla asked.

"Oh, no," Escondido said. "Captain, get ready to fly out of there."

"What's it doing?" I asked.

"Converting mouth cannons," Escondido said in awe. "It's getting ready to shoot or spray paint."

Sweat stung my eyes. I didn't have enough deodorant for the duration of the game. Unless I got out soon.

"WHOA!!!!" All voices at once blared into my earpiece.

"What?" I asked. "What?!"

"Captain Kamaeleo is eliminated," said Diamonds.

"Really? How?" I asked.

"And…the Seeker is moving on. One house away," Diamonds said.

"Kamaeleo was distorting light in a tree branch across the street," Escondido said matter-of-factly.

"Don't warp light around multitudes of objects in motion," said Dr. Bird, rehashing an old tutorial lesson. "Bent light is more obvious with independent motion."

"And then there was nine," said Harla. No one would say anything further about how Kamaeleo got out, or why everybody yelled at once. I was stuck imagining gruesome, horrific situations in which the mechanical insect caught its prey.

* * *

At Escondido's suggestion, I watched a movie to pass the time within the hot water heater. Once Wall-E and Eve saved the day, I heard something.

"Is there somebody in this house?" I asked Diamonds.

"Captain, there are approximately 150 houses within the playing field," Escondido answered. "What are the chances one of them is in that house?"

"Um…eight in one hundred fifty?" I answered.

Harla added, "That's a little over five percent."

"Don't get testy, Captain," Dr. Bird's terse voice said. "Sarcasm won't help the situation. Describe what you're hearing."

"Well, it's muffled, but it's footsteps. A person's. Not the Seeker's."

Diamonds asked, "Based on how loud the footfalls are, maybe we can eliminate Miss Mars?"

"Yeah, it's louder than she'd be," I agreed.

"So, it's Stab Whisper, The Warrior, Mist, or Spectrum," figured Diamonds.

"And Mist ain't aggressive," pointed out Harla.

"We can't take that chance." Escondido's voice was apologetic. "Captain, I suggest evasive maneuvers."

"Sure." I wasn't wild about moving. "Escape out of the back

quietly?"

"I was thinking about something a little louder," said Escondido.

Sure enough, Diamonds was right about the running water working in the house, as well as the double safety seal of the water heater. So, according to her directions, I emptied out the interior water tank, and blew out the pilot flame underneath. I turned a knob, and the tank filled with gas.

I hid behind a pallet of bricks in the corner of the basement, leaving one tiny block of the Throne, smaller than a Rubik's Cube, below the hot water heater.

BOOM!

Even having known the blast was coming, with my helmet on, and behind a solid chunk of brick, the explosion was disorienting. Dust filled the room with brownish grey clouds. Everything was in sunlight, and there was a hot-water-heater-sized hole up through all three stories and the roof of the house.

I converted the Throne to the floatboard. "OK, Diamonds, where to?"

"Hold, Captain," they said.

I stood ready on the floatboard in the sunny, dusty basement, hovering. I tapped my foot.

"Captain, it appears there was activity in the area already," Escondido explained.

"So? What does that mean?"

"Stay there, Captain," Harla said. "Aggressive contestants coming up on you."

"Well, if they're headed my way, shouldn't I run?" I asked.

"Can't risk it," said Escondido. "They're right on top of you. Pick a spot, hide, and see if your upstairs friend gets caught."

"Don't use light warp in the dust and smoke," reminded Dr. Bird

"Where's the Seeker?" I asked.

"Engaged in a chase about a quarter mile away."

"How many contestants are heading my way?"

"It looks like three, plus the bogey upstairs," answered Diamonds.

"Captain," said Escondido. "One of them's the General."

Chapter 28

Great, not only were there other participants right upstairs, but they were probably working together under the jerk who hated me. Shaking off the image of the general in his mech suit flying at me, it was time to get to work.

Controlling my breathing while moving fast, I converted the Throne to a series of small piles throughout the room, blending in with the ones already there in the unfinished basement. Then I got in the fetal position, hiding within one of the piles of bricks, and focusing on shallow breaths and slowing my heart rate.

Footsteps fell upstairs, now more audible with the hole in the ceiling. The basement was thick with dust, tickling the back of my throat and my nose hairs as I struggled to control my breathing.

With a THUD, an invisible person landed, a cloud of dust puffing off the floor. The footprints of the camouflaged contestant appeared. I breathed as slowly as possible through my nose, feeling my breath push and pull at the sweat pooling on my upper lip. An itch from the dust, almost a pinching sensation, developed deep in one nostril.

I could track the camouflaged contestant by his footsteps, drawing a trail between the brick piles, until he stood right in front of my brick pile, not a meter away. A pile of bricks to my right toppled; the invisible contestant must have kicked them. Another stack of bricks next to that fell over. Then the one next to that. He was pivoting, kicking each of the brick stacks surrounding him. And the last piles to kick were pieces of the Throne.

The tickle in my nostril grew. I blinked, scrunched my nose, and stretched my upper lip, trying to make the little itch go away, but it didn't work. I was going to sneeze. I held my breath.

The piles reminded me of buildings, breaking apart as they tipped over. Slowly, I tugged the minicube cat ear so I could pinch my nostrils. The footprints in the dust rotated to face me within the pile of bricks.

The tickle of a sneeze took over now, and I inhaled tiny seizing breaths, not knowing how audible they were to the competitor in front of me. The whisper of dust from his invisible foot followed up from the floor and out, reaching out to touch my tiny building of bricks. Sweat poured down my face. My shoulders pulled up, my eyes scrunched shut, and I prepared myself to sneeze and flee.

Suddenly a voice rang out. "We got Spectrum."

The line of dust hanging from the invisible foot stopped in midair for a moment. A new footstep appeared as the contestant stepped back and spun to face his co-conspirator. I felt a small amount of relief, but my heart was still pumping so fast it hurt.

"The target is secured?" the brick-kicking contestant said.

The other voice, from a contestant most likely hovering, mocked the brick-kicker, "Yes, 'the target is secure.' Who talks like that? Come on. The idiot hid in a house he didn't realize had a faulty hot water heater."

The footsteps pivoted again, away from me in the other direction. Once they got under the hole in the ceiling, they disappeared, and I heard a thud on the floor above. I heard his voice trailing off say, "Remind me when the game's over to get my water heater checked out."

With a heaving sigh, I relaxed my shoulders and wiped the sweat from my face. I sneezed with my whole body, making a big achoo noise whiplashing my head forward so fast my cat mouth shut and snot spotted the inside. I felt cold and shaky and still in danger, even with the conspirators gone.

"Gesundheit," said Dr. Bird.

"Great job, Captain," Escondido exclaimed.

It didn't feel like I was doing a great job. I thought I was going to be sick and swallowed back a sour taste.

"Who's 'we'? Why is he saying 'We got Spectrum'?" asked Harla.

"That's an admission of cheating," said Dr. Bird.

"Running voice recognition to audio from the Ball," announced Harpreet. "Stab Whisper and The Warrior. Definitely those dudes."

"He said, 'We got Spectrum,' like they got their whole fam working on this," said Harla.

Following what they were saying, I felt numb to it, like I was in the middle of a slow-motion car accident, and the passenger was talking about the weather.

"Think it's the other dude, Mist?" asked Harpreet. "All them dudes are using the same technology with those suits."

"Not Mist," said Escondido. "They'd want to keep the conspiracy small. Less likely to have a double agent."

"You can't know that!" said Harla. "Everyone could be in on this. This could go all the way to the top. The Secretary of Defense could be in on this!"

"I'm muting everyone," Diamonds said suddenly.

Silence. I breathed for a second, realizing my shoulders were tight again, my teeth clenched since the invisible brick-kicker first landed in the basement. Among piles of bricks, the hole in the ceiling poured a spotlight onto footprints and dust motes.

"Captain, how are you doing?" Diamonds asked. That damn even voice of theirs. Sometimes I couldn't tell if they cared if I lived or died.

A lump showed up in my throat, and I felt my lip quiver. This was too much. I was up against a freaking SWAT team with futuristic tech. I was going to die out here.

A tear settled onto my lower eyelash, dangling with my breath. I wished Grandad was here. I was mad he wasn't, that he left, that I wouldn't be able to ask the General what really happened. And I was mad at myself for being so selfish and making this about me. But I couldn't say any of that to Diamonds.

"I'm OK."

"OK, good. I'm unmuting Bird."

"Hey, Captain. I know you've been through a lot today," said Dr. Bird sweetly. "I'd like you to take some time for yourself, do some breathing exercises, maybe some meditation, drink some water, and eat something before you move to the next hiding spot."

"The area is clear for the moment, Captain," said Diamonds.

"I suggest getting a vantage point and hide on the roof. Leftover heat from the explosion will mask you."

So, I gathered the brick piles that made up the Throne, and flew up to the roof. I converted the Throne into an extra chimney. I sat on the roof, eating a sandwich, a granola bar, and some weird chicken-flavored paste Dr. Bird left for me, accessing my human mouth through my wide open cat mouth.

The afternoon sun shone down onto the roofs, all black shingled, making patterns of yards and trees; a line here, another line there, making up the battlefield. In the distance, I saw the figure of the Robobug, bobbing up and down above the roof line. From here, his eyes couldn't be seen, but I knew they were there.

Diamonds must have read my mind because she said, "Captain, I'm employing projector zoom on your helmet to give you a better view of the Seeker."

And just like that, I could see the action from four streets over like it was happening right in front of me. Robobug, walking on its hind four legs, was spitting out a rapid fire of paintballs at a black-clad figure who was tumbling, flipping, and swinging out of the way.

Shinobi.

The ninja figure hopped up into a tree, dodging a string of paintballs. He leapt again, swinging around a branch onto a nearby roof. He slid down the roof and onto a shed, which he rolled off of straight into a sprint. A jagged line of paintball fire followed his trail.

Robobug continued lumbering after, and then the shed exploded.

BOOM!

It wasn't like in a movie, there was no ball of fire. It just...

popped. The green plastic roof jumped a foot or three in the air, and the doors violently flapped open. But up close, the blast was enough to knock the Robobug off balance, bending one of its back legs. The giant Seeker fell back, then steadied itself on three other legs. By the time it had its wits about it, the ninja was gone.

It was quite a sight to behold, and Dr. Bird warned me about my heart rate spiking. So I ran the doc's breathing exercises as I chewed my granola bar.

I shouldn't have been doing both. A chunk of granola caught in my throat, and I felt my neck close and a tugging within my lungs. I couldn't breathe. My body convulsed into dry heaves and attempts to cough. My skin went cold and sweat poured down my face and ribs. Time slowed, or my thoughts sped up, and I grew sad realizing I'd never get to see Grandad or the rest of my family, or the team, or Diamonds, ever again.

Then the chunk of granola came up and out, bouncing down the roof off the house.

I almost died. In the middle of this battle. I almost died while eating a granola bar. I laughed so hard I about peed myself.

"Captain, are you OK?" Escondido asked, but I was laughing too hard to respond.

Chapter 29

By the time I'd finished my sandwich, granola bar, and chicken-flavored paste, the Seeker had clambered over a nearby roof and disappeared into yet another manicured yard. I scanned the area, waiting for his mantis face to reappear over the dark roofs. If it weren't for the dark shingles, I didn't think I'd be able to see the autumn-tree-colored Seeker.

And for a moment, the Robobug's head rose above the houses, only it was a quarter mile in a different direction than I thought it was going. I dusted crumbs off my bomber jacket.

"Okay, Diamonds. Let's pick another hiding spot."

"I was looking at the compost bins some of the houses have. You can hide inside the Throne disguised as one of those. They have heat coming off decaying plant matter. There are more water heaters, of course, and most houses have chimneys, for a much tighter fit."

"Compost bins it is. Where do I go?"

"Well, that depends, Captain. Do you want to avoid the Seeker, avoid contestants, or avoid any conflict between combinations of the two?"

"Take us away from all the action," Escondido butted in.

"South by southwest."

Following Diamonds' instruction, I flew the Throne between houses for a block or two before finding a house with a compost bin. Diamonds was right, they were perfect. Five foot by five-foot cubes , emitting a little bit of heat from rotting compost, and I could bury any excess Throne parts underground. The smell wasn't great, but I could stand it.

On the opposite side of the wall from the real compost bin, I sat in the Throne, facing the postage stamp backyard with its stone platform, grill, and lawn chairs. This backyard didn't have a tree, and it felt nice in the warmth of the sun.

Movement flickered in the corner of my eye. But when I looked, I saw nothing. Just the west side of the backyard fence—red-painted wooden slats, green grass, and blue sky.

I studied the grass, used the minicube helmet to zoom in on the individual blades to see them move in the breeze, and there it was. Light distortion. The grass had an unnatural curve in it that moved with my eye.

"Guys," I whispered over the comms. "Someone's in this backyard with me."

"That's impossible. I have most players accounted for," Diamonds said, sounding busy. I imagined them scrolling through monitors, counting.

"Most?" Escondido asked in a disappointed tone. "Who is it, then?"

I slowed my breathing, inhaling through my nose, fighting against my heartbeat growing faster and faster.

"Let's see…" Diamonds' even tone rattled off, "The cluster of three by the park should be the two soldiers with kidnapped

Spectrum. I see Shinobi in some bushes, and Mist is patrolling streets near the out-of-bounds perimeter."

"What about the General?"

"No idea. I lost him a while back. I haven't had eyes on the Martian since gameplay started." There was a pause, and then Diamonds said suddenly, "There it is."

"There what is?" asked Harla.

"Do you guys not see it?" Diamonds asked. "It's right in front of you, Captain. Just zoom."

Sweat beaded on my forehead. I zoomed my view and squinted, staring at the point where the grass met the house's siding until I thought my eyes would cross.

And then I saw it. Floating in the air, maybe the size of a baseball, on the side of the next house over...the eye of the chameleon. The clone's scales were beige with dark grey in horizontal stripes to disguise it against the siding. Its tail draped over the fence, blending in with the vertical wooden slats. The tip of its tail shone bright green against the grass.

I said quietly, "Y'all see this?"

The chameleon's scaly eye was on me. Minutes passed, just us staring at each other.

Diamonds broke the silence. "Captain, we have a set of bogeys headed your way."

I heard movement down the street. Yelling.

Suddenly, the Throne disguised as a compost bin rocked as something hit the side of it.

"What was that?" I asked Diamonds, trying to see whatever hit my hiding spot. Outside, I heard running. Two sets of feet.

"Confirming three bogeys," said Diamonds.

"I only hear two," I said. "What was that noise?"

"They've still got Mist."

"No, the noise over here. What hit the Throne?"

Suddenly my view went dark. I should have been able to see the yard through projector mode, but something coated the outside of the compost bin. My stomach tensed. Did the Throne lose power? Was this what happened when it overheated?

"What's going on?" I whispered, tempering the panic in voice.

"Gross. Chay-Z just got slimed!" said Harla.

Diamonds clarified, "Captain, the chameleon has attacked you. And it, a couple bogeys, and the Seeker are all headed your way."

Chapter 30

"We're going to give you a view of what's going on, Captain," Diamonds said on the comms.

Harpreet whispered the command, "Remote control viewscreen of the exterior, minimal delay."

A screen popped up within my little box, the fake compost bin, showing a wide, sweeping view of the playing field–a rolling sea of geometrically-spaced black rooftops, peppered with treetops. The shot zoomed in closer and closer, to a cluster of houses, and then to one particular backyard, where I was hiding.

Suddenly, a pink line shot from the neighboring house, over the wooden fence, onto one of the box bins. I could just make out the Chameleon's tongue stretched out to my compost bin, like a string of pulled-apart chewing gum. Suddenly, from the end of the tongue, black liquid erupted, coating the bin.

"Nasty, dude! Bro got squid inked!" Harpreet yelled out, way too excited.

"Genetically modified clones is just wrong," muttered Harla.

My compost bin was now covered in black ink, and instantly the tongue shot back into the chameleon's mouth.

"So what triggered its defense mechanism?" I asked, afraid of what the answer might be.

Almost in response, a body clad in white flew up and over the fence, landing with a THUMP like some heavy rag doll.

It was Mist, and he wasn't going to be standing anytime soon. The NASA captain was either dead or knocked out. I assumed if he were dead, he'd be out of the game, and Diamonds would have informed me. His all-white uniform was spotted with grass stains, soot, and blood.

Then someone in a light bending suit, moving too fast to keep invisible, scaled the fence, landing next to the incapacitated Mist. Mist's dead-weight leg seemed to lift in the air on its own, then his entire body supernaturally lifted into the air, doubled over. The invisible light-bender heaved Mist's body over his shoulder, jogged across the yard, and threw the unconscious body over the next fence.

Breathing heavy, the light-bender muttered to himself something I couldn't understand, like some deranged person. He scrambled over the next fence. He was afraid of something, and I got nervous thinking about how I'd do against something that scared a soldier.

"Why doesn't he just fly over the fence?" Escondido asked, oblivious to whatever danger was driving the light-bender.

"His jet's dead?" Harla asked.

"If his propulsion system is too loud," Harpreet thought out loud, "firing off a jetpack could attract unwanted attention from..."

As I tried to listen over the team on comms for the kidnapping light-bender running through the next backyard, I heard someone following instead. Or rather, something with booming footsteps.

Diamonds interrupted, "The Seeker is right on you."

FOOM!

The noise came from right outside my little hidden box, and I waited for the video feed to catch up with the noises outside.

A leg like a flagpole stomped into the yard, shaking the ground, sending my teeth chattering. Up this close, I could see the hexagonal pattern coating the Robobug's limb, no larger than dimes, each a different shade of gray, blue, or brown. There was a mechanical grind of metal on metal when the Seeker moved, and then the next flagpole leg landed in the next yard over with another booming noise.

I craned my neck to see the Seeker's glowing eyes, but the sun obscured my vision. I did see its gun mandibles, moving like fingers coming out of its mouth, firing paint pellets into the next yard. A man screamed. The Seeker, almost three times as tall as the house, continued firing while stilt-walking to the next yard.

I didn't have time to exhale before a shape moved through the wooden fence. Not a shape, but this amorphous, undulating cloud, like a thick swarm of bees, or one of those flocks of birds that move as a blob. The swarm continued across the yard, flying not a foot away from me inside the disguised Throne.

ScatterSwarm.

And then all of the bees vanished. Cloaked, projection mode, bent light, or something, but I could no longer see them.

The Seeker returned, stepping his flagpole leg back into the yard, bright eyes looking about frantically for the movement of the hi-tech cloud of nanotechnology, its mandibles spraying throughout the yard. Paint bullets pelted grass, splashed on the lawn furniture, and just kept coming. Closer and closer.

My breath seized in my chest, my wide eyes following the stream of projectiles. Even if he shot the ground in front of m e and it splashed onto the Throne, I would be out. We would be out. The whole team. And I'd be no closer to finding out what happened to Grandad.

The paintballs, making a purring sound in the midst of the automatic firing, suddenly stopped.

Through the screen within the Throne, I couldn't tell what had caught the Seeker's attention. Then I remembered the inky black shape in the corner of the screen was me, within the ink-drenched compost bin. The Phasmodea-X Seeker was looking right at me, bright eyes glaring down, uncertain of what the dripping black box was, but certain it didn't belong.

The Robobug straightened a mandible out to form a gun barrel and fired a tiny wad of liquid tagging solvent, no bigger than a chewed-up piece of gum. I heard it land above me in a soft wet PLTHK sound.

The Seeker had tagged my vehicle.

I was out.

It was over.

Chapter 31

I let out a grunt of relief as the weight of the world lifted off my shoulders. We were out. I had survived the game, thank science, even if I had lost. Even if I came in second to last place. Even if I hadn't found Grandad.

But then doubt came into my mind, overtaking the sense of relief. It was over. And not just the MC Squared. The hunt for Grandad was over. The relief left as the monster of sadness closed its grip around my neck, squeezing my tears up and out my eyes. I had failed. I'd never know what happened to him.

On the monitor, in front of the ink- and paint-covered Throne disguised as a compost bin, something had gotten the Robobug's attention, drawing it out of this yard. In two steps, the Robobug was up and over the house, leaving a dent the size of a coffee mug in the ground. I stared at the hole and felt super alone for a second, not even the chameleon around anymore.

"You're not out yet, Cap!" Diamonds called out.

"What?" I asked, my stomach tightening again.

"That solvent hasn't hit the Throne yet." Escondido pointed

out.

"Solvent?" I asked, not following.

"The paint! The tagging substance! They ain't got you yet, Cap!" Harla said.

I perked up. "I'm not out?"

"Not yet," said Diamonds.

"Do we shift into something else?" asked Escondido.

"Not with the Captain inside!" answered Harpreet.

"Is there an emergency hose?" asked Dr. Bird.

"Dunno, maybe the fire sprinklers will work?" suggested Harpreet.

"Muting," Diamonds said. They cleared their throat and returned to their calm, quiet, usual tone. "Captain, the splotch of paint, or tagging solvent, is sitting on top of a layer of clone's ink. Floating really. Until that solvent touches the surface of the Throne, you're still in this. Now, carefully and slowly, we need you to open the lid of the compost bin."

My hand shook as I placed it against the aged wood surface, or at least the Throne pretending to have an aged wood surface, then pushed up and prayed to science.

The sound of the team was too much for the comms, just a cacophony of noise, and I couldn't read whether the team was happy or devastated. After what felt like forever, I could see the black box moving on the screen, the lid folding upward. And the singular, tiny pixel of blue paint slid down the black surface of the open box lid, and off onto the lawn.

As the team's cacophony settled, I heaved another sigh with my entire body, genuinely happy I wasn't out. We were still in the game. I still had a chance to find Grandad.

Falling back onto my butt, the lid closed above me, and I laughed out loud. The whole team joined me, and we all trailed off to soak in the relief of the moment.

In silence, I hydrated, ate some more chicken paste, and ran through Dr. Bird's breathing exercises. A deep, snoring breath was interrupted by the comms.

"The Warrior is out," Diamonds said.

"Oh, naw!" cried out Harla, actually sounding pretty bummed. "gon' miss you, The! See you at the crossroads."

Dr. Bird said, "I imagine carrying the weight of another human would slow your flight down considerably."

"But Mist was out cold, though," Harla pointed out, "How good you got to be to wake up and get away that quickly from a stick bug attack?"

"I think the ScatterSwarm is an evolution of nanotechnology NASA built a couple years ago," said Escondido. "It was an emergency measure, like our quantum airbag. In case the Phasmodea-X crashed, the bots would be deployed to catch me and carry me to safety, while keeping me camouflaged through light-bending."

"Them bees can carry someone?" Harla asked.

* * *

The sun was starting to set, and the golden orange quality of the sky made the siding of the houses glow warmly in their cool blues and grays. It was quiet for a moment, both over the comms and on the playing field. Overhead, bats flapped around in the darkening sky while the alternating glow of lightning bugs appeared in the evening air.

"Is everyone gone?" I asked.

"The coast is clear, Captain," Diamonds answered.

"Where am I staying tonight, then? Here?" I asked.

"What's wrong with the compost bin disguise?" Escondido asked.

"He can't lay down!" interjected Dr. Bird.

"OK, OK," Escondido said. "So what are we thinking?"

"Well, as the sun goes down and so does the temperature," Harpreet said, "the Throne's heat signature is going to be easier to find."

"We should stay away from hot water heaters," Escondido said, "In case someone put two and two together and goes house to house checking basements."

"Houses, in general, is too obvious of a place," said Harla. "Why not go house to house? As a Seeker, or whatever cheating gang is out there."

"Diamonds," I asked, "how about someplace up high?"

"Like a tree branch?" they answered.

"We need Captain to have something comfortable to stretch out on," Dr. Bird said. "And I'm not cognizant of any horizontal space in any of these houses that could mask your heat."

"I guess, like, one tanning bed left on would be a little suspicious," Harpreet joked.

"What's a tanning bed?" Harla, Diamonds, and I asked at the same time. I could hear Dr. Bird laughing in the background.

"I could survey the area for signs of burrowing animals," said Diamonds, trying to be helpful.

"I say we hover the floatboard by an electrical box," Escondido suggested.

"Wow. That's actually a real good idea," admitted Diamonds.

"Yea, good job, leader guy," said Harla.

"Why's everyone so surprised I had a good idea?" Escondido asked angrily. While Diamonds found an electrical box hot enough, Escondido continued, "I want everyone to think about this possibility of conspirators cheating."

"The possibility?" Harla asked. "It went down right in front of us!"

"There's no denying some cheating has occurred," Dr. Bird agreed.

Escondido continued, "And we have the footage and audio for proof. But there is the possibility one of the two conspirators was The Warrior."

"Captain The Warrior," Harla corrected, as the cat helmet display filled with directions to the nearest electrical box. "To be a conspiracy, it technically got to have three or more participants."

"You know what I mean!" Escondido said, holding back anger. "There may have been two cheaters, and one is out. So the one that's left is on his own, just as if he wasn't cheating. Hopcfully it's an cvcn playing ficld again, and oncc thc gamc is over, we can bring our footage and audio of cheating to the Secretary of Defense."

Wow, the Secretary of Defense? I didn't know Escondido knew people that high up. I wondered if I was going to meet the Secretary of Defense. Was he at the Ball?

"But if there were more conspirators?" Harla asked. "Are all of them still in the game?"

"That's what I want everyone to think about," said the team leader.

* * *

In a quietly humming field of warped light, laid out on the floatboard for a bed, I set my plan for the General—how I could talk to him, what I would even ask him about Grandad's disappearance. To be honest, the guy scared the crap out of me. When I closed my eyes, I kept seeing him, only now in his green camo Optimus Prime—no, Megatron—aiming that cannon hand at me and firing.

Eventually, I drifted in and out of sleep for about six hours or so, hovering fifteen feet in the air by a telephone pole at the edge of the neighborhood. The board bobbed in the air above two big cylinders that sent cables and telephone lines sprawling in all directions. It reminded me of a nest.

Diamonds' calm voice woke me. "...of concern. Approaching contestant movement of concern, Captain. Captain?"

"What is it?" I asked groggily.

"SHHH!" Diamonds said with a sense of urgency. "Bogeys, Captain. Two of them."

"Where?" I whispered.

"Up Mountain Trail Road. Your three o'clock. I don't think you can see them yet."

The sky had some light to it, a grey before dawn, but everything else was black and invisible if it wasn't silhouetted. My helmet view shifted to thermal to see down the oak-tree-canopied road.

"There they are. I can positively identify..." Escondido said, trailing off. Then with fear in his voice, he whispered, "No, it can't be."

Chapter 32

I searched the area with thermal vision. Sure enough, there were two people. One red form, the shape of a big bulky person, walked down the middle of the street. And next to him, in a cloud of tiny signature dots, another contestant floated in the air. Captain Spectrum and his Scatter Swarm.

"Spectrum? He was the one the cheaters abducted, right?"

"That's right, Captain," Escondido said, his voice oozing disappointment.

"Then how is he one of the conspirators?"

"I don't know," Escondido answered, and I could tell he said it through clenched teeth.

"Who's that he with?" I asked.

"Mist," he spat the name.

The two figures were nearing my telephone pole, and I switched my helmet back to projector mode that zoomed when I squinted.

Grey morning touched the east face of everything, lighting the two figures. The floating guy, wrapped up in white with reddish brown slashes of what looked like dried blood, sat reclined, three feet in the air, his swarm not visible. Neither of them was camouflaged, although Mist, the one walking, held onto the four foot by ten foot rectangular camo shield normally mounted on his vehicle.

"Where's the dude's motorcycle?" asked Harpreet.

"And how come they ain't cloaked?" Harla thought out loud.

"Is every contestant a cheating conspirator?" asked Dr. Bird with a frustrated, questioning sigh.

"Muting," whispered Diamonds.

I could hear one of the men talking too loud for the game, although I didn't catch every word. "Is this Oak? We should start…"

The two men looked up at my telephone pole, and I ducked back behind the floatboard. I breathed, reminded myself of the lightwarp, then peered back down. A cross of green street signs sat two feet below me; that's what they had been looking at. My body tensed as I peeked over the floatboard, staying within the light warp field.

"I can't pick up what they're saying," Diamonds whispered through the comms.

I couldn't answer without giving away my position. I was already afraid my heartbeat was audible. Sweat developed in my armpits and ran down my ribs.

The two men turned and continued down another street.

"Couldn't hear everything," I breathed. "Something about Oak Street."

Ten or so feet ahead, still walking away, Mist cupped his hands around his mouth and raised his voice, "I SAID, 'THIS IS OAK STREET. WE SHOULD START TALKING LOUDLY!'"

My chest went cold, and I ducked against the floatboard. My ears were about an inch dug into my shoulders. I scrunched my eyes, prepping for the moment either of them made a move, and I tensed my legs, ready to bounce to my feet and surf twenty houses away in a blink. I tried to keep my intense breathing quiet.

Spectrum answered, also yelling, "THEN LET'S GO DOWN OAK STREET WHILE YELLING!"

The two meandered up Oak Street, still un-camouflaged, yelling about nothing in particular.

"Captain," Diamonds said, "Dr. Bird says you need to relax."

I took some deep breaths and collapsed back onto the floatboard. "What are they doing?" I asked.

There was a moment of rustling and whispers the comms didn't pick up.

"Really?" Diamonds asked somebody in mission control.

"What'd they say?" I asked them. Someone on the team was talking, but the comms were still muted.

Harla's brassy voice broke through, over-pronouncing the words like it was the most obvious thing in the world, "They're fishing."

"What do you mean…" I trailed off as I heard it. In the quiet of the morning, there was a swishing sound. Like a tree in the wind, only it was one singular tree that was swishing. Just down the street, just behind the competitors, one tree's leaves moved in unison.

The two contestants walking down Oak Street stopped in front of one of the houses. They threw military hand signals to each other, then split up, Mist continuing down Oak, and Spectrum with his swarm floating back my way.

The tree swooshed once more, and then fell. Well, it didn't fall, it split; a portion of the trunk split off, then…stood up? Robobug, the enormous grotesque machine that it was, successfully hid from the two conspiring contestants, me, and even Diamonds, disguised as some monstrous split trunk.

Down the street, past the Seeker, Mist cloaked as he engaged his projector shield. Spectrum stopped about a house away from my telephone pole, close enough to yell out to. His swarm cloud lowered him to his feet without a command and encircled him. The nanobots surrounding Spectrum rotated and increased speed, orbiting the white-clad contestant in a frenzy.

The Phasmodea-X's eyes burned bright in the low morning light. Its dexterous mandibles came to life, presenting multiple barrels, all aimed for Spectrum, the swarm now spinning about him like a miniature tornado.

The first paintball fired missed low. The next missed to the left. A stream of paint pellets then poured from the Seeker's mandibles, but none of them hit the contestant.

"He's created a force field of wind," Escondido said, impressed.

"Is that legal?" Harla asked. But if she didn't know, no one did.

Suddenly, a stream of paintballs aimed at Spectrum diverted in his wind, curving upward to fly up at me. Four pellets pelted the cylindrical electric box at the top of my telephone pole, a couple feet beneath me. I swallowed a scream.

"Captain, get out of there," Diamonds said.

"I'm getting!" I answered, scrambling to my feet, already leaning forward to put the floatboard into motion. Turning down Mountain Trail, in the opposite direction from the conspiring contestants, I engaged light warp and dipped low to the ground to avoid the paintball fire.

It was too late once I saw the warped light speeding towards me. The nose of my invisible floatboard collided with Mist's cloaked motorcycle.

I, however, flew forward, hit the ground, skipped along the asphalt, and then was in the air again for a moment. A pain in my knees and elbows burned as my world tumbled over and over and over. I didn't know which direction the motorcycle went, I didn't know which direction was up, pain stung my shoulders and elbows, and I flopped onto my back as I slid to a stop.

Everything went quiet, and I saw the motorcycle straighten itself and continue down the street as the silver floatboard tumbled onto the sidewalk.

"Captain!" someone yelled out, but it sounded far away. A high-pitched whine was louder, closer. This is what people meant when they called it a ringing in their ears.

"Captain!" someone else yelled. Or maybe it was the same person.

I felt shaky, like I'd just hit a baseball with an aluminum bat, but all over, not just in my hands. Through the piercing ringing, I could barely feel my body: shaky, cold and hungry. I laid still for a moment. When I moved, pain stabbed at my elbows and knees.

"Get up!" said several voices. Or was I hearing double? Was that a thing?

"Get up!" said another voice, but not from the comms.

The voice was from real life, from the playing field. A man wrapped up in white grabbed my elbow. Spectrum? He lifted me from the pavement, pulling my arm around his neck. My legs struggled to work, kicking at the ground with minimal success. He practically carried me, dragged me, along Oak Street.

Rushing.

Running.

Spectrum kept looking over his shoulder. So I looked behind us. I shouldn't have.

Chapter 33

Phasmodea-X was chasing us, several houses away, as we hobbled away as fast as we could. Paintballs poured out from the Kaiju Robobug. The self-driving motorcycle ran figure eights around its legs. The Throne, again the antique chair, was flying to catch up with us, barrel-rolling to attract the Robobug's fire while avoiding the paintballs.

With the motivation of a giant robotic insect chasing us, my legs started working again. Spectrum and I ran side by side, enveloped by a cloud of spinning nanobots.

Something pushed at the back of my knees, and for a moment I thought the Robobug was stepping on me. And then I was scooped into the air by the Throne. I looked back to the ground to see the swarm overtake the blood-striped Spectrum, orbiting tightly around him, lifting him into the air, and then cloaking.

The Throne flew me safely into the air and out of range as the Seeker screamed up Oak Street, chasing after the motorcycle. The self-driving vehicle drove off in the other direction, slow enough to allow the Seeker to keep up. Bait.

"I don't get it," I managed, catching my breath, "Why'd he help me if they're cheating?"

"I'm not sure…" Escondido admitted.

"I say we go back, follow them guys, and watch some fishing," stated Harla.

"Are you mental, dude?" Harpreet's voice cracked. I could hear him sweating from here. "You want a contestant to chase *after* the Seeker?"

"Why would contestants go fishing in the first place?" I asked.

"Usually," explained Escondido, "they're pointing the Seeker in the direction of other contestants."

"So maybe Spectrum was just getting revenge?" Harla asked. "Get back at them for kidnapping him? For cheating?"

"So, NASA's captain might *not* be cheating?" Escondido asked.

"He's still working in tandem with other participants," Dr. Bird pointed out.

"He saved me," I noted. "Maybe his…their plan is just to clear the game of all the cheaters. Start over fresh with players who follow the rules."

The line went quiet for a second, and I could only hear the metallic stomping of the Seeker as a soft thump in the distance.

"Do we know where they're headed?" I asked, hoping my navigator would answer. "What's up Oak Street? Diamonds!"

"Oak Street dead-ends at the park," Diamonds said, their voice wavering a bit, taking breaths between sentences. "By the pond."

"OK, Captain, what are you thinking?" Escondido asked me. But the floatboard and I were already in motion. No time to see if Diamonds was okay.

I flew over a line of houses two streets south of Oak, just to give the Seeker and the bait a wide berth. I could see its upper thorax pushing through the trees, its bright eyes trained ahead of it. The yellow morning sun reflected off the pond by the playground, right where they were headed.

I put on my thickest Southern accent and said, "Well let's get down to the pond and watch us some fishing."

* * *

The park was shaped like a lightning bolt—one large rectangular strip of land, then another narrow triangle plot coming off, its end wrapping around the pond. North of the body of water, at the bend in the lightning bolt, was a playground of colorful plastic pieces.

Taking a page out of the Seeker's playbook, I found a tall oak tree by the pond and hid as a branch of the tree trunk. Even though I was still at a safe distance, I took no chances, running a bit of the Throne, disguised as a root, along the ground to vent heat exhaust in the cool water.

The sun was breaking the horizon by this point, and the orange glow of the sky took on pink hues, fiery red around the growing sliver in the east. The orange sky had a dulling effect on the sidings of all of the matching houses. The roofs somehow were darker, as if the contrast on the houses was turned up.

I heard the motorcycle before I saw it. Tearing up Oak. Whatever high-tech muffler the vehicle had in stealth mode was disengaged when I collided with it, because that chopper

211

roared. Engine noises echoed across the pond. Then I saw its headlight.

"Dude's got his headlights on?" Harpreet asked. "Isn't that a bit much?"

"Ain't no dude," Harla said. "Driving its damn self."

It was zig-zagging down the street, definitely not at full speed. The motorcycle, or whoever was controlling it, was waiting for Robobug to catch up. And catch up, it did.

The Seeker shambled down the street, pushing trees out of its way like waist high bushes. But instead of firing paintballs out of his gun barrel-mandibles, out poured a steady stream of paint, like from a garden hose. Like the thing was puking everywhere.

A sloppy crisscrossing trail of blue paint followed the motor-cycle down the street as it headed toward the playground. As Oak Street ended into Park Street, the motorcycle turned, but not onto the other road. Instead, it drove onto the playground, kicking up wood chips as it cut between a couple swing sets. Its headlight shone in my eyes.

The self-driving motorcycle was headed for me, and lumber-ing behind it, burping a stream of blue paint from its mouth, was the thirty-foot insect robot.

"Should I move?"

"No, Captain! It's too close," warned Escondido. "We haven't seen the stick bug move in the open yet."

The stick bug, scurrying on its four hind legs, ran into the clearing of the playground, past the tree-lined street. Then all six of its flagpole legs hit the ground, and it crawled, gaining on the motorcycle almost instantly.

The Seeker's eyes shone as blue dripped off his mandibles down its body like a gruesome photo negative. I flinched within the Throne tree trunk. The stick bug skittered not a hundred feet away, the motorcycle bearing down on me.

I saw something large and white within the stick bug's mouth, and it fired. A small missile, about the size of a celery bunch, flew, leaving a trail of smoke, closing the distance to the motorcycle.

The motorcycle swerved.

The missile was coming straight for me.

At the very last moment, when I could see the little white projectile clearly in the bright morning sun, it turned, headed after the motorcycle circling the pond.

The Seeker stood a few feet away from my hiding tree, watching the missile locked onto the little vehicle roaring around the pond, back toward the playground.

The motorcycle didn't make it to the playground.

Hitting a patch of soft sand, the wheels lost traction. The missile made contact, bursting into a cloud of blue paint, covering the motorcycle and spraying the playground.

A few feet away, the playground came to life. The two sides of a red and yellow plastic slide scissored, folding in on itself. One of the ride-able characters on a spring, this one a purple octopus, flickered and fizzled, revealing it was a projected image. Two competitors in their vehicles leapt back to avoid the missile's blue blast.

"That's the General and Stab Whisper," said Escondido.

The stick bug skittered away from my tree and toward the playground, planting one telephone pole leg after another, one step splashing in the edge of the pond. It stopped.

Its dinner-table sized head tilted in confusion. Its enormous eyes suddenly changed color, glowing a fiery red. The entire focus of the robot changed as it followed a submerged tree trunk, the Throne's trunk, from the pond up to the false tree trunk. The empty, soulless red lights seemed to look through the Throne's fake bark, right at me.

Chapter 34

The insectoid head tilted again as it studied my hiding spot. My skin went cold, and I felt the goosebumps against my pilot's gear. Behind the towering Robobug, on the playground, wood chips sprayed out, and the yellow and red slide launched into the air. The colors faded to green camouflage, and I recognized the General's mech suit, flying with jet propulsion coming out of his feet.

Holter's take-off drew the Seeker's attention. But for one split second, I felt the stick bug's red eyes move back from the playground and fall on me. Like it was staring into my soul with its empty luminous eyes before it skittered away, following the contestants.

I sighed so hard, I thought I'd be sick. My body was shaky, my gut nauseous. Was the seeker somehow more dangerous? Like when superheroes' eyes glow red when they're under an evil spell? Something had changed in the robobug with its eyes. And I didn't want to find out what.

"They teamed up to get the General and his men out!" Escondido said happily.

"Great," I managed to say without vomiting.

"Don't you see?" Escondido said, still way too excited. "We can work with them. Once we get the General and his men out, we can have a real competition."

"Are you kidding me?!" I was done clenching my fists or jaw or biting my tongue. Done holding back the anger every time I felt helpless on this team, everything I didn't say those days leading up to this messed-up game. Done feeling like a video game character the team was playing back at mission control. I screamed, "I'm barely surviving out here as it is. 'Work with them'? What are you thinking? Do you want to get me killed or are you just stupid? I'm not working with anybody except my team, and all we are doing is keeping me alive! I'm a kid, not some fighter pilot!"

I yelled so hard my throat was raw, and I was out of breath. I was certain he was going to yell back, maybe even kick me off the team, make me surrender right then and there. Instinctively, my face fell to stone neutral, the expression for in trouble or in the middle of some argument. My automatic reaction as I waited for Escondido to throw it all back in my face, to fire me on the spot, to forfeit on the team's behalf.

Instead, he quietly said, "You're right, Captain. I'm sorry. Bird, check in please."

I couldn't believe it. I wasn't getting chewed out, much less kicked off the team.

"How are you, Captain?" Dr. Bird asked in her no-nonsense tone. "Are you bleeding anywhere?"

After removing my jacket and gloves, I patted down my coveralls to find any cuts. "I don't feel any blood. Lots of bumps and bruises. I got an egg growing out of my elbow."

"You have an egg growing out of your elbow?" Dr. Bird

asked, her voice going high.

"Something my dad says. I have a big bump on my elbow."

"On a scale from one to ten, how bad does it hurt?"

"I don't know, a three, maybe a two."

"OK, do me a favor and find all of those bumps on your elbows and knees, and anywhere else, and give them a squeeze. Push on each of your ribs and your clavicle, too. It might hurt a little, but tell me if the pain spikes to a nine or a ten."

I poked and prodded myself, but the pain didn't jump past a four.

"Good. Nothing's broken, then. Are you hungry?"

"Yeah."

"Have you peed this morning yet?"

I was too embarrassed to answer.

"Well, you need to go have a bathroom break, eat something, then in fifteen minutes or so, hydrate," Dr. Bird said.

"I will, Dr. Bird, thanks. Diamonds?" When there was no answer, I called again, "Diamonds?"

"They've been gone for a while, bro," Harpreet answered.

Dr. Bird cleared her throat and said, "Diamonds took a minute, sir. Since the encounter at the playground."

My jaw tightened at the news. I knew what it meant for them to 'take a minute.' A panic attack. Over the game. Over a new captain dragging the team down. A panic attack that was all my fault, and I wasn't there to help.

I pulled my phone out and started texting, erasing like eight corny messages until I settled on, "*I m OK. Hope u r,*" and sent it. I texted them again, this time, just the word, "*Over.*" I did a quick Dr. Bird breathing exercise and refocused.

"Hey team," I asked, "Does anyone know if all the houses have running water?"

Harpreet answered, "As far as we can tell, bro."

"Can anyone pick out a house away from the action where I could eat and get a bathroom break?"

"Over by the park?" Harpreet suggested.

"The park's been a hotbed of action," Escondido said.

"How about smack dab in the middle of the houses?" asked Harla. "Like Washington Street?"

"Isn't that where the guys are?" said Dr. Bird. "The general's men?"

"Northeast of you, Captain," Diamonds' even tone answered firmly. "Corner of Pine and Creek, 140 Creek Road."

I couldn't help but smile. "Thanks, Diamonds."

The even tone of the navigator answered dryly, "Just doing my job, sir."

I warped light and flew the floatboard northeast to Pine and Creek while the comms stayed silent. Things weren't right with the team, and I couldn't get past feeling bad about losing my temper earlier.

"Escondido?"

"Yes, Captain?"

"I'm sorry I yelled at you."

"It's OK. You were right, Captain. I lost sight of our priorities."

"I still shouldn't have yelled."

"Apology accepted. And may I say something, keeping in mind we're still in a very live and dangerous competition?"

"What is it, Escondido?"

"You have had an impressive first day, sir."

"Thank you, sir."

"I'm proud you're my captain."

The other seven spoke up in agreement.

My cheeks burned, and I felt the lump in my throat again, but this wasn't some monster of sadness. It was happiness, or joy, or just plain contentment. And also stress and sleep deprivation.

* * *

That shower was everything. It was like I was covered in a film I didn't realize was itchy until I scrubbed it with a washcloth. It even felt good to wash my hair. Dr. Bird and Harpreet hid a travel bag of shampoo and soap in the Throne, and I didn't even care it made me smell like lilacs. The flight suit coveralls were moisture wicking, so I washed it, too, and it came out dry.

Getting out of the shower, I found a clean towel hanging on the wall, and I wondered what this neighborhood was. Did whoever ran DARPA just evacuate the area? I opened the medicine cabinet, and everything in there—toothpaste, toothbrushes, shaving cream, deodorant, perfume, makeup—was brand new, unopened. There was a price tag on my towel. For the first time, I questioned who was running this competition.

"Captain, bogey coming your way," Diamonds said. I was really getting tired of that sentence.

I hid underneath the Throne, currently a loveseat in the living room, and got dressed while crouched within.

"Who is it?" I whispered.

"Shinobi," answered Diamonds.

I put the cat helmet on, already displaying a view of the street, I guessed in front of the house. The street had a canopy

219

of trees, yellowing leaves shivering in the wind.

"What am I looking at?"

"This is one of the four views I have of the playing field," answered Diamonds. "Zoomed in, of course."

"But where's the bogey?"

"He's right there. In the trees."

But it was just a view from over the roof of this house, a big canopy of trees blocking the street. I looked for a person dressed in black but saw nothing. The wind shook the leaves and branches swayed and dipped. Then I saw. Just a clump of leaves that moved with the bowing of branches. Except this clump of leaves, moving with branches and bowing to the wind, flowed from one tree to the next.

Then the clump stopped, staying in one tree. "Diamonds, can you zoom more?"

There, within the trees, on one branch, was the ninja. His black outfit was dark green in bright daylight, and he had covered himself in twigs and leaves sticking out of the wrappings on his elbows and knees. He hung from all fours beneath the branch, glaring into a nearby house. He removed something from his leg and put it up to his face. It was an old spyglass.

"What house is he looking into?"

"Well…" Diamonds cleared their throat. "That would be the house you're in, Captain."

Chapter 35

I nside the Throne's disguise as furniture, I freaked out over the comms. "He can't see me, can he? He can't see heat signatures, and he wouldn't know what a loveseat even was, right?"

"Calm down, Captain," Dr. Bird said.

"Easy for you to say, you haven't just been noticed by one of the greatest assassins in history!"

"Get a hold of yourself, boy! It's your smell," Harla said.

"I didn't think of that," said Diamonds. "Modern soaps and chemicals must smell very foreign to someone from ancient Japan."

"Super interesting, guys," I said sarcastically. "How does that help keep me from getting killed?"

On the screen, the ninja put away the spyglass and grabbed something from his waist. His arm shot out like a blur, and glass broke in the next room over followed by a THUP.

I leaned within the loveseat to see down the hallway, where a ninja star stuck halfway out from the wall.

"He's just trying to scare you, Captain," said Escondido.

"Well…" I said, my voice cracking, "The man's good at what

he does."

"He just wants to flush you out, sir," said Diamonds. "He doesn't see you, but can smell you're in there."

"Probably thinks you're one of the dudes who kidnapped him and brought him here."

"Harpreet, enough," Escondido said.

Harla said, "He's right, though. That ninja catch the Cap, ninja thinks he one step closer to freedom."

"Captain, please do some relaxation breaths," said Dr. Bird. "Everyone else, stop telling the Captain what you think the ninja is going to do to him."

"Wait, is that a bow and arrow?" I don't know who said it, but they were right. The ninja had a bow and arrow in his hand, aiming it right into this house!

"Where was he keeping it?" Harla asked.

THWIP.

On screen, the ninja loosed an arrow from a taut bowstring.

THUNK.

Right next to the ninja star, a small black arrow shot into the wall, making me jump. A thin rope, the width of a phone charger cord, hung from the projectile. Onscreen, the ninja ran the other side of the rope over a branch, pulled it tight, and tied it. In the hallway, the rope vibrated with a thrum, pitched higher and higher as the rope tightened.

The ninja reached out and grabbed the rope, hanging upside down, hand over hand, walking himself over, like an orangutan at the zoo.

"What should I do guys?" I asked.

The entire team replied at the same time.

Escondido said, "Run."

Harla said, "Stay put!"

Dr. Bird said, "Calm down!"

"Oh!" Diamonds said, surprised, then calmly added, "Never mind."

"Never mind?" I whisper-screamed. "Never mind what? Never mind getting killed by an ancient Japanese warrior?"

They answered with one word: "Seeker."

Just then, as the ninja was halfway across the rope to this house, a white dot flew into the screenshot and burst into a cloud of blue against the dark green warrior.

Diamonds zoomed out the image for me, and there, in mottled black to match the roof shingles, were the neck, arms and head of the giant robot stick bug, perched atop the house next door, shuffling its mandibles.

"Shinobi is out," said Diamonds.

The ninja screamed and fell to the ground, rolling on the grass and writhing in pain.

"Wait, did the Seeker just hit Shinobi with," Escondido said as if he were afraid to be right, "a projectile of corrosive tagging solvent?"

"What?" I remembered the term from the guide, but it wasn't anything we'd practiced.

"A missile full of acidic tagging solvent," Harla recited from the rulebook. "Made for vehicles. So you don't just wipe it off with a squirt of wiper fluid. Historically used quite sparingly."

The Seeker scrambled over from its perch on the house next door to stand above its victim, regarded the flailing human on the ground for a moment, and then looked around. The glowing eyes passed over the window of this living room, but I stayed quiet within my loveseat, hoping the Throne wasn't putting off too much heat.

Then, the Seeker continued down the street, lumbering

while combing the neighborhood.

The moaning and wailing outside subsided, and I asked Diamonds, "Is the coast clear?"

"Cap," Harla interrupted. "You got to get out of there. Ain't safe at the scene of an incident."

I ignored her. "Diamonds?"

"The coast is clear, Captain."

I jumped on the loveseat and rode it down the hall, through the window destroyed by a ninja star and an arrow, and hovered outside of the second story window, floating above the ninja's body.

I swallowed hard, then asked, "Is he…dead?"

Dr. Bird said quietly, "Engineer, zoom in, please? Thank you. Yes, Captain, Captain Shinobi is no longer breathing."

I descended. The smell was atrocious, like burnt meat and chemicals. As if someone dropped a hamburger into a mop bucket. The body was making a sizzling sound and the clumps of blue foam bubbled and swelled.

The fabric had fallen to cover the ninja's fierce eyes. I knelt beside the body.

"Captain, what are you doing?" demanded Escondido.

"Don't touch that corrosive foam!" shouted Dr. Bird.

With my gloved hand, I reached for the fabric hiding Shinobi's face, and the ninja's clothing collapsed, empty. The black wrappings resembling the contestant's body had been hollow. Shinobi was gone.

"Damn, he's legit," Harla said.

A scream broke out behind me, the words foreign to me. Repeating over and over.

I turned in time to catch a glimpse of pale flesh streaked behind a nearby house. Screaming in pain, Shinobi dashed away with hair in a ragged bun, black thong-like underwear, and boobs.

Everyone over the comms gasped.

"She's legit." Harla said in a dreamy whisper.

"She's lucky to be alive," said Dr. Bird.

"Captain," said Harpreet, "I got a translation. Captain Shinobi was repeating, 'There is no honor here. There is no honor here.'"

"What'll happen to her?" I asked.

"She's out," said Escondido. "They'll trap her in a field to remove her if they have to."

Stunned, I said, "She was used for a game she didn't even understand, and she about died for it. Either the Phasmodea-X is malfunctioning, or…"

"Or shooting corrosive foam at a person wasn't an accident." Escondido, likely tired from two days of action, let out a sigh. "How many people are going to die playing this game?"

My blood boiled at his words. It was as if the lump, the monster of sadness in my throat, jumped up to my brain, only it wasn't making me cry. It was making me mad. I gritted my teeth and said as calmly as possible so as to not lash out at Escondido again, "My Grandad's not dead."

Without another word to the team, I commanded the loveseat to shift into the floatboard and hopped on, tearing out of the subdivision probably faster than necessary, up and over the trees and houses. I had Diamonds mute the comms for one minute so we could talk.

"I need an emergency communications jelly bean thing."

I had to talk to the General. And I finally had an idea how.

Chapter 36

There was movement out of the corner of my eye. I commanded to zoom views, but through my cat helmet, the image was shaky. I had expected it to be like the video feeds Diamonds gave me. The Seeker, head and shoulders above the tree line, lumbered to a standstill. Its brown thorax faded lighter and lighter to a tan, then a fiery orange, then a mottled mosaic that blended in with surrounding trees.

I wondered how much longer the team would be muted.

Then, the Seeker took off, ducking beneath the trees and houses, like it was diving into water. As it chased whoever it was chasing, its head reared and lifted into vision every so often like Jaws' fin.

I leaned and flew the floatboard after them. Once I closed within a few streets, Diamonds said carefully, "We advise you don't get closer, Captain."

Instead of moving forward, I moved around, circling the Seeker from a distance, hoping to catch a glimpse of whoever was getting chased. Seemed like more fishing to me. Whatever the bait was, it was now cloaked.

Seeing the direction they were going, I flew ahead, looking down to see where they were driving the giant robot.

Then I saw her. Little Miss Mars, playing hopscotch on the sidewalk. The Robobug headed down the street, scuttling straight for the little girl.

Diamonds said nervously, "Captain, we advise you get out of there."

I asked, "What happens if she gets hit with a missile?"

There was no response. I leaned in, descending toward the Martian girl, the giant robotic stick bug now at the end of the street, not twenty houses away.

This time, Dr. Bird spoke up. "The Seeker is supposed to use paintballs against players wearing their technology."

I remembered another of Grandad's sayings: 'And what does 'supposed to' got to do with anything?'

Stopping, I hovered not twenty feet away from the Martian girl. The stick bug, six or so houses down the street, perked up, its geometric head snapping to stare at her.

My skin crawled.

"What if what happened to Shinobi happens to her?"

"I don't know, Captain."

The Seeker scurried quickly, not two houses away, but I stayed there hovering, paralyzed; I watched helplessly. Miss Mars reached the end of her hopscotch squares, but instead of turning and going again, she looked up and waved…at me.

But I was supposed to be invisible…

A cloud of dust blew in from a nearby yard, sweeping the girl off her feet, and carrying her out of the Seeker's path. "Mist!" I cried out.

The Seeker's red eyes followed the swarm and Captain Mars as they flew into a nearby house.

The revving of a motorcycle engine broke through the air. Uncloaking, Mist drove his motorcycle, tearing down the street, between the Seeker's legs. The giant insect swiveled and crawled after them.

Mist reached to the front of his vehicle and removed the enormous rectangular shield, lifted it with his right arm, then swung it out, yelling with all of his might as he punched at nothing.

The General's stealth three wheeler pixelated into visibility, skidding onto its side from the hit of the Fracture shield. Mist hit the brakes, the motorcycle squealing as it slid sideways to a halt, and he dropped the vehicle, running back to the crashed General.

The Seeker unleashed a flurry of paintballs from its mandibles, and they splattered against Mist's shield.

"Captain Mist is out," Diamonds said.

Captain Mist didn't care, still marching to the General's tipped-over three-wheeler, the General himself climbing out of the shattered window of his mech's cockpit.

"Why?!" Mist screamed as he clocked the General in the jaw with his free hand. The Fracture shield, powered up to repel the paint bullets, protected both contestants from getting hit. The General was still in the game!

With a rigid dignity, the General stood straight in front of the wreckage of his stealth tank, now pelted with blue. He stared down Mist. The motorcycle soldier removed his visored helmet and tossed it onto the yard. A big white guy with a brown military cut and angry eyes, he whispered a command and the motorcycle took off down the street loudly. The Seeker followed after, leaving the players to fight.

Just as the General opened his mouth to answer Mist,

something, or someone, clocked the old guy across the face, knocking him to the ground. The General, no longer under the protection of the Fracture Shield, ran off for the shelter of the nearest house. Spectrum got to a knee, shaking off a little blue paint as well as the punch, as the light around Stab Whisper un-warped, revealing the Halo cosplayer in a boxer's stance.

Stab Whisper laughed at his downed opponent and threw a couple practice punches in the air. Behind him, a cloud of dust formed and consolidated, forming an oversized fist. The Halo boxer turned just in time to get punched into the air by the swarm. Their master, Spectrum, came walking from behind a nearby Elm Tree. The cloud of nanites flowed to Spectrum's arms, merged together giving him protective gauntlets of the tiny merged robots. He put up his dukes to Stab Whisper. Mist, polka-dotted with blue tagging solvent, sprang to his feet and ran into the nearby house after the General.

That's when the brawl started.

Chapter 37

There was a rumble in the distance, and I could see over the rolling hills, storm clouds were on the way to cover the mid-day sun. In his dingy white, Spectrum put up fists reinforced by the ScatterSwarm and merged into metal boxing gloves. Facing him, Stab Whisper squared up in his matte grey Halo costume. Meanwhile, in the next yard over, a big picture window shattered as the General tumbled through. Within the house was the blue-speckled Mist, dramatically dusting off his palms. He was savoring this.

Back on the lawn with the elm tree, Spectrum and Stab Whisper collided. Spectrum in his mucky and bloodied white bodysuit took wide swinging shots, trying to keep this a brawl so he could use his reinforced fists. Although Stab Whisper had limited movement from the hard casing of his outfit, he dodged and blocked each punch, clearly much more adept at hand to hand combat.

Meanwhile, the old General, without his armor or mech suit, ate reinforced punch after punch. Mist yelled out as he planted his hands on the old man's camo uniform, "What was the plan? What were you going to do with my brother?"

His brother? Mist and Spectrum were brothers?!

Stab Whisper was dodging the weighted jabs and uppercuts by Spectrum, then grabbed him by the arm and tossed him over his shoulder onto the ground.

On the other lawn, the General yelled, "You're not even in the competition!" Mist held him up by the lapels before decking him in the jaw.

I wasn't the only one paying close attention. Across the street, in a picture window, partially hidden by a curtain, was the little alien head of Captain Mars. The oversized lifeless black eyes on the girl's mask tracked from the action on the lawn up to me, seeing straight through my bent light, watching me watching her. I swallowed hard.

"Does that creepy little girl see you?" Harla asked.

The sky darkened as the fights continued. Spectrum and Stab Whisper kept at it, Spectrum throwing nanobot-reinforced punch after punch, Stab Whisper using kicks, chops, and throws to keep clear of the heavy hits. The General, on the other hand, was getting the stew beaten out of him by the already-out Mist.

The Robobug burst through a house nearby, crawling out the front of the house as it burst. Its glowing red eyes searched the wreckage. The Seeker showed little to no interest in the four men fighting a few houses away. It scampered to the next house, running head-first through that home's picture window into its first floor.

"What's it looking for?" Harla asked.

I waited for Escondido to answer, but he seemed too enthralled with the fighting, repeating a barely audible, "C'mon, c'mon."

But before I could tell Escondido to snap out of it, I realized what the Seeker saw. Not two houses down, in the path of the Seeker's trail of destruction, was Captain Mars, still watching me from within her oversized alien head.

"Why rig the game?" Mist demanded of the General, bludgeoning the officer, who didn't attempt to defend himself.

I surfed the floatboard down to Captain Mars' window.

"What you doing, fool?" Harla barked at me as I hopped off the silver board and sprinted into the house.

The robobug crashed out of the house next to us, just as I came running out, holding the lightweight Captain Mars.

I leapt onto the floatboard and flew down the street as I heard the mandible gun barrels of the Seeker spit their paint bullets after me. Crouching, I pushed the floatboard as fast as it would go without risking my balance.

Diamonds changed my display. I could see the seeker chasing me and steered toward the brawling contestants down the street. Using the view, I led the Seeker toward brawlers, three of whom were still in the game. In clockwork motion, the giant insect cocked its head to shine bright red eyes onto the yards full of fighting. Strings of paintballs flew from its mouth, raining onto the fighters.

The hand to hand fighters were splattered first, both yielding as they were pelted blue. Along with the hits of paint bullets splattering them and thumping their uniforms, rain began to fall.

The unrelenting stream of paintballs crossed into the next yard, shooting a line of blue into the grass along the way.

With the Fracture shield across his back, Mist had the General just where he wanted him, held up by his own uniform, at Mist's mercy. As the string of blue fire got to them, Mist activated the Fracture shield and pulled the General underneath it, saving them both.

Diamonds said, "Enhanced audio."

Then, along with the pitter patter of a steadily increasing rain, I heard Mist say, "Why? Why'd you rig the game? Why do you want to win so bad?"

The General laughed in response. "I didn't want to win. I wanted to shut it down!"

"And that's why you tried to kill the ninja? And you'll kill the dragon, the boy, and the girl, too? That's why you killed SteelCut?"

The breath caught in my chest, and my hand went to my helmet mouth. Would the General admit to it? Maybe I didn't even have to talk to him...

The old man laughed again raggedly. "No, but I'd skip your funeral."

"Admit you rigged the game!"

"I admit I rigged..."

Mist tightened his grip on the General's shirt.

"I rigged my discarded gear!"

The General's ten-foot tall mech robot, camo green drenched in blue splotches, crashed into the thick neck of Seeker. Like a T-Rex attacked by a raptor, the beige stick bug flailed and swatted its front mantis arms as the mech latched on. The Battlesuit didn't punch or fire at the Seeker, wasn't even attacking. It just hugged the giant's neck as the engines blasted out of the bottom of its feet, driving them both into the ground.

The General used the opportunity to unleash a series of precise hits and kicks onto Mist's face, chest, and gut. The old man had been playing opossum. He hauled ass into the nearest house, just as the Seeker got back to standing.

After I surfed the floatboard up the street and away from danger, the team began using the comms again. "Stab Whisper and Spectrum are out," Diamonds said like she couldn't believe it.

"And then there were four."

But all I could think was how glad I was the General was still in the game. I still had my chance.

I heard another little girl's voice. This one different still. "LAND NOW."

But this voice didn't come from the jellybean comm link. This voice was little Miss Mars', only the voice didn't come from her helmet. It came from within my own head. But instead of thinking about how weird that was, all I could think was, "I should land now." I knew it was mind control, and I didn't care. I obeyed the voice.

Chapter 38

Lightning flashed and illuminated the darkened house, interrupting my hypnosis for an instant and making me jump. Sleepwalking toward something, following the voice, I didn't remember climbing the stairs. Through the hallway lined with framed photos of a family I'd never meet, I walked, following Miss Mars farther into the house.

Clouding my thoughts and controlling my actions, she spoke without turning to me. At times her voice came from her, but sometimes it was coming from inside my head. I tried to shake it off, to stop listening, even to run away, but it was like something was steering me, like a controller with a stuck joystick. I was out of control. Like some zombie, I followed Captain Mars down the hall lit from rain-streaked windows.

"Captain? What's going on? Your blood pressure has dropped, and your heart rate is way too calm," Dr. Bird said from somewhere.

"YOU SHOULD MUTE THE TEAM," the Martian said inside my head.

"Diamonds, give me a whole-team mute for ten minutes."

"Captain, are you sure?"

"Do it, Hunt!" I screamed, surprising even myself at how angry I sounded.

"OK," their tiny voice replied.

Somewhere ahead of me in the house, Miss Mars stopped. I stopped, too. Frozen with fear at whatever her plan was for me.

"Why aren't you afraid of the Seeker," I asked, "when it doesn't have a brain you can control?"

"Oh, Mr. Creepy-Crawly's got a brain, alright, Kitty." Miss Mars' voice came from the room ahead, muffled by her mask. "There's a man back there behind that mean old stick bug, far, far away. But if I try real hard, I can get to him."

"There's a man driving it? So a man tried to kill Shinobi?"

Then the powerful voice inside my own head, "ENOUGH. TELL ME ABOUT WHAT POWERS THE THRONE."

That's when I noticed my floatboard behind me, bobbing midair, powered by the Lack.

"WHAT IS THE LACK?"

I remembered the story Harpreet had told me about a late-stage nuclear fission trapped in a quantum vacuum suspended by ionic, magnetic, and gravitational fields.

"WHAT? WHAT DOES THAT MEAN?"

Harpreet had talked about Captain SteelCut in his shiny metal Cowboy hat wandering the multiverse.

"WHAT DO YOU THINK THE LACK IS?"

I hoped the Lack was the gateway to another dimension, but deep down I knew it wasn't. It was just radiation. My heart dropped and my knees about gave way when I realized I thought the Lack was just a nuclear blast suspended in time.

I knew Grandad was dead.

I laid back, collapsed, really, flopping onto the floatboard. I felt like I was going to throw up. Then I felt the firm grip of the sadness monster tightening around my throat. The world spun around me. I would never see Grandad again.

From the other room, the sing-song voice came again, muffled by the alien face. "I've been looking forward to playing you in this game, Chase. Oops! I meant Captain Kitty! You've been playing so well. I'm very impressed. We all are. I've played thrice, and I'm already bored. The fun part is the players; the Seeker just gets in the way.

"SteelCut was the most fun to play with. I couldn't read his mind. I couldn't make him do things. But you know what I think? I don't think he's dead. I just think he's soooo good at hiding, he found the ultimate hiding spot. The Lack."

The room stopped spinning, and I managed to sit up.

Miss Mars stood two feet away in her dirty doll dress, her alien head tilting in curiosity. "Did you know how susceptible to subconscious suggestion you were, Kitty Kiddo Captain Chase? Very easy to hypnotize, very easy to incept, very easy to steer. And now you won't know what's real and what's in your head for the rest of the game, Kitty Kiddo Captain Chase!"

And then, in her same sing-song voice, she chanted, louder and louder, "Kitty Kiddo Captain Chase! Kitty Kiddo Captain Chase! Kitty Kiddo Captain Chase!"

"What are you doing?" I mumbled, still feeling like I got hit by a truck, emotionally and mentally.

"Kitty Kiddo Captain Chase!"

"She's fishing," Diamonds said into my earpiece. "Captain, get out of there now!"

"Kitty Kiddo Captain Chase!"

I didn't hear Mr. Creepy-Crawly, or rather, the Robobug

Seeker until he was crashing through the house.

My recent life choices had led me to see many houses, all much nicer than my one-story home, get destroyed. Robots, drones, hot water heaters, all do quite a number on even the best-built house. But nothing prepared me for the feeling of an earthquake, then realizing that instead of standing inside, you're on the edge of the wreckage.

We were still standing in something that resembled a house, a couple of the frames on the walls hadn't even fallen, but there was now a sheer drop-off from the second-floor into... nothing. Rubble. Like we were in a house sliced in a cross-section to film a sitcom.

I'd forgotten about Miss Mars for a second until the lightning flashed and I saw the silhouette of the alien head and floofy dress. Through the filter of rain, she looked up fearlessly, right at the Seeker.

Standing on his hind four legs, the Robobug was gargantuan up close. It dwarfed the two-story house, and with the pouring rain, it was tough to see its face clearly. Just the glow of the lifeless robotic eyes.

Tagging solvent poured from its mouth onto Miss Mars, black in the red light of the Seeker's eyes. But there was no screaming or smoke. No smell of burning flesh and chemicals.

"Captain Mars is out," Diamonds said. "Captain please get out of there."

But I was frozen. Couldn't move. I just stared up, the falling rain haloed its face in glowing red.

And with two lumbering steps, it was above me. I could barely make out the movement of its gun barrel mandibles spasming.

I heard Diamonds' voice again. "Chase, run."

That snapped me out of it, but maybe too late. I was trapped, right below the Seeker. Nowhere to run.

I stepped forward into the drop-off.

There was nothing ahead of me, no floor for my foot to land on, just a mangled pile of wood, pipes, furniture, and photos below. Just a destroyed home. And I fell forward into it. Straight for a jagged four by four pointing up at me, poised to stab me through the chest.

Chapter 39

As I fell toward the wooden skewer, I knew it would happen. The sharp end of the broken four by four rushed up at me, but then I felt the pressure on my back, my butt. Like I was being pushed. Like I was being held.

The Throne scooped me out of the air and into the rainy night.

In a flash of lightning, I saw the monstrous Seeker, tagging solvent pouring from its mouth, turning to follow me as I fled into the safety of the night sky.

"Captain, there's a missile on your tail," Diamonds said.

Two streets away from the Seeker, the missile still pursued me.

I was surprised I wasn't scared. I was tired of being scared. Heck, even in this game, I was tired of hiding. Something had replaced my fear: determination.

I steered the Throne to the ground, hopped off, and commanded it to shift shapes. The majority of the Throne followed me on foot, hovering as the antique chair. Behind me, the missile crashed into an explosion of blue paint as it ran into a fraction of the Throne, which had morphed into a Juniper bush. I kept walking.

"Where are you going?" I heard Escondido's voice for the first time in a while. But there was no use explaining. They'd just try to talk me out of it.

"Dude, you're shifting too much," Harpreet said. "She's gonna overheat and start stalling out the next time you try to morph."

"I know," I said as I came to the wreckage of the brawl. The houses had been blown out by the Seeker scurrying through them to find Miss Mars. I passed the broken picture window Mist had thrown the General through, chunks of lawn tossed around like an invasion of moles.

I walked up to the house I'd last seen the General escape into.

"Ain't no way he's still there," said Harla, understanding what I was doing.

Pushing open the door, I hoped she was wrong.

Muddy footprints stood out on the wooden floor and white carpet. I imagined how mad the homeowners would be if one of their kids caused such a mess. I chuckled and followed the footsteps, although I didn't need to look to see where they led.

With a creak, I opened the door to the unfurnished basement. The Throne hovered behind me as I made my way down the wooden stairs, my footsteps muffled by mud and rain. I continued on the concrete floor, then stopped, the Throne pulling up to hover beside me as we stood before the General's hiding spot, the hot water heater. But the General didn't have the Throne to help him in and out of the big white cylinder. Probably just copying my hiding spot from earlier.

Laughing, I gave the command for the Throne to shift into a jaws of life.

"Cap, she's gonna stall," Harpreet said. "This morph'll freeze her up for at least ten minutes."

"That's fine," I said, loud enough for the contestant within to hear. "I've got something to say to the General."

Lit by the orange light, the antique wooden chair showed its gridlines, which grew wider and then stopped. The grinding sound of a car out of gear came from within. It stalled.

"General Holter," I said, "I know you're in there and still in this blasted game. And I don't care. I don't care about your stupid game anymore. I don't care if I win, or if I lose. I only care about getting the rest of the contestants out of this alive. That means you, me, and the clone.

"My plan was to give you a comm link, so we could talk. So I could ask you a bunch of questions, so I could prove my grandad was alive. But he ain't alive. You killed him. You've been sabotaging this game for who-knows-how-long just because you miss the good ol' days when your men won every year. I'm here to tell you, the old ways ain't better. My grandad's ways were better.

"Everything my grandad built could have helped people. The Throne could keep soldiers alive and keep civilians safe in the right hands. Instead, this Throne is the closest thing Grandad has to a real tombstone. All because you don't like to lose."

"Enough!" a muffled echo came from within the hot water heater.

Fear came back like an arrow to my heart. The Throne was still spasming mid-shift, not becoming the necessary jaws of life anytime soon.

The white cylinder of the water heater bent with a rumble and the screeching sound of tearing metal. A gloved hand tore through the outer shell of the appliance.

Luckily, the General wasn't used to hopping in and out of hot water heaters like I was. Tearing through the metal barehanded takes time. So, I spun around to scamper back up the stairs and out of the house.

But waiting for me at the front door out in the driving rain, standing taller than the first floor of the house, was the blue-splattered Battlesuit of the General's.

Chapter 40

An orange warning light flashed between the Battlesuit's shoulders where a head may have been. Through the patter of rain on my helmet, I could hear a man's voice coming from the mech. "Warning. Equipment Failure. Discarded equipment malfunction."

"I know that voice," Escondido said.

It was the General, only through a speaker.

With a crow hop, the damaged mech suit stepped forward to grab me. On instinct, I jumped back, the oversized robot arm tearing through the door jamb like it was balsa wood. Moving faster than I was thinking, adrenaline and self-preservation pushed me to run through the house to the back door. By the time I'd gotten outside, the blue-splattered Battlesuit was landing in the backyard.

The General's voice spoke again through a speaker in the mech. "Chase Hawkins!"

There was nowhere to go. Soon the General would make it out of the hot water heater. The Seeker might be here before that, and for all I knew, maybe whoever controlled it worked for the General. Maybe the Seeker's mission was to kill me next. I couldn't fight the Battlesuit, and the Throne was still in the basement, stuck mid-shift. All I had was my uniform and my cat-faced helmet.

My helmet. The minicube.

I took the cat head off, and whispered into it, "Floatboard" before tossing in front of me.

This piece of equipment hadn't been shifting constantly over the past two days. Midair, it flashed orange as it fell, forming a skateboard-sized floatboard. I hopped on and flew past the mech suit's swiping.

"You missed!" I yelled. But instead of flying into the rainy night, I flew back around at the mech.

"Captain, what are you doing?" Escondido asked, his voice tinged with fear of the answer.

I didn't have to answer; Harla did. "Luis, ain't you been paying attention?"

The mech suit took another swing at me, and another. But the smaller floatboard reacted quickly, and I flew circles around the thing.

That's when I heard the booming footsteps, freezing my guts solid. Straight out of my childhood Jurassic Park nightmares, the giant Seeker stalked us in the rain, lit by the sporadic flash of lightning.

In one last orbit, I swiveled around the Battlesuit and away from the monstrous Seeker when, from the back door of the house, what appeared to be a man-sized glass marble rolled in the rain.

The crystal ball effect.

Easily dodging the mech again, I floated up to meet the towering Seeker, a misty cloud of red surrounding its eyes. "Come on!" I yelled at it. "Let's play!"

245

"Get out of there, Captain! This isn't a game," Escondido cried out as the Seeker's mandibles straightened and took aim.

"It is if you treat it like one," I said, hearing Dr. Bird's voice in my head.

The stream of paintballs fired. I dove off the side of the floatboard, as the projectiles missed me and poured into the crystal ball. The minicube's quantum airbag deployed, temporarily suspending me in a sparkly cloud.

The General, who'd just been bending light below me, appeared, now soaked in blue. He looked up at me in the airbag and said, "It can't be. That's how he died!"

That's how who died? I tried to find meaning in the General's words. But then Harpreet's emergency protocols kicked in and the minicube, now a small chair, scooped me out of the air, just in time to miss another string of paintballs.

The Seeker was right on me. There was nowhere to go but back into the house.

After flying in, I hopped off the minicube floatboard at a run, morphing it back into my cat helmet, while somewhere behind me, the General repeated in disbelief, "That's how he died!"

Sprinting back down to the basement, I hoped the Throne had finished morphing. The second I opened the door, I was hit in the face with a blast of heat. It got hotter and hotter down the stairs, closer to the Throne, hopefully a floatboard. No such luck. Just bright orange coming from a floating jumble of cubes.

"Deploy the quantum airbag," I commanded them.

"Deploying gravitational field."

One of the slow-motion cubes emitted a sparkling cloud, an amorphous blob floating out between me and the Lack. I fished the commlink jellybean out of my pocket, and tossed it through the quantum airbag into the glowing radiation of the Lack.

That's how the General saw Grandad disappear into the Lack. That's how he thought Grandad died—safe inside of a quantum airbag.

A thunderous crash deafened my ears. The entire house shook as plaster and wood fell in chunks from the ceiling. But it wasn't the Throne causing the rumble. The basement roof peeled back like the lid of a sardine can, and water poured down. The Seeker stood above me, its two clawed arms picking apart chunks of the house.

Its dexterous mouth aimed barrels at me.

The room without a ceiling, rain pouring through, grew cold. The orange light behind me had faded.

Where the stalled shifting cubes once floated in the middle of the room, was now a free-standing wooden door.

I heard the stream of paintballs, like angry purring breath. My hand jumped to the knob.

Voices exploded through the comms all at once.

Harla yelled, "No, fool!"

Escondido warned the door could lead to out of bounds.

Harpreet said I didn't have protection against radiation to return.

Diamonds just said my name.

I turned the doorknob and pushed into the orange light and the wave of heat. Another sparkly cloud surrounded me, shielding me from the door's radiation, and I stepped through.

* * *

The sky was dark, but orange was everywhere. Not ambient orange light, everything—all the walls, the floor, even my hands—glowed orange, shining. I waved my hand in front of me, leaving orange trails. I opened up my helmet and could breathe.

But I was still there, in the basement, on the other side of the freestanding door, everything giving off orange.

Only, everyone from the game was gone. General Holter, his suit, the Seeker…all gone.

But I wasn't alone. A figure descended the cellar stairs, giving off yellows and oranges difficult to look at directly. I couldn't make out the face, but I recognized a gesture. He scratched the left side of his mustache and shuddered with a laugh.

The ground fell from beneath me as my body went numb. Like I was floating. Or falling.

"Well howdy, Kiddo."

Grandad.

VI

Part Six

The Lack

Chapter 41

"Took you long enough," Grandad said, smiling and scratching the right side of his mustache.

It was him, actually him. Captain SteelCut, dressed just like he was in the footage for the last game, in Powers, Limited coverall, boots, and gloves. His cowboy hat was missing, showing his thinning Einstein head of hair.

We stood in that same basement, ceiling and roof ripped off, orange light everywhere.

Uncertain of what to do, I wanted to hug him. I wanted to cry. I wanted to deck him in the jaw for leaving. Instead, I asked questions, unable to stop. "What is this place? Where are we? Is this some dream? Are you in another dimension? Are you already dead?"

Grandad smiled with sad eyes in a way only old people have earned. "I don't know, Kiddo, but come here."

The old man hugged me, and I felt him. Solid, not a ghost, still bony, but warm and alive. His knobby fingers brushed hair out of my face. He even smelled like Grandpa, Irish Spring and WD-40. Tears poured out of our eyes. I had done it. The smile spread wide on my face but gave way to crying in a way

I just couldn't stop.

"Oh, how I've missed you, Kiddo."

"I missed you!" I said into the wet shoulder of his coveralls.

"And I'm sorry I kept all of these things from you. The Throne, the game, Todd Fowler..."

"It's OK, Grandad. I'm sorry I haven't done better at the game."

"How's it going? What day are you on?"

"End of two, I guess," I sniffed back snot and wiped my eyes with the bomber jacket's wrist. I took a big breath to let it all sink in.

Interest grew into a glint in Grandad's eye as a smile pushed up at his mustache. "And how many's left?"

"Two, I guess."

His mouth fell into an O, then stretched back to a smile. "Hot dawgit, Kiddo. You're a natural!"

Stopping myself from smiling with him, I shook my head. "No, it's been terrible. There were two different groups of cheaters, and a woman almost died while I watched, and I keep losing my temper. I yelled at Escondido."

Grandad broke into his boisterous, high pitched laugh and I felt my shoulders relax. I took an uneasy deep breath and managed to laugh too.

"Old puss-face Escondido, huh? He on the team? Used to call him Esco the Grouch!"

We laughed for a while until we didn't, and a quietness held between us. "It sounds like you're doing great and you don't know it."

Then Grandad switched over to his storytelling voice, wagging a finger to let me know he was setting a parable up. "Man fishing in a boat on a lake. Another man, in the water, splashing and causing a stir, yells up at him, 'I cain't swim! I cain't swim, help me, help me!' Man in the boat calls back, 'Whaddya call that you're doing now then?' and then casts his lure right back in the lake."

I nodded and smiled, happy to listen, to be able to listen, and understanding this moment was precious, even if I didn't 'get' the parable.

"Is this place your lake now, Grandad?" I asked, scared this fishing story was his way of saying he had to stay.

"I don't rightly know. Best I can tell, it's some kind of dimension layered within ours, made up of the trails of energy within subatomic particles. But I can't be sure."

I laughed. I couldn't help it, it just bubbled up.

Grandad joined in chuckling, but asked, "What is it?"

"Well, if you don't know what it is, and you're the smartest guy I know, and you've been here for six months, we don't have a prayer of figuring it out!"

We both had a good laugh for a spell. Grandad said, "Come on now, I ain't the smartest guy you know."

"Sure you are," I said.

Of course he was. Grandad was always the smartest, it was just a fact, just like it's dark at night, or the sky was blue, or high school sucks. Grandad's a super genius.

"I do okay, but you know Harpreet, right? He's smarter than I am. Heck, maybe even Harla. Diamonds, too, in a way."

I thought about the team, back in mission control, waiting and not knowing what was happening. Pangs of guilt crept up, urging me to hurry, to get back to the game, back to leading the team.

"Here we go!" Grandad said suddenly. The orange light leeched away, and everything faded dark. My body lurched, like riding a roller coaster, then I stumbled to the ground, landing on all fours. After that, like the beginning of the Lion King, the orange light crept back on. We were in a small room, with tables and desks and seating for eight or nine people. Monitors and computers were everywhere.

Grandad was beside me again, exclaiming, "And you just figured out how to travel in the Lack!"

"I did?"

Within the room of orange workspaces, blue figures emerged, ebbing and waning like shadows of mist. Standing out in orange, they sat in silence, but I could see them arguing with one another. One patted her head compulsively.

Grandad continued, "You thought about someone. An anchor, kind of. A connection to someone in the real world. You can see them. It's how I watched you from here, Chase."

One misty blue figure, the most solid one, stood up from a seat and ran toward me. I braced for impact, but it passed through me, like a blue hologram, running out of the orange room.

"You're connected to your team," Grandad said, observing and figuring it out as he said it. "I was only connected to you."

My dreams. The moments I wanted to give up but heard him whisper my name. It *had* been him. And now we...*I* was connected to the team.

"This is...mission control." Around the room, the misty figures were arguing, pointing at each other while standing. My team.

I followed the path of the most distinct blue figure, the one that walked right through me. They were in the hall, sitting with their back against the mission control wall, looking at something in their hands.

"Who is it?" Grandad asked.

"Diamonds," I said.

"What is she doing?"

"They," I corrected. "They're texting. Me."

I don't know how, but I could feel Diamonds, too. In a vague way, I felt what they were feeling. A rising panic. A surge of tightness in the back, between the shoulders, up the neck. Cold sweats. Helplessness.

Grandad's voice was excited and rushed. "Hot dawgit, kiddo, you're a natural! You figured out traveling in the Lack in minutes! Took me days! You're already finding connections to the real world. That took me weeks. You're going to be great here!"

"I have to go back," I said as I realized it.

"Well, you can't go back," Grandad said as if he were surprised.

"What?"

"How? You have more quantum fields? The one you're in is already diminished. You're soaking in radiation from the Lack right now."

My mind raced. He was right. I hadn't taken it into account getting back. The quantum airbag was weakening by the second, which meant I'd be taking on radiation before I knew it. I figured Grandad would have the equipment, some kind of plan to get back, but he didn't.

There were no hidden Throne safety measures, no hair-brained schemes based on half-cocked theories. There wasn't $20 worth of inventions in the whole danged Lack. All I had was this cat helmet.

Holy Crapola, I forgot the cat helmet was the minicube.

"What if I use the minicube?!"

"For what?"

"To take us back?"

"You can't use a portal to the Lack within the Lack. You're already here. And we don't have the airbags."

"But I could make a radiation-tight suit and take the door back."

That meant going back alone. The monster of sadness made it to the Lack and choked me, tears flowing freely down my dirty face. I couldn't help but cry.

But not Grandad. He had a look of pride. Old SteelCut scratched his mustache, thought about it for a second, and then let out a big sigh. His eyebrows tilted up in a plea as he whispered, "Stay."

The word knocked the air out of my lungs. It hit me like a ton of bricks. It shifted the axis of the world.

Grandad, maybe sensing my uncertainty, kept talking, "Stay, Chase. Stay with me here and let's figure this place out. Harness its energy. Learn to control the Lack."

He needed me. Not that he loved me or missed me, or spent the same time trying to get back to me as I spent to find him, he plumb needed me to figure out the Lack. I *was* good at this, all of this. Maybe everything I learned from the team about the Throne, about the Lack, had prepared me for *this*, got me ready for this place, whatever this place was.

We'd figure it out.

He smiled with his orange glow, his soft old eyes.

Behind me, the misty blue figure threw the object they held and buried their face in their hands. Diamonds' body shook as they sobbed. Imagining a life here was hard to do, playing with the laws of physics, experiencing things no other person ever has. Not to just invent, but to *explore*. With my Grandad.

Isn't that what I always wanted?

I'd be a scientific pioneer. No more bullies or grades or high school or sports or awkward feelings about boys and girls.

No more parents fighting. No more hiding. No more science project, no more team. No more teasing from Harla.

No more time with Diamonds.

I swallowed hard. Even though I knew it was impossible, I pleaded, "Come back with me."

"I can't," he said.

Closing my eyes, I could barely bring myself to whisper, "I know."

But I couldn't open my eyes to face him. We stood feet away from one another, but in my heart, Grandad was already gone. Forever.

Right then and there, I had my chance to say goodbye. All I had to do was open my eyes and speak. But it was too difficult, it hurt too much. I blocked him out, blocked the whole room from my mind, forgot about mission control, even Diamonds, hard as it was.

Then I pictured the freestanding door. And I traveled.

Back in the basement, still in the Lack, I opened my eyes to the freestanding door giving off orange light. The cat helmet shifted into a thermal hazmat suit I zipped myself into. Then I walked through the doorway, out of the Lack and into the blinding brightness.

VII

Part Seven

Finish the Game

Chapter 42

"Captain? Captain, are you OK?" Escondido's voice was ragged. Back on the other side of the door, the reality side, rain poured from the night sky into the wrecked basement.

"Yeah, I'm fine," I said to the team. "How long was I gone?"

"A couple of minutes," Escondido said.

I asked, "And it's down to us and the chameleon?"

"And then there were two," Harla answered.

If the game was still on, the chameleon wasn't safe. "Where can I find them?"

Then, from the corner of the rainy room, laughter began as a rumble. A low, bubbling hiccuping coming from the body slumped in the corner, so still I hadn't noticed him. Laid out with his blue splotched head propped up against the cinderblock wall, his leg askew at an unnatural angle, was the General.

The General.

"Kiddo SteelCut, throwing away his first MC Squared championship. Your grandfather would be ashamed of you."

"I'm not too sure about that."

"Why not wait it out? Let the bug paint the Triceratops."

"Because the bug is using corrosive missiles." I paused for effect. "Just like you ordered."

"Captain, the Seeker's on the move," Diamonds said into my ear.

"Is that Esco the Grouch? Telling you what to do?" the General asked, before his voice went breathy and high, without any care. "Not my orders, not that it matters. Nobody controls any of it anymore. There's always a game within the game."

I tuned him out and focused on what had to be done. "It's time to end it," I said.

"End what?" The General asked.

"I wasn't talking to you, *sir.* You're out," I said.

"Damn," Harla said. "Captain, you sexy when you talk like that!"

Glad the team couldn't see me blush, I commanded the door to the Lack to morph back into the floatboard, hoping it had cooled off. It shifted with no problem.

"Captain," Harpreet interjected, "I don't know how many more smooth shifts she's got left."

"Diamonds, any idea where our clone friend is?"

I was already steady on the floatboard before Diamonds could answer, shifting the minicube back from a nuke suit into my cat helmet. "I don't have eyes on him."

I asked, "Where is the Seeker, then?"

"North side of the pond, headed for the playground. Oh, there he is, Captain," said Diamonds, their voice tinged with sadness knowing my plan. "I see where the chameleon is. Hidden in the playground. Go get him."

Escondido asked, "Are you sure? I don't see anything…"

But I was already off, leaning into it, accelerating and climbing higher into the air, over the trees and houses.

"You're pushing it, bro," Harpreet warned. "Expending all this energy is going to slow shifts."

"It'll be over soon," was all I said.

"What's happening?" asked Escondido, the confidence in his voice slipping.

"Let Cap do his thing," Harla said, like she was comforting him.

In the driving rain of the playing field, I sped east on the floatboard into the brightening grey right before dawn, right for the north end of the park. The board flew so fast I felt my footing give, and my boots slipped back on the board's slick surface.

"Magnetizing boots," Diamonds' soft voice said.

"Thanks, and Harpreet?" I asked, yelling against the noise of the wind in my face.

"Yeah, Cap?"

"The Throne's secret safety devices?"

"Yeah?"

"Is one of them teleportation goop?"

"Yeah, Bro, the cube's got goop in case emergency teleportation is needed."

"And is it against the rules?"

"No, it's good Captain," Harla answered me back.

Ahead, the monstrous robot was lumbering around the small pond toward the playground, its shining red eyes visible from this distance, locked on their target.

"Captain, you're coming in uncloaked," Escondido warned.

Past the line of houses, I flew into the open air of the park, the Seeker a couple hundred yards away.

"Engineer, can you give me some light?" I asked.

The floatboard glowed white. My cat helmet lit up the falling rain around me. I slowed to a stop, hopped off, and waved the board over my head, screaming to distract the Seeker.

"Hey! Over here!"

It wasn't taking the bait, its red eyes still focused on the playground, not veering from its path.

"How much goop we got?" I asked.

"Two tanks' worth if you combine it," Harpreet answered. "Should be enough for the chameleon or the Phasmodea-X."

"What are you doing, Captain?" Escondido asked with a tinge of desperation in his gravelly voice.

"Split the Throne up. A tank of goop stays with me. I'll take a little floatboard. A tank goes with a decoy Kiddo."

"Cap, the Seeker pulling out the big gun," Harla warned.

Sure enough, within the Robobug's mouth, the blue-stained mandibles parted to make way for a white missile, the biggest one yet. Maybe enough corrosive tagging solvent to kill the chameleon.

As commanded, the floatboard split, some morphing into my doppelganger, some shrinking into a smaller floatboard, the rest converting to tanks to hold all of the emergency goop.

We split up, the doppelganger running for the nearest house, while I flew after the Seeker, a tank of goop strapped to my back.

As the giant robot came to a stand still, its missile tongue trained on the playground, I closed in and opened the hose valve to spray goop at the Robobug. I had to save the clone from that corrosive missile.

Starting with the eyes, I generously gooped its head and

spiny thorax before hosing its stilt legs. It thrashed and shook about as I corkscrewed around the thing, filling the dewy morning with the smell of cotton candy.

"Captain, the clone's on the move!" Diamonds said.

In the pre-dawn light, I could barely make out Furcifer the chameleon. Disguised as a yellow plastic slide, the colorful figure scurried away toward the pond.

"How's number two doing?" I asked, referring to my doppelganger.

"Destination portal ready, dude," Harpreet said.

Emptying the rest of the tank into a puddle in front of the Seeker, I gave the order "Engage."

I never knew the goop-gate gave off light. The silvery sludge lit up, illuminating the whole Robobug as it fell into the puddle, sinking like it was in quicksand. It fell through the goop and into the house my doppelganger had hosed.

It slid further into the puddle, but just before its silver sludged head submerged under the spacial lubricant, the Seeker fired the missile from its mouth.

I gasped as the projectile streamed over my head, leaving a wake of white smoke, headed right for the chameleon. But then, it passed over the scurrying chameleon. It flew with a PLUNK into the pond.

I was confused, but just for an instant.

"He's going to make that pond one big acid bath!" Escondido said.

I pivoted the floatboard to follow after the giant clone, surging through the air, pushing the Throne to its limit. The chameleon scrambled toward the water as blue clouds of corrosive solvent bloomed throughout the pond.

"You ain't outrunning that chameleon," Harla said.

"I don't have to," I replied.

I commanded the board to increase to full speed. The sudden acceleration sent me tumbling off the back of the board and onto the wet grass.

"Captain!" someone yelled, as the ground and the sky tumbled. I hit my back, then my butt, then my limbs, all at once. Everything flashed red. Then I was in the dark.

I rolled to a stop, but the world kept spinning. I tasted rust with a thick tongue.

"Captain," a voice said again, maybe the same voice, maybe someone else. Maybe even saying more.

"Captain."

Against the spin of the world, I pushed myself up onto my elbows.

I tore off the cat helmet. By that time, the morning sky was almost blinding. The pond water was an unnatural bright blue.

I shook dizziness from my head, desperate to keep the sky straight up and the ground down.

"Captain."

Then my eyes focused, and there they were.

The Throne—the floatboard, my inheritance from my Grandad—sliced through the air in an arc, gaining on the running chameleon...then speeding over it, past it, and diving into the water with barely a splash.

"Chase," Diamonds pled.

The voice snapped me back. I could hear and see. It hurt to breathe.

I felt...cloudy. My neck stung. I couldn't put weight on my left arm. But I had to finish the plan. I had to stop the Seeker from hurting anyone.

"Shift to Throne," I commanded, my voice hoarse through the comms.

"She's going to stall!" cried Harpreet.

"Captain, what are you doing?" cried Escondido.

"Using the power of the Lack to save the clone," I managed to say before falling back to the ground. I groaned as the wet earth hit my ribs.

Within the still water, the cloud of blue tagging solvent lit up from beneath as the pond roiled and steam bubbled up.

"She's freezing up, stalling, mid-shift!" Harpreet yelled.

Glowing orange illuminated the billowing blue cloud from underneath as the surface of the water frothed like some rabid dog.

The chameleon skidded to a halt, his scaly reptile digits gripping the slick grass at the pond's edge. Right there, the acidic water sank as the pond drained, bubbling. Blue retreated farther and farther, more and more discolored mud showing at the edges, until in the middle of a grey crater, in a fog of steam, the antique chair stood.

The Throne sat covered in a blue film, shooting sparks and fingers of smoke until squares of the chair pixelated and changed color, the stealth mode of the vehicle failing, the corrosive tagging solvent eating away at Grandad's invention.

Cube by cube, the Throne malfunctioned, as the antique chair flickered into an exaggerated chair shape made up of gray blocks peppered in blue. Like something from Minecraft, only instead of perfectly squared cubes, my stealth equipment was melting under the blue tagging solvent.

"Captain," Diamonds said, "you are out. Game over."

The chameleon turned and ran back toward the safety of the playground. It had no idea of the pond full of corrosive liquid it just avoided.

My arms gave out beneath me. The wet ground slapped me in the face. I realized I was smiling because a split in my lip hurt. For some reason, that tiny pain made me laugh.

A voice called out angrily. Maybe Dr. Bird. I remember thinking I didn't care if she was mad at me as I drifted off into unconsciousness.

Chapter 43

Groggy.

My thoughts…thick.

Eyelids, heavy.

A hospital room. Hi-tech. 3D readouts. Someone in the corner.

Back to sleep.

Captain Mars, or maybe just a blurry nurse.

Someone still in the corner. Can't see.

Was I sleeping already?

Tongue is thick. Heavy. Dry.

Corner Empty. Someone else in the room. Hoodie. Button-up.

Todd Fowler?

Said something I didn't catch. "Been watching me"?

Something else about support. Then a smile. A pat on the shoulder.

He leaned in and whispered. Stern, almost angry. "Secret," and, "daughter," and, "portal," and then, "I will, I promise you."

Time passed, but maybe not.

Fowler was still here.

Angrier.

No. Not Fowler. Holter.

His words steady, like a machine gun. "Hated your grand-dad… Respected the Hell out of him… Don't recognize the game anymore… Don't know who's in charge… Screwing up. Civilian loss of life is unacceptable."

He wiped the corner of his eye. Squinting and halting my breath, I concentrated, trying to follow his words. "… a promise that day to your Grandad once I failed to save him with the net gun. I would make the safety of contestants my number one priority, even more than winning. Someone drove the Seeker to see the attack lizard as a vehicle. Someone could have killed that Japanese mercenary. Someone shot corrosive missiles at her, at the chameleon. Trying to stop them, I may have gone…a little far."

The uniformed figure stood, more worn than dangerous, snapped to attention, and saluted. "I look forward to working with you, Captain. Thank you for saving the lizard. Of course, he may be the one chasing us next game."

But the General stayed.

Only he didn't. It was someone else.

Then nothing.

Did I black out? I didn't feel groggy.

Someone here.

Miss.

Gone.

Medics in full white hazmat suits crowded over me.

I drifted off.

* * *

I woke up on a cot in a blank white room, no furniture on the white floor, nothing on the white walls, white sheets covering me. And somehow, someone had changed me into a surgical gown, also white.

I didn't recognize the room, and figured this was somewhere in DARPA HQ.

I headed for the door, surprised at how good I felt. There was no stinging in my elbow or knees, and my ribs no longer stabbed with pain when I inhaled. My body felt tired and weak, but not pained.

I turned the white doorknob.

The door opened to the hangar back at Powers, Limited, complete with most of the team, still in black suits. Diamonds spun around first and their face lit up.

"Captain!" Everyone yelled at once and rushed over. Escondido clapped, Diamonds and Harla hugged me, and Dr. Bird pushed in front to inspect me. She admonished me for not staying on the gurney, declared I probably had some bruised ribs and maybe a deep bruise in my left elbow, then let people hug me, but instructed them to do so gently.

Harla tousled my hair and hugged my neck. Dr. Bird stood behind me rubbing and checking out my back until Escondido came in for a handshake. I stood as straight as I could and shook his hand. But the tough guy veneer was gone. With tears in his eyes and a huge grin too big for his face, Luis Escondido pulled me in for a hug.

Then everyone was hugging, and the lump in my throat came back, but I didn't mind. For a moment, my eyes met Diamonds', and I thought I was going to lose it. My breath caught in my chest when they leaned in and planted a soft kiss on my cheek. My face flushed, and I couldn't fight off the smile taking over.

Changing the subject, I mumbled, "How long was I out?"

"You look great, Captain," Escondido said.

"Injuries sustained are surprisingly minor," said Dr. Bird, reading a tablet at the base of the cot.

I cleared my throat and asked, "What day is it?"

"Are you feeling OK, Captain?" asked Diamonds with their hand on my chest, sitting me back down on the hospital bed.

Harpreet said loud and slow, "Can you tell me who the president is, bro?"

"How long was I out?" I asked again, realizing the team was wearing dressed down white shirts with loose ties and sleeves rolled up. Even Escondido had a five-oclock shadow.

"Like...an hour...?" said Escondido.

"Like less than an hour, fool!" Harla laughed.

"Less than an hour?" I tried to make sense of it. Had I imagined Holter and Fowler's visits?

"Just long enough for the council to render a decision," said Dr. Bird, seriously.

"What kind of decision?" I asked, feeling dread in her words.

"The bad kind," said Escondido. "Everyone accused of rule-breaking was found guilty."

"All of the General's men," said Dr. Bird.

"Stab Whisper, The Warrior, Kamaeleo and the General," listed Diamonds.

"All them bros," added Harla.

"Spectrum and Mist," said Diamonds.

"And..." said Escondido, driving Diamonds to finish.

"You," Diamonds said like the words hurt them.

"I'm guilty?" I asked, sucker-punched by the news. "Of like a crime?"

"Oh, no, Captain," said Dr. Bird. "You're just suspended. For the Spring game."

"Turns out the Lack is considered out of bounds," said Harla, almost gently, even though I knew she was thinking she'd told me that when I was about to go into the Lack.

I let it sink in. I was willing to throw everyone's hard work away just for one more moment with Grandad. And what did it get me? I had let everybody down for nothing.

Harla looked down at me, eyebrows tilted like she was reading my mind. But her pity made it worse. It'd be easier if everyone were just angry at me for getting us disqualified.

* * *

When it was time to hose down and scrub the van, Harla spoke up, so tired she smiled easily, her guard down under her puffs of hair escaping her braids.

"Can I talk to you for a second, Captain?"

Too tired to be surprised she called me Captain, I was happy to get out of van-scrubbing duty, but was unsure whether I should let the team do the dirty work.

Escondido nodded. "You can take this one off, Cap."

Harla climbed into the van, and I followed, closing the door behind me.

"There's something I wanted to talk to you about, Chay-Z…" Harla played with her fingers nervously. This sounded serious, and I felt my chest tighten as I put the clues together.

Harla had trusted me with theories about Grandad, things she even kept from Diamonds. She always took the opportunity to sit near me or touch my hand. And, of course, her teasing me must have been a way to hide her true feelings.

I'd had difficult conversations before, getting rejected by the girls in my grade, and I recognized the same nerves in Harla's fidgeting and lack of eye contact. My mind swam. I didn't even know if I had feelings for Harla. But no one had ever confessed feelings for me before. I acted like I didn't know where the conversation was going and nodded and smiled encouragingly.

The hose hit the outside of the van with a loud HISS so suddenly, we both jumped, then laughed at ourselves.

"Call me Chase? Please?" I said, trying to take this seriously.

"OK, Chase," Harla said like it was difficult to pronounce. She looked down at her hands as she spoke, searching for words, "I…"

After she stuttered again, I said, "I think I know what you're going to say, Harla."

"You do?"

"I do."

"When'd you find out? Who said? Diamonds?"

"No one told me, Harla, I just…I guess I figured it was going to eventually happen."

"That's real nice to hear, Chay-…Chase," she corrected herself. We both laughed, the inside of the van darkening as the last window was sprayed with goop. The thud and woosh of the brushes punctuated their conversation.

"So you're not mad?" Harla asked.

"Why would I be mad?" I asked.

She flashed a grin. "Because I'm going to beat you!"

I about had a heart attack right there. I'd never had a girlfriend before, but that didn't sound like something I'd be into. Plus, Harla seemed to be putting the cart ahead of the horse. "You're going to beat me?"

"Yeah, I'm going to do better than second place. Next Game. As a captain. Wait. What did you think I was talking about?"

"You're going to be a captain next year? "

"Yeah. What did you think I was talking about?"

"Do you know what team?"

"Not yet, hopefully ours," Harla said, grabbing me by the shoulders and smiling. "Chase, stop changing the subject. What did you think I was talking about?"

Her hands were surprisingly strong, and I felt her pull me towards her. Nobody had ever tried to kiss me before. I panicked; I didn't know what to do. For a moment, I tilted my head and moved in, but then my thoughts went to Diamonds. And I knew whatever Harla was thinking, I didn't want it.

"Harla, I can't kiss you."

"Excuse me?" She raised her voice suddenly, like scolding a child.

"I don't like you like that. I think you're a great friend and an absolute genius at—"

"Hold up, cornball, why would you think I would want to kiss you?"

"It's OK, Harla," I said supportively, thinking of what a good friend should say. "You'll find someone who has feelings like that for you back…"

"I'm gay, fool!"

"Oh," I said, then realized Harla hadn't ever been teasing me all along to flirt with me. She was teasing me because she was pissed I had her spot. Everything Harla ever said to me suddenly made more sense.

The van doors opened in unison, and the whole team piled

in. My skin burned with embarrassment. I must have been redder than the Seeker's eyes. Dr. Bird noticed and asked, "Captain, are you alright?"

Dr. Bird reminded me to buckle up as Diamonds set up the laptop in front of Escondido, shooting me a smile through his rearview mirror. Harla drummed against the headrest behind me. I smiled. My team.

* * *

"Mom?" I called out, walking into the house. I was only gone for three days, but the house felt...different. The smell hit me first, like dust and wood and off-brand Febreeze. But it looked different, too. The curtains seemed dingier, the furniture looked more worn and out of date. The place was a little bit of a mess, with Mom's books and Dad's mugs all over the place, and I felt a little embarrassed as Dr. Bird and Diamonds followed me in.

Mom met me with a big hug, and I was eight years old again for a moment, in Mom's arms and safe. But Mom felt smaller in my arms now, and I wasn't eight years old anymore.

"Mom, you know Dr. Bird."

Mom smiled and shook her hand.

"And this is Diamonds."

"Diamonds?" Mom said, arching an eyebrow as she shook their hand.

"Yes, Mom, Diamonds Hunt," I said shortly, stopping her before she said something embarrassing.

"So," Mom said, sitting everyone down, in her drawl that

seemed more pronounced than I'd remembered, "tell me all about it, how'd you do? Did you get to meet Mr. Bigshot Fowler?"

"It was…" I searched for an answer that wouldn't take an hour, my wandering eyes going to a smiling Dr. Bird before landing on Diamonds then flitting away. "Fun. It was a lot of fun."

"That's it?" Mom asked incredulously. "Fun?"

"Chase did really well," Diamonds said, without looking up from their hands in their lap.

"Did you?" Mom sounded surprised.

"During gameplay," Dr. Bird answered, "we placed second."

"Second? Out of…"

"Ten. But retroactively, we were disqualified."

"Disqualified?" My mom's hand instinctively splayed on her collarbone, although she'd never owned pearls to clutch.

I rolled my eyes that Dr. Bird had let it slip. Mom was going to make a whole deal out of this.

"I got suspended for a technicality," I said, picking the dirt from under my nails at the edge of Dad's chair.

"Cheating?" Mom was suddenly serious, her voice dropping low. "Is this going to affect Chase's school credit?"

"No, ma'am." Dr. Bird went into calming mode, putting her hands out, smiling and nodding as she said. "Chase's infraction was a mistake in gameplay, not cheating. Merely…stepping out of bounds. Plus, most of the other teams were suspended on much more egregious breakages of gameplay rules."

"How many teams ended up placing?" I asked, realizing the number of captains suspended for conspiracy.

"Three," Diamonds said. "Captains Furcifer, Mars, and Shinobi."

"Champion, and two runners-up," said Dr. Bird. "But I wished to speak with you about Chase's school credit…"

"He's still going to be credited for his work on the project, right?" Mom asked.

"Of course, of course. What I wanted to speak with you about, and you'll get a formal proposal with paperwork backing it up, is privately tutoring Chase."

"Like…homeschooling?" Mom was confused.

A jingle of keys and stomping of boots meant Dad was home. And after all I'd been through over the last few days, my stomach still clenched, and my skin went cold. I was scared of Dad reacting to the team in his house. Or seeing me.

But Dad took two steps in the room, and instead of disappointment at strangers in his house, warmth spread across his stubbly face in a big smile.

At me.

At seeing me.

In two giant steps, he took me in a big hug. I felt tiny. Not younger, like I did with Mom. I just felt small and weak next to Dad. But I knew as he hugged me, he meant it. He'd missed me. He kept his big paw on my shoulder as he asked what we were talking about.

Dr. Bird, maybe remembering how contrary Dad had been in the first living room meeting, took a quick inhale and gave her spiel. "Powers, Limited would like to pay for your son to have a private tutor, specializing in math and sciences. Through practical experience, internships, apprenticeships, and a metric ton of lab work, the goal is to get Chase a full ride to any college of his choice."

"And what all this cost?" Dad asked, still smiling with an arm around me.

Mom rolled her eyes. Dr. Bird's head tilted for a moment, then she inhaled to speak again, even though she already had answered the question. Diamonds cut her off. "Powers, Limited would pay."

"Excuse me, and you are?" Dad asked, the tone of his voice adding an aggressive edge to his politeness.

"Dad, this is Diamonds Hunt." I felt my cheeks getting hot.

Dr. Bird said happily, "Currently my pupil."

"Hi, Miss Diamonds," Dad said, "You also work for…"

"It's just Diamonds, Dad," I said, interrupting him in my politest tone.

The muscles on his face let go of the smile a little, and he said, "Excuse me?"

As I moved my neck to look him in the eye, his hand slid off my shoulder. I tried to speak lightly, like it was no big deal. "It's just Diamonds, Dad. No 'Miss.' They have different pronouns."

Shrugging, he shifted in his seat and said, "Hey, I was just talking to the young lady."

I knew what he was doing now, and it was annoying. Taking control of the situation. He messed up talking about her again, on purpose. Like a bully would.

And I knew it wasn't personal against Diamonds, this was Dad chewing me out in front of company. But I didn't care, I wasn't going to let anyone talk to, or about, my friends like that.

"Dad," was all I said, as I held eye contact with him for what felt like an hour. I just about passed out from nerves, waiting for him to say something, or to change his face to say something without talking.

And I didn't care if he did say something else or if I mouthed

279

off and got in trouble. Heck, I didn't even care if he tried to embarrass me any more in front of my friends. I was done hiding, ready to exchange words with my father.

Instead, he got to his feet with a groan. "Diamonds, Dr. Bird," he nodded, "if you excuse me, I got a bent muffler in the garage I need to repair."

Once he walked out the room, I exhaled, my shoulders relaxing, my jaw unclenching. I looked over at Diamonds, who held my gaze, smiling a tiny secretive smile.

Dr. Bird went on to explain the nuts and bolts of private tutoring to Mom, as Dad banged on his muffler in the garage.

What a weird three and a half weeks it had been. Not weird — bonkers. I tried to list everything, categorize, and file it. The game, the contestants, the explosions, everything I'd seen. Even some of the cool stuff I managed to do, saving a little girl and a big chameleon clone, fighting mechs, and trapping a Kaiju stick bug.

And there, on the couch, Diamonds moved their hand on their lap, then over more to graze mine. My thigh could even feel the heat from their slender fingers. As I blushed, I couldn't put a name to what I was feeling, or what it said about me.

Dr. Bird made a corny science pun and everyone forced laughter, then she went back to her pitch for tutoring services at Powers, Limited, training year round for the game.

My eyes still on their hand, I let out a silent giggle, just a flutter of realization. This was how life was now. It was all so...so...*unreal*.

It was all real, wasn't it?

I thought back to what Captain Mars said about me. "Very easy to hypnotize, very easy to incept, very easy to steer. And now you won't know what's real and what's in your head for the rest of the game."

None of it was hypnotic suggestion from Captain Mars, was it?

It's not THE END for Chase, Diamonds, and Harla!

They need you (yes, YOU) to REVIEW NOW!

Please support this story by leaving a review at your online book retailer.

The following is a sneak preview first chapter from

Miss: The Girl in Disguise
Book Two of the Hide & Seek Chronicles

"Do you even know who you're looking at, mean lady?"

Captain Miss whipped her head around the room. She must have been looking for the source of the voice.

And for the umpteenth time, I wished it was me in that game. If I could see what the Captain was seeing, the illusion she was trapped in, then I'd know how to help her out of it. Then I'd actually be useful to the team.

"Yeah, Captain Mars. Emily, right? Aight, Emily, I'm gonna kick your butt as soon as I find it."

The giggle came from everywhere in the room; none of our sensors in Mission Control could pinpoint it. That creepy, echoing giggle, ran down my spine.

"Well, of course me, silly. And my team, and your team-"

She blipped into existence on our video feed of the cavern, an oversized, bright green alien head on a girl wearing a flouncy dress. She had bent the light around her; that was a new trick. Now every contestant could bend light, it seemed. Her big, slick black eyes looked into the camera, and her tiny, breathy voice squeaked excitedly, "Hi, Chase. Good Kitty."

Hearing my name turned my stomach, and being called "Kitty" by that manipulative little... Well, I guess I was losing my composure, so I could imagine what this was doing to Captain.

Disappearing again instantaneously, Captain Mars - Emily - taunted Captain some more. "Who else do you think is listening? Is watching? While we play. While we train. When we have to sit up straight at the dinner table? Someone is always watching you, mean lady, and you know it."

"Oh, I'm about to get real mean up in here."

Dr. Bird leaned back in her chair, covering her mic, and whispered, "Captain's pulse is rising, and I'm not even sure she can hear us right now."

One wall of the cavern was wet brown rock, but most of the rest of it was an enormous root structure. Captain Miss, our captain, in matte black covering her head down to her clunky rocket boots - also matte black and rising up to her knees - stood wide legged, arms out, looking ready to fly away or throw a punch. In her mind, she wasn't in the mud under a giant Amazonian tree. She was mostly likely trapped in some painful memory, nightmare, or phobia, mentally tortured by the cute little girl.

"But you can't tell anyone, or they'll think you're a crazy mean lady."

"Shut up," Captain barked.

Taking on an overly-calm tone, barely above a whisper, Dr. Bird said, "Captain, if you can hear me, take a deep breath. In through the nose, out on a six count...close your eyes. Close your eyes."

In their effortlessly smooth voice, Diamonds alerted us softly. "It's not working."

Hearing their voice was automatically comforting for me, at least. I've been suspended from captaining for six months and even I needed to take a breath, unlock my jaw and remove my tongue from the roof of my mouth.

"Diamonds, you talk her down," I say. They did it for me, hopefully they could for Captain.

They cleared their throat, looking at me across Mission Control, lit by the wall monitor in whitish-bluish. I got that feeling again, all loosey goosey in my legs but also somehow all tensed up everywhere.

"Breathe." The word lasted several seconds. I swear to God I felt wind in my face when I heard them say it. "Breathe."

They repeated again and again as the little alien girl circled Captain Miss.

Dr. Bird whispered, "It's working."

As they repeated themselves, Diamonds changed the view on the wall monitor to thermal, this one from a different perspective, looking at them through the tree. There was Harla's silhouette in red, arms and legs out in readiness. There was another red figure in the tangle of roots.

"Breath, Harla, breathe. She's on your two o'clock, twenty feet ahead, four feet up. Breathe. Two o'clock, twenty feet ahead, four feet up. Breathe." It was a meditative rhythm.

Maybe even hypnotizing.

Harl- Captain Miss somersaulted forward in the mud, coming up in a perfect kneel and flinging a single cube from her rocket boots. The cube splashed underneath the hidden alien girl, then flashed a blinding light. It then rumbled with booming bass, rippling the surface of the water. Above, in the ropey cascade of roots, the air rippled, revealing the girl in a poofy dress and alien head.

"Crap!" The dainty voice was muffled behind the alien head.

Wrapping her arms in the roots, sitting back and pointing her heavy boots at the girl, Captain Miss went full mean lady.

"Flame on right," she commanded, and a streak of fire streamed out the bottom of her boot. She sprayed wide of Captain Mars but burnt away a thin cluster of roots. Once the fire kicked off, Captain Miss said, "Airblow. Left."

And Captain Miss blew Captain Mars out of her hiding spot out into the open, splashing down into mud. Mud inky with the tagging solvent of the dragon seeker. And that tagging solvent ruining her flouncy dress meant she was all but officially out.

But the Captain waited to move. "Where's the Seeker?"

Diamonds' tone warmed up. "North-Northeast, thirty feet up. Visual?"

"No, thanks. How long until another ink spray?"

"Hold please."

Of course, Captain Miss had already blipped out of sight, her rocketboots bending the light around her.

All was deadly still.

"Captain Mars is out. Final three."

Go to ZJeffries.com and sign up for the newsletter to read Miss: The Girl in Disguise now!

Special Thanks to:
My wife and daughter
Jess Clapton
Taylor Anderson
Liz DiNorma
Michael Chandler
Evan Engle
Kim Garvey
Ben Dawson
Margaret Casner
Robyn Lustbader
The Muppets…not *The* Muppets, but shout out to them, too
Mikki Noble
Charlie Knight
Edgy Writer's Workshop
My parents and family

` Printed in Great Britain
by Amazon

63424752R00167